Tom McCulloch is from the Highlands of Scotland. He currently lives in Oxford with his family. With his first novel, *The Stillman*, he became an Amazon Rising Star.

By the same author
The Stillman

A
PRIVATE
HAUNTING

Tom McCulloch

SANDSTONEPRESS
HIGHLAND | SCOTLAND

Published in Great Britain by
Sandstone Press Ltd
Dochcarty Road
Dingwall
Ross-shire
IV15 9UG
Scotland.

www.sandstonepress.com

The publisher acknowledges support from
Creative Scotland towards publication of this volume.

ISBN: 978-1-910985-15-1
ISBNe: 978-1-910985-16-8

Cover design by Blacksheep, London
Typeset by Iolaire Typesetting, Newtonmore
Printed and bound in Great Britain by Clays Ltd, St Ives PLC

For my grandfather, Bert, and
the Good Doctor Graeme Ainslie, my brother.

You must let fall body and mind.
Ju-ching

One

His dead aunt was a psychopath. Fletcher didn't know this back then. She fitted the types he read later in the Hare checklist: grandiose sense of self-worth; cunning; lack of empathy and self-responsibility; short-term marital relationships (four times married). The village was still full of her. He tried to concentrate on the house across the road and the man within but all he could think of was her. A God-awful woman. He almost braced himself for the familiar slap.

Blasphemer!

Yet a religious hypocrite too, first in church and first to judge. She could piss right off. And Him too.

The changes didn't bother him, Parker's Ironmonger now the café he was sitting in, Donati's chip shop a sandwich bar, the play-park with the treacherous Witch's Hat roundabout in-filled with red-brick flats, so many aspirational conservatories built into back gardens.

Merry England-dom, his aunt called it. Fletcher could smell it, the pretentious pride of the petty bourgeoisie. He looked round the dreary café, wondering again what he was doing here.

His aunt wouldn't like him staring out the window like this. *Goggling,* she would call it. Not that it stopped her. The image was bold in his memory: his aunt at the bleached nets, peering out. Fletcher would creep up on her but she was never ashamed at being caught, only annoyed he'd interrupted. *Get away*, she'd say, *shoo*, a greedy woman who couldn't share.

He never complained. To complain was to invite another slap. He'd listen to his aunt's surveillance report at the dinner table, his uncle barely listening, his little sister bored; *Mrs Jones, what's in all those packages...? Mr Soames was round at that tart Angie again... the Browns were arguing, surprise, surprise...* In this way Fletcher found out what he hadn't been allowed to see, his imagination filling the gaps. Sometimes his whole life felt like that.

'You want a refill?'

Fletcher looked up. The man was about forty. Behind the sagging face and disappointed eyes were echoes of someone remembered. The question was repeated, the words only now reaching him. *Do you want another?* He looked down at his long-finished coffee, eyes moving to the little black flecks in the sugar bowl. He wanted to count them again.

'Well?'

The clock on the wall said ten fifteen. He'd ordered his coffee at eight thirty. One hour forty-five minutes ago.

'Yes,' he decided. 'And a teacake.'

'A teacake?'

'No butter. Just plain.'

'Dry?' The man's eyes flicked across his face, lingering for a moment on the untidy beard.

'A dry teacake.'

The man ambled back to the counter. His trousers were black and a bit too short, Fletcher's shiny grey and too long, as if he had shrunk. They made him angry and he made a priority of getting rid of them as soon as the opportunity arose. He fidgeted with the zipper on his black bomber jacket, buttoned right up to the neck. His head bobbed above and he wondered what it looked

2

like. Maybe a sweaty red apple, on the turn, his cropped hair like grey mould.

Fletcher had time. The saggy-faced man didn't know this. If he chose, and Fletcher might, he could sit in this café all day. He'd learned patience in a way the man would never understand. Nor the few customers, none of them, who came and drank and ate and pissed and left. They didn't try to hide their stares at the bearded man with the bomber jacket and shiny trousers. It didn't matter to him. They could point and laugh and none of it meant anything.

The patch he'd cleared on the window was steaming up but the house across the street still vaguely visible. The man was in there, crying maybe, he could be a secret depressive. Or on the toilet, a bad curry the night before. Fletcher hadn't had a curry in a long time and considered having one later, there was an Indian takeaway up the road that hadn't been there before. A newsagent's too, and a scruffy hairdresser's with a sad-eyed teenager.

The waiter returned with his coffee. At 11 am he bought another. He would buy twelve more over the next three days, sitting at the same table by the window. The longer he sat there, the more he assimilated the changes. It was all about reconnaissance and interpretation. He had a long-developed ability to easily step into a new scenario. Skilled, he thought.

By day two he was familiar with the new shops and houses, by day three the café felt reasonably comfortable and by day four he'd established the regulars. The man in the house across the street had also come into a clearer focus. Fletcher had seen him many times now, each sighting another reminder that his role in life was to offer his bollocks for a regular kicking.

The front garden was an overgrown mess. This didn't bother Fletcher at all, unlike the living room light. It was

3

always on, a fact that annoyed him almost as much as his shiny trousers.

There was no need for that light given the dazzling sun of this long, hot summer, *the best in fifteen years* he heard the saggy-faced waiter say. He wanted to break in and switch the damn thing off. Instead, he wrote LIGHTS in big reverse letters on the steamed-up window. The coffee was good. Fletcher savoured it, counting how long it took the LIGHTS to fade, slightly unsettled that it didn't completely disappear, a phantom lingering behind the fresh steam.

Two

Jonas Mortensen lay under the cold water. Both arms floated free. No bubbles from the mouth.

Say a stranger, a beautiful woman, a beautiful naked woman, was looking down on him. What a strange introduction. Never mind how this woman came to be in his bathroom, that was irrelevant, just imagine what she'd make of it. She was probably thinking about cause and effect, the series of unknown choices which could only have led to this moment. She'd study the face, wondering what his final thought might have been, perhaps his mother, his first pet, the love that got away. A one-eyed children's doll? The possibility was remote.

Jonas decided to breathe, his corpse-like serenity erupting into splutters and coughs as he rose from the water in a near panic. Two minutes twenty-three. He had no idea why a forty-five-year-old man did this other than he liked the feeling of inordinate happiness that grew alongside the burning urge to breathe. And c'mon, he was a professional. He had a handle on it, *control*. Like free-divers who knew the optimum depth, Jonas always came up in time.

He sat breathing heavily, staring at the dripping tap. His head hurt a bit, maybe from these obsessive thoughts about the doll. A scuffed, grubby face, long black eyelashes around the right eye and the left eye missing. A ragged white dress with a lacy design around the collar.

It had been said, and Jonas wouldn't disagree, that he was a man of *eccentric impulse*. It explained the decision to do the loft insulation at the height of summer and, by extension, explained the doll. At least, the appearance of the doll, not the *reason*, which was very different.

He'd seen the pile of carpets in the far corner of the attic many times. What he hadn't done was take any notice of them. But today, to fit the insulation, he did, pulling them aside to find a shoebox. *Clarks*, said the lid. He hesitated before opening it. It was the setting. A dark loft, skylight sun angling through dust. It might have winked, lying there in its little cardboard coffin.

Despite the cold bath he was sweating within five minutes. Thirty degrees for over two weeks. High humidity. The whole village seemed edgy, a collective desire for a decent night's sleep.

He padded naked into the living room and realised he'd left the lights on again. They frustrated him hugely, these forgettings, his complacent contribution to the dooming of the planet.

An exhibitionist urging took him to the net-curtained window, just as a group of girls from The Hub passed. None looked in as his gaze moved to the strip of cracked slabs and feral vegetation that was the front garden. He kept it that way deliberately. Told Gladstone in the café he liked to see what the weeds would do *next*. Gladstone just frowned; the dude lacked wonder.

'How *you* doing, doll-face?'

He slumped down on the armchair beside the wood-burning stove. The doll stared back with its one good eye. He'd sat it on a stool, opposite the chair on the other side of the stove.

'I've got you pegged as a pessimist but I don't know why. I apologise if I'm doing you a disservice.'

Jonas stared for a few more moments then looked away, around the burglary scene that was the living room. Scattered books, wood shavings and bits of twine, dirty mugs and magazines, even a bit of old toast beside the log basket. The mess was so demoralising he fled into the kitchen, the stacks of dirty dishes making him back straight out. He'd have to clean up before he got a cleaner.

Back in the living room Li Po stared out from the Chinese scroll painting hanging above the mantelpiece. Quietly admonishing, as ever. What did a poor man have to do to please that guy?

* * *

The crew picked him up at midday. Eggers was driving the yellow Iveco tipper, Boss Hogg beside him. Davis and Johnson grinned in the rear seats, nudging each other like the school-boys they'd been until a few weeks ago. The day before, he'd caught them doing wanker signs behind his back. Daft lads, that's all, Jonas's nature as benign as mulled wine in the snow.

Eggers wanted to know why he'd taken the morning off, sparking a spirit-leaching conversation about insulation that lasted the length of the journey up to the works site. Eggers had all the answers, naturally. *There's grants available, you Norse plum, and if you'd come to me...*

Potholes.

Always the potholes. The politician who solved the pothole problem would be more loved than Mandela.

Today's fix site touched the sky. Flatlands-style, two hundred metres up! He smiled when people here talked about *hills*. He knew black tarns and eagle peaks. That spook in an empty valley. The tremors here were different. Limestone plateaus. Big sky and ghost winds.

And places like this.

The Rollright Stones. Three bows for karma, do enough terrible jobs and the diamond eventually sparkles. They peered back through hawthorn as Jonas set out traffic cones on the single-track. Two hundred metres away in the opposite direction Eggers did the same. Safe-zone set, Boss Hogg chain-smoked rollies until that mysterious moment of action.

Jonas waited. He lay in the middle of the circle, splayed like an angel and staring up into depthless blue. He had been to the stones a few times. Every visit made him think of Big Haakon, that childhood fulcrum, Larvik's pre-eminent drinker in a town with more than its fair share. He pictured him, the maniac who revealed *the old ways*, six foot five and army surplus combat trousers, whirling a faded Black Sabbath t-shirt as he danced the Neolithic ring in bare feet, round and again, a sudden sense of falling upwards making Jonas close his eyes, the blue becoming ever-shifting kaleid-o-colours abruptly shattered by *move your arse, you lazy fucker*.

Boss Hogg put Davis and Johnson on the sweep and shovel, Jonas and Eggers on the stop-go lollipops.

Top result for the J-Man, too hot to be messing around with tar, so watch the cars and wave to the drivers, who all waved back but one. Souped-up Subaru, young male, braking to a last-second halt. Boy Subaru made the mistake of revving and Jonas looked over his shoulder. Way down by Eggers on the other end of the fix site a cyclist had appeared. So Jonas held the lolly on red, Boy Subaru rev-edging but impotent, stranded until the cyclist passed.

Somewhere on blue a red kite mewled. As if to remind him not to take the bait, to let go the contempt of Boy Subaru, whose eyes said, *forty-five years old and you're holding a road sign in the middle of nowhere? What happened?* Well, young man, nothing had happened. I, Jonas Mortensen, have come to be. I have come to be here. That is enough and that is *all*. He smiled and

8

closed his eyes. The southerly wind was warm and Boy Subaru's after-fug was soon evaporating, the engine fading. The world re-asserted. There were elderflowers to be collected. Jonas picked them as the hours passed, twirling the occasional lolly.

When he got home the one-eyed doll hadn't moved. Lazy swine, he thought, then realised that the doll could do whatever it damn well wanted. It *belonged* here, much more than Jonas did.

Six years he'd lived at End Point. And someone once told him the house had been empty for seven more before that. All of which meant One Eye had been skulking in the loft for at least thirteen years. He should be deferring to the *doll*, breaking out his best little tea-set and baking some tiny cupcakes. Maybe then she'd let on who hid her away in the old shoebox.

'What do you say to that?'

The doll said nothing.

'You want some dinner?'

The doll chose that moment to fall off the stool.

It made sense.

Jonas believed that everything, animate or not, was interconnected, a meld rather than separate elements, connected one to the next. The whole, essentially, was more than its sum, a unity in itself. But lower the highbrow and Jonas was a pragmatist. So, instead of a fraught existential struggle breaking out as he pondered the meaning of a one-eyed doll falling off a stool at this particular moment on eternity's rollercoaster, he started laughing, so loudly that his neighbour missed the dramatic last line on *Eastenders*. Then he made dinner. For one.

* * *

9

Cleaner wanted. Call Jonas on 07871 399747. Jonas had worked hard to be known only as Jonas but hesitated before he posted the advert through the Post Office door. The *assumption*. It nagged a bit.

Lee and Danny nodded hello outside the village hall. Through a set of windowed doors on the inside, another fifteen or so kids milled around. The noise increased exponentially as he opened them, a mix of laughter, shouting and pulsing 'Grime' (Danny had explained).

Mark waved flamboyantly from the kitchen. Long-time organiser of the youth club, The Hub, a man more camp than a field full of wigwams. Beside him were Wendy and Greg, fifty-something divorcees conducting a secret affair that everyone knew about. They had that usual *just finished off* look. An auburn-haired woman Jonas hadn't met before was drying cups.

'You still on the plants?' asked Mark.

'Flora. Think of margarine.'

'I prefer butter.'

'Very funny.'

'The old ones are the best, Jonas, like you.'

'Time to give these damn kids some roots,' said Jonas and let out a roar of '*shuuuut UUUUUUP!*'

Five years he'd been volunteering now. The accounts, some admin, and he organised the annual trip to an outdoor activity centre. But the bushcraft was the main event. As Mark once said:

'You can make fire? How cool is that?'

What was even cooler was that the kids went for it without sarcasm. The present was app-ed up, dreaming in digital. Bow-drills and star navigation should be as appealing as Chlamydia.

Jonas was thrilled. He was *still* thrilled, five years on. He taught them and he taught them well, having once upon a distant time been a teacher. And while he'd never be their friend he kind of wanted to be. Better a

10

friend than some cool uncle figure, trying to get down with the kids, although a whiff of either meant the credibility bomb went boom. Disastrous, no way back to the normality that was fifteen teenagers milling around on a Friday night, discussing the often toxic members of the Umbellifer family and their hollow stems.

'Know the plants,' said Jonas.

'Dig it,' said Danny, who'd recently blossomed from a fourteen-year-old gangle-kid to a fifteen-year-old Johnny Depp-type with just enough angst to blind him to the female appeals.

He passed Jonas a CD. DJ Fresh.

'Why, thank you kindly, sir.' Jonas scanned the room and picked out Eggers's two kids, Laura and Eloise. Zero chance of seeing their father helping out at The Hub. *Too many porridgy do-gooders*, he once said. Lacey was down by the stage. She smiled his way, gave a little wave.

Jonas loved these kids, he surely did, that wonderful openness which should be bottled, sold as precious balm and the world instantly transformed. An ongoing project was *wooden-spoon-making* for crying out loud. How could that compete with iPhones and Instagram for teenage attention? But it did. Lacey still couldn't get the crook knife technique and came over with an exaggerated pout. Jonas smiled and stood close behind her, leaning her forward and placing her elbows on her knees. *Carve away from the body, see, slow and easy.*

Later, he ducked out for a smoke, looking up to a crescent moon. The kids. They knew how to find south now, just imagine a line connecting the horns and extend it down to the horizon.

But north, *north* was where it was at, whatever *at* might be. He moved his gaze to the Big Dipper, Merak and Dubhe, the two outer stars in the bowl, following a tick-tack line north to Polaris.

What an epic sky. Crammed with a trillion stars

11

but never called messy. So why was his house? He pictured the mess growing and growing, his private universe expanding towards inevitable entropy. Again, Jonas regretted the cleaner advert. And once more he didn't.

'I should take responsibility.'

The auburn-haired dish-washer paused as she was stuffing the rubbish bag in the bin.

'But I'm a lazy, lazy man.'

Jonas walked, round by the nature park. 10 pm passed, the moon through birch lighting the path. He sat down and leaned against the old yew and wondered about late walkers. There may be a few.

Hello there!

They would be surprised, sure, but not spooked. It was summertime, people *indulged*. If coming across a smiling man under a tree at ten o'clock on a summer night was not exactly a given, it was at least much more explicable than on a winter's night, when a meeting moved the threat from eccentric to sociopath. Jonas should come back on December 21st, wait for the walkers with a fire-torch, two lines of mud smeared under his eyes.

He laughed and clapped his hands. The night sounds immediately stilled. He counted sixteen before the creatures stirred again; a blackbird's short burst of song, something in the rhododendrons to his left. The breeze rose and thin saplings moved in the darker distance on the other side of the reedy meadow. Like people dancing, witches making ritual preparations for tomorrow's *Jonsok*. Did they know he was here? Did they watch? He'd raise a glass to them when he got to *The Black Lion*. The final part of his own ritual. The Hub, the nature park, the pub. Some would find banality in this but Jonas knew when to extend the parameters.

Last year he'd bivvied in the woods when the first snow came in January, swum in the river in midnight July.

'So, who's coming?'

'Open house as ever.'

'You having a barbeque?'

'When have I not had a barbeque?'

'I wouldn't know.'

'Well, why don't you come one of these years then, Sam? Be good to get some new faces there.'

'You Vikings like your meat, eh?'

'Like a bit of meat myself.' This last from Clara, a hand on Jonas's shoulder as she passed, an exaggerated wink suggesting a *history*, a sometime affair that existed only in her head.

Old Sam missed it, lost in contemplation. Tiny sweat bubbles on his nose. 'I remember that from Orkney. The war. There was always meat. Lamb or beef. Always a bite of meat.'

Jonas smiled. Five minutes for Sam to turn the conversation to the war, his posting to the northern isles for the Arctic convoys; bannocks and local hooch, farmers' daughters in cold barns.

'I liked it up there. Always felt at home, you know. I don't know what you're doing down here.'

'I'm not from there, Sam. You should know this by now. I was born in Larvik. Worked in Bergen.'

The old man knew, of course he did. He just wanted Jonas to keep providing the cues, give him another way back to 1943. Jonas liked these rituals, the quick raise of Clara's eyebrows, *here we go again*. Too much was flux. Time should be always found to circle back.

Sam's eyes glittered. 'Knew a fisherman in Stromness. Helluva boozer. He'd worked the Shetland Bus. You have to hand it to those boys, pitching across the Atlantic with guns and money for Norway. No protection, not

13

like us on the convoys. Cold as Death's bad brother but we had the Navy port and starboard. Nothing like that for them. I'm boring you again.'

'No, you're not, Sam.'

The old man went on, walking again the Stromness cobble, a sky even clearer than tonight's, this young southerner who only knew hedgerows and hawthorn, the lap of gentle rivers, keen to stay awhile in a different landscape because he'd seen the connection between Rollright and the Ring of Brodgar, felt the satisfaction in knowing these stones were thrown up at the same time, all over northern Europe, warm with this comfort and whisky as he picked a way through the reels and outside to the cold, hunching his neck into the heavy jumper, Graemsay across the water, where croft-monsters castigated drunken husbands and belonging never ebbed with the tide, and what about him, could he make this place his home, as the Viking ships had come ghost-sailing round the point and made it theirs?

'Those northern lights. You know them too, Jonas. Colours in the sky like God's at the watercolours.'

He bought Sam another pint.

'There was a girl too.'

'Isn't there always! I'll see you at the party?'

'Sure you will. Sure.'

But Sam wouldn't come. Jonas glanced in the window as he left the pub. The old man in his usual chair. Walled in. The bar he never left and the past that wouldn't let him be.

'Jonas!'

Eggers weaved towards him from the smoking shelter. A few faces peered out. People he didn't know and a couple of lingering looks. One of them turned away and spat on the ground.

'Chinese,' said Eggers.

'Eh?'

14

'Getting a Chinese.'

They walked. Eggers had managed eight pints in the four hours since Hogg had dropped him off at *The Black Lion*. He told Jonas he didn't like going home, back to her and those crappy TV shows and sure, getting pissed didn't help, made it worse prob'ly, but what was really worse, Jonas, hmmm, you tell me man, sitting there sober as and wanting to scream, or taking the fuckin initiative and off to the pub and I know, I know, it means an argument but an argument means I can get *away*, upstairs, and you're lucky Jonas, lucky to live *alone*.

'Maybe I am.'

'You ARE!'

He left Eggers spring-rolling outside the Jade Dragon and wandered home, to stand in the living room as the eco-bulbs gradually revealed the bomb site. Yep, old Jonas sure was lucky.

What woman could resist?

JJ Cale helped him tidy. Steady background beat, the Roksan separates and Wharfedale speakers he hadn't skimped on, Bose surround-sound like a blues-womb. This got him thinking about women again, or the lack thereof. He slumped in his pants and cracked a beer. How long had it been? Would there ever be another if they could see him now?

Clara crept into his mind and he contemplated for a while, got a bit hard before leaping up. Old JJ sure liked the women, songs like incantations that had him horny for Clara for crying out loud, so get over there and change the music. Had to be something less suggestive, *Jonsok* was coming so maybe something pagan-fringed. But Death in Vegas was too dark, DJ Fresh too frantic, the bass shaking loose his internal organs, gotta look after this old body.

He settled on the Rolling Stones, *Beggars Banquet*, in honour of old Martinsson. He used to blare out The

Stones when they were sitting in his kitchen knocking back the *akevitt* before heading down to the beach bonfires. Ah, *Jonsok*. The celebration of the summer solstice, the final defeat of winter's darkness by the Sun God. Jonas's parties were an import, sure, but some imports catch on. *Jonsok* would follow where boom boxes, breakdancing and the mullet had blazed a trail. Five years ago only three people came to his first party. That was fine, that was cool, no one really knew him then. The next year seven or so, a few kids from The Hub.

Then *fourteen*. A watershed. You can't impose a tradition; it has to be earned. Look at Morris dancing. The foot-bells didn't start *shs-shshing* overnight. Someone did it once, maybe for kicks. But do it again and again and you get a tradition. Hence Jonas's open door and the midnight bonfire, the flames fanned until the dawn. Just like home, almost. At home he wouldn't be the automatic figure of fun, or disdain, as he was to the men outside the pub.

At home, he would be something else altogether. They didn't need to know about that here.

Jonas had almost blown it from the start, his September arrival too sudden and too keen. Blame the mushrooms. And the beech nuts and blackberries, the rosehips and rowans. So why *not* a foraging walk? He put out flyers, introduced himself at the supermarket, the Post Office, and the café, thrusting leaflets into one bemused hand as he shook the other. In a misjudged burst of enthusiasm, he handed some out in *The Mucky Duck* on a Friday night. A few young guys made fun of him. Asked what the fuck he was doing here.

Only Mark turned up, his interest genuine, as was his suggestion that Jonas do something at The Hub. And Jonas's disappointment at the lack of interest in the walk evaporated.

He bumped into the guys from *The Mucky Duck* again, early December. Walking along the street a hard-packed snowball hit him full in the face. He tried to laugh it off but they followed him, shouting *Down With Thor*, the snowballs hitting harder, laughter becoming cruel.

Thor.

Or the Viking.

Sometimes even strangers would shout out. How's our local Viking? How's it goin, Thor? One time a woman came up to him at the fete and asked him to show her his mighty hammer. The boyfriend was not best pleased and sometimes even gods have to make a swift exit.

But hey, some of the locals had nicknames: Crooner Joe, Randy Clara... It was a sign not of difference but of belonging. A nickname meant you were a *character*. If they wanted to call Jonas Thor or the Viking then what's the problem? He was so much of a local he had *two* nicknames.

'I should be flattered.'

The one-eyed doll was unconvinced. Sat there on the speaker, shifting with the throbs of Bill Wyman's bass. He didn't know what to do with the damn thing. Re-inter it in the loft? There were thirty new centimetres of insulation up there so at least it'd be snug. Dithering meant no decision and the doll would soon be subsumed into the mess. He'd have to hide it during the cleaner interviews. It was probably an HR rule. Prospective new employers and single men should not, repeat *not*, reveal one-eyed dollies to the interviewees.

'Confucius said that. Does Li Po agree?'

Like the doll, the figure in the scroll painting above the fireplace said nothing. He and Eva had bought it on their honeymoon in China from a wizened old man outside a Taoist temple. That gleam in his milky eyes, Jonas had never decided if it meant 'got you, round-eye sucker' or 'this painting will bring great merit'. He edged towards the latter. As had been pointed out, and as Jonas himself would likely agree, he was a trusting fellow, mystically-inclined.

He put his nose close to Li Po, who kept on sweeping the jetty in front of the lakeside pagoda. There were a few trees in the background, a hint of high misty mountains, and nothing to suggest that the figure was indeed the famous Chinese poet. Then again, there was nothing to suggest that he wasn't. Jonas had never told Eva that he often stood in front of the scroll, imagining himself as a Taoist monk, living free and solitary with Li Po's spontaneity.

Some things, truly, should remain unsaid.

Anyway, Jonas had long decided he wasn't cut out to be a wandering Taoist poet. Cultural determinism was the final nail, the idea too quixotic even for Jonas, a man brought up in the land of salt cod and trolls. Not that he then shunned Li Po. That would be rude. As rude as having snowballs hurled at him. He'd turned the other cheek but one hit him on that side too.

Three

Fletcher was talking to a man called John Smith. Probably the most common name in the country.

He wondered if this was the man's real name, or whether he couldn't be bothered making up something more interesting, like Jean de Havilland Smythe. Then again, in this part of the world you could actually run into someone with that name. He'd heard a posh mother trilling for her children in the supermarket the other day: *Zebedee, Xenephon, come along now!*

He usually avoided pubs, or found himself escorted out as soon as he entered. Some had told him he stank. All granted themselves the right to stare. But tonight he felt confident and confidence was key. You had to decide that you belonged. Still, even though Smith had no way of recognising his name, his first instinct was to claim another. Taylor or Davidson, Brown. Instead, out came Fletcher. He told himself he was just imagining it, the hesitation before Smith said *pleased to meet you*, the flicker in the eyes.

'You want another?'

'Sure.'

'That's what I like to hear!'

Fletcher watched him go and looked round. He'd chosen this table in *The Black Lion* deliberately. NW corner, 180° sweep from the main door to the toilets, the bar in the middle.

The pub was busy, the heatwave driving people out of doors. None of them knew a thing about real heat, how it crawled across your body like ants and left a rash in the crotch. Their ignorance was like a test. Again, he told himself to relax, as they were relaxing, a few cold beers to cool down; women in cotton dresses bulging at the stomach, men with cargo shorts and Nikes, ankle socks white as their legs. Back and forth they went with their slopping trays.

Smith returned. Fletcher studied his close-cropped, military-style haircut and imagined a DVD collection of movies by bald Hollywood action stars: Bruce Willis, Jason Statham and Vin Diesel. His favourite film was bound to be *Top Gun* and he was probably gay. He talked incessantly about himself, as if afraid that when he stopped he might disappear. Fletcher had met many people like this, socially maladjusted and given to envy.

'Look out, here he comes. The *Viking*.'

'Eh?'

'Guy by the door. He's a Norwegian. Jonas Morten-something.'

'What about him?'

'He has these parties.'

'What kind of parties?'

'Wanky ones.'

'Wanky?'

'Thinks he's popular.'

Smith burbled on. Then he started saying other things, insinuations that were much more interesting. But when Smith started repeating himself he decided to leave, Smith following him outside for a smoke. He headed up the street but as soon as Smith turned away Fletcher doubled back. When Mortensen emerged, he was watching from the shadows beside a plumber's van. He saw Smith spit on the ground just as the Norwegian passed.

Fletcher followed Mortensen back to End Point. The dusk light gave a smoky poignancy to the house. Echoes

20

of the long gone. Children who had once played, men and women who had died. In time he might uncover all these stories. No one else knew the house like Fletcher did.

Built in the 1920s, End Point had once been just that, the last house of the long terrace on the north-eastern side of Pound Lane. A road had now been built alongside its eastern wall, allowing access to a new, red-brick estate. On the other side of this access road, fifties semis and the occasional bungalow stretched down the remainder of Pound Lane.

When Mortensen opened the front door Fletcher continued on, following the pavement around the gable end. At the end of the wall was a low fence and behind that a line of thick Leyland cypresses hid the back garden. Fletcher looked round then vaulted the fence. Keeping to the trees, he turned two right angles until he was in the south-eastern corner. The cypress was thinner here but the dark heavy. Only a floodlight could pick him out. He peered through the fronds. A large stack of bonfire wood had been piled in the middle of the lawn. To his right was a ramshackle shed and a tall wooden fence, giving privacy from the neighbours. Crossing the lawn would leave him exposed to any overlooking window for about three seconds before he reached the sun room that led through to the kitchen.

Ten minutes later Mortensen opened the sun room door. He bowed deeply to the garden, almost as if acknowledging Fletcher, then stepped onto the grass and settled into the Lotus position. Fletcher remembered meditation once being described to him as *positive distraction.*

When Mortensen went back inside Fletcher stayed in the trees. He could pray, he thought, feeling his aunt's squeezing grip on his shoulder, pushing him onto his knees before bed.

As I lay me down to sleep...

His little sister in the top bunk, peering down on his humiliation. A chip off the old bitch, Iris never had to be reminded to say her prayers. Fletcher saw her on the lawn. She sat down where the Norwegian had, a very serious look on her face but trying hard not to smirk. She lifted her hands up high, thumb and forefinger making a circle and the other digits splayed, a parody of Fletcher's Buddhist gestures. She said *ommmm* and then came the laughter, as she had laughed at him last night in The Skull, like *what on earth are you doing here?*

The cypress shifted in a quick breeze, his sister's face hidden and revealed again. His stomach cramped, heat in the face. He had time to brace for the sinking. He had time to sit down and be glad of the dark and no one to see him but her, always her. He called it the Watching.

You cannot understand. My being here. All you know ended at the age of fourteen. You are trapped in childhood. Hopscotch and school-days. Holidays at the seaside. Two pence shuffle and crazy golf, you loved crazy golf, always pestering our uncle. Up at seven and can we play now, can we? You're delighted I've made camp at the old crazy golf course down by the river. One of the best in the land, they said, once upon a time. And I see you there as back then, club in hand. You're aware of the older girls, hanging out with friends and not parents, but not too aware, a year or so removed from full-on awkwardness, from going down to the beach, under the salty timbers of the broken down pier to smoke and drink cider, feel the hands of the boys wander downwards, down there, down there, that place you are not sure of, drowsing to the calm dazzle of the silvered sea and watching the pedalos, the pedalos like swans, beautiful swans. And that other girl in a far-away land, she too deserves crazy golf and pedalos, surely everyone does! Although she would understand so little of it, being a child of strange customs, mud shacks and flies,

22

stabbing winters and broiling summers. As I too understand
so little of her, finding her only in the familiarity of you. I see
your childhood in her eyes as she lies in the dirt of Sangin
bazaar, I see your memories flicker in her eyeballs before
they roll back that final time. Seaside and crazy golf. She's
remembered! She's remembered those holidays. She loved
them! So far away now it is painful, long before today, this
cold winter morning, long before her dark hair fanned out on
rust-coloured ground among the warm spilling grey of her
brains and her bright, bright, fourteen-year-old blood.

Four

Orange light beyond closed eyes. Don't open them, Jonas, don't turn the soft glow into the hard yellow dazzle of the morning sun. He still wanted the dream. To let in the light was to lose it.

He was back in the Beaujolais, a cartoon-coloured return to his first job after getting sick of the building sites of Copenhagen and drifting south, west. Acres of Gamay grapes, an infinity. A blood orange sun like malevolence made visible. He was picking impossibly fast, his hands a blur, overflowing baskets lining up. As he moved along the vines he heard a whimpering, somewhere near. The noise began to put him off, hands slowing, trying to place the sound.

Axel Johansson appeared, ten years old, telling him to pick up the pace, it was being *noticed*. But Jonas had recognised the sound and stopped picking altogether. The klaxon started in the distance and he saw the black uniforms hurrying down his row. He ran into the vines, following the whimpers and found it, a rabbit in a snare, whimpering louder when it saw him.

Then the uniforms were beside him, laughing at the rabbit, great belly laughs like they'd never seen anything so funny. The rabbit's tongue lolled as Jonas dug his fingers under the wire around its neck, blood on his hands and now an uncanny, human-like scream, little feet pumping the air as he finally managed to get the wire free. *Leave it*, the uniforms shouted, suddenly furious. But Jonas kept his eyes fixed on the rabbit because he knew if he even blinked it would not be an animal but a child, bloodied and dying on the ground.

Then, as ever, he blinked.

Jonas opened his eyes. He'd dreamed about the rabbit for decades, the one he had shot with Axel's .22, wounding it horribly but not killing it. Axel had to finish it off, holding the rifle one-handed like Schwarzenegger, putting a slug right through its eye. For a long time the dream had locked into this gruesome metamorphosis from rabbit to child. Such was the price.

★ ★ ★

'How's the head?'

Eggers ignored him.

He'd picked Jonas up forty minutes late, said nothing on the drive to the stones and now slumped beside him like a bayoneted dummy. Boss Hogg had sent them to check the tar and clear the cones. 9 am they'd got there and now ten. Eggers's fault they hadn't left the truck.

'Jackie.'

'What! What do you want?'

'How's the head?'

'Why? Why do you need to know that?'

'Just concerned.'

'The Nigerians are still partying,' muttered Eggers.

'Why Nigerians?'

'They're noisy.'

'So are lots of people. You being racist?'

'You think I'm being racist?'

'Maybe. Maybe I think you're being racist.'

'Fine. Just leave me alone.'

'Italians are noisy too.'

'Oh for Christ sake.'

25

'Swedes might be the worst though. I remember this one time on holiday down by Varberg when we –'

'Shut up!'

'So you don't want it, then?'

'What?'

'A little pull-you-up.'

'What are you *talking* about?'

'Sorry, sorry, a *pick*-you-up.' It amused him. Getting words wrong deliberately, just to annoy Eggers.

'I'm not listening to you anymore.'

Jonas reached into his rucksack and, with a flourish, produced the bottle of *akevitt*. 'But it's *Jonsok*!'

'The hell is *Jonsok*?'

'Don't you listen to anything I say?'

'Give it here then.'

Eggers took the bottle. And soon as he did sip his face drained. For a while he sat very still and very quiet. Jonas awaited the barf but Eggers kept it down. He took another sip, another.

By ten thirty Eggers was drunk again. Jonas watched him clamber onto one of the stones, shouting *I'm sitting on a standing stone, I'm* sitting *on a* standing *stone!* He gave Boss Hogg a wide berth when he appeared in the pick-up around midday and told them to *get the fuckin site cleared this side of Christmas, ok?* They nodded, watched him go and ignored him.

Jonas walked the hedgerows. He filled another bag with elderflowers and dozed in the circle, waking to the sure sense of being watched. Just echoes, no one there but the gnarly old stones and a reinvigorated Eggers, dancing alone on the far side of the circle, the truck radio blaring.

The dream drifted back. The rabbit and the child, the blood, all that was expected. But Axel Johansson? Jonas hadn't thought of him in a long time. His first true friend. Inseparable at primary school, they drifted apart at secondary. By their final year they contemplated each other across a distance they would never again bridge. The poignancy was apparent even to a seventeen-year-old Jonas, whose default setting was ruthless condescension.

'Meatloaf!' shouted Eggers.

'No. Too theatrical. Sounds like a West End show.'

'Not the music, you twat! The food. Tonight. You making meatloaf?'

'Wait and see.'

Jonas stacked the traffic cones. Neat piles of five. How satisfying it would be if every aspect of his life slotted away like that. It must be possible to achieve a generalised neatness. He had the ability. Take *Jonsok*, the care he took with the *smorgasbord*, the smoked salmon and pickled herring, Jarlsberg and *knekkebrod*. Each element was set out just so.

He learned this from his mother, who spent hours, days even, preparing the food then fled before the gannets descended. She'd head down to the beach to sit and watch the sea, the bonfires. His father would come staggering along drunk, or maybe just the loose pebbles giving way under his feet. He remembered watching them, hand in hand in silhouette, disappearing into blue falling night, a secret so open he had no way of grasping it. Their affection was embarrassing, a first glimpse of an unsettling universe he knew nothing about.

Axel once noticed them kissing. 'Look, Jonas, *look*, do you think they're going to have sex?'

Ah, Axel. A happy-go-lucky boy, stilled by adolescence like the night extinguished birdsong. Yet an unexpected teenage hit with the ladies. Jonas remembered him with girl after girl, arm in arm on the lunch hour promenade. Not the top level chicks but the Cs and Ds, the lesser-noticed, the plainer and the gauche, who Jonas found out would bloom late and well, streaking

27

past those whose beauty peaked at sixteen and down-hill ever faster from there.

A reunion was in order!

Follow the songline, revisit the tales. Get back home and onto Facebook, search down Axel Johansson and pick up the phone. Imagine the delight on the end of the line as memory's flashbulbs began to pop: the farmer's gate falling, falling, *down*, dumping them in the mud and cow shit; the button they tied to a string and taped to old Zetterlund's window, tip-tapping from the dark; his father telling him *this isn't a second bloody home for Axel*.

Jonas felt a surprising heat in his cheeks. Still that anger towards his father, thousands of days gone by. He hated telling Axel to go home because home was a frightening place. His dad worked the boats. A big guy. *A fisherman and a fighter*, he told Jonas once, when he was still allowed to go round, before Axel's mum spent a week in hospital. Anyway, getting in touch with Axel was ridiculous, the sudden brain-fart a treacherous mix of too many hours in the midsummer sun, the guilt of passed time and some subconscious desire to atone for not even saying goodbye when he left for university in Oslo.

The past. It sucked like the tide. But what are you left with when the waves recede? Empty shells in an open hand. He thought about the sea as he threw the last of the cone stacks in the back of the Iveco and drove up the road to pick up a suddenly re-appeared Eggers.

'I finished the booze.'

'Where have you been?'

'I climbed a tree. I haven't climbed a tree in *yonks*.'

'What kind of tree was it?'

'Big one. Big tall fucker with leaves.'

'Leaves, eh?'

'It's a *tree* innit?' He started to laugh.

28

He couldn't imagine Eggers doing nostalgia. You had to leave home for that but Eggers never had. Only distance created the melancholy, like thoughts of the sea made Jonas again think of his father, tumbling through his childhood like a plastic bag on a winter beach. The only thing Eggers got melancholy about was when the free show ended on the sex-cams.

'So what about it? Is there gonna be meatloaf or not?'

'You'll have to wait.'

'Tell me or I won't come!'

'You always come.'

'Not this time!'

Jonas smiled. Today, he liked Eggers. Rather, at this precise moment of today, he liked Eggers.

Later, it may be different. His thoughts of Eggers ranged in a spectrum from deep hate to horror to distaste to neutrality to *whatever* to like to delight to love. Right now, perhaps, as Jonas drove to the depot, glancing at Eggers with his feet on the dashboard, a cigarette and a boozy smile, pointing out this place and that, perhaps right now *like* was edging into *delight*.

How could it be otherwise? The afternoon *was* a delight, the yellow fields and the old pubs, the limestone cottages and the hedgerows. It felt like belonging and belonging was good. If he mined a deeper sense of it from Eggers, the man who had never left here, then strike down the fool who sought happiness in a place that once wasn't his home but now was.

'I like this place,' he told Eggers.

Eggers looked at him. 'And?'

'I just do.'

'What the fuck do you want me to do about it?'

'Nothing!'

'Knob end.'

But Eggers was laughing and Jonas was laughing and he could *see* it, *belonging*, not just in Eggers but later on, in the warmth in Lomax the butcher's eyes as he handed over the hamper of meat and fish, and in the banter with the off-licence boys as they loaded the beer slabs into the cab of the truck. Commitment to a place. It was a practice. Just ask Li Po. But you can no more belong to a new place in a few months than you can make fire with damp tinder. And *yessir*, Jonas knew how to make fire. All those evenings round at Haakon's and Jonas's parents with no idea; burning the fingertips, honing the craft under the big man's expert eye.

* * *

Cannonball Adderley welcomed the first six guests. Dizzy Gillespie and Stan Getz the next seven. Just after 9 pm Sun Ra sound-tracked the breaking of the party record. Sixteen people!

Then more people. And *more*. Jonas beamed and stopped counting because he didn't need to. It pleased him on a near-molecular level to see these people enjoying themselves, eating at the *smorgasbord*. The six cases of Ringnes beer the off-licence had sourced were fast-disappearing. His buzz was already respectable and two *akevitt* shots with a red-faced man whom he'd seen but never spoken to gave it an edge of impregnability.

'I'm Jonas.'

'I know you are. I'm Dave, work in The Hand and Shears.'

'Good to know you Dave.'

'Good to know the Viking.'

Jonas saw the smirk but decided it wasn't a smirk. There was no need for it, and because there was no need it couldn't have happened. He wanted to like all these people, every couple and clique, the kids from The Hub, trying not to enjoy themselves too much; the parental units at an appraising distance; Greg and Wendy, the

30

permanent flush revealing the obvious storyline; Eggers and the pub boys, half-cut when they arrived and sawn through by nine; the primly woollen Grandees of Village Life like Mrs Hawthorne from the village hall committee.

'You will not believe *this*,' said Mrs H.

The little group glanced forlornly at their empty glasses and across at the winking drinks. As one, they patiently turned their faces. Mrs Hawthorne, commanding obedience since 1958.

'I was at Sands Hill doing a risk assessment for the Beaver Cub walk. I parked the car in the car park and – '

'*Careful*,' said some innocent interloper who didn't know the protocol. 'I was there once and you – '

'*Anyway*. It was only four o'clock but there were a few cars, more than I would have thought. Then I noticed there were a few men huddled round one car. When I got a bit closer I saw a girl with hardly any clothes. On her knees and.... can you *imagine*? How could I take the Beavers there?'

Glances were exchanged.

'*Beavers* don't belong in a place like that.'

Feet were looked at.

'Beavers should *not* be exposed to *that*.'

Jonas had to flee. An *instant classic*, a story that people would tell for years and it happened *at his party*, that time Granny Hawthorne, because she must be called Granny even if no one called her that and maybe Jonas would start it off, another tradition born of the Norwegian, he of the parties, the *nickname giver*, so Granny Hawthorne said *beaver* a dozen times until silenced by a sudden explosion of laughter. To this day she'd have no idea why.

'Uncle Jonas.'

He gave Lacey a sideways glance. She'd appeared half an hour ago, alone, no sign of her parents. Fourteen

31

was a bit old for the uncle thing. He wondered if she was mocking him.

'Is it time yet?'

The wheedling little girl routine annoyed him, the flirty edge a touch unsettling.

They walked hand in hand into the garden. Jonas wanted the boyfriend to be watching. Spencer P. But there was no sign of the kid. A few regulars from The Hub started clapping and whistling.

'Go Jonas!'

'He's the firestarter.'

'Twisted firestarter!'

Before Jonas began he gave a little bow to the crowd. Then he reached into a bag of straw and formed a clump into a ball. Next, he picked up his willow bow, wound the cord round a nine-inch wooden spindle and placed a small piece of bark under a v-shaped cut in the rowan hearth-board. He stepped firmly onto the board, fitting one end of the spindle into the groove in a small wooden bearing block and the other into a similar groove on the hearth.

He could hear Big Haakon whispering. *Long easy strokes, son, like with a woman.* After a few strokes Jonas built up the bow speed, the smoke beginning to wisp now, furry shavings building in the v-notch. A few faster strokes and he put down the bow and picked up the bark, gently fanning the ember to a red glow. He carefully tipped it into the ball of straw, holding it up and blowing, softly, *softly*, then hard and *looong*, the straw suddenly bursting into flame. Then the bonfire itself, the straw ball setting off the cedar branches that he'd stacked in the centre, filling the night with a crackling sweetness that quickly became a roar, the woodpile dry as old dust and the flames licking high and rising as people stepped back and now oohs and aahs and nice

32

one Jonas and didn't everyone love a bonfire. Lacey took Jonas's hand again and he stared at her for a few moments, watching the flames dance in her eyes.

And midsummer's night began to curl at the edges, like the twigs on the edge of the bonfire, the alcohol flowing and the laughter rising with the little orange embers into the dark blue sky, the *Jonsok* sky that would right now, east and across the North Sea, be blanketing the Skagerrak, smoke-hazed from the fiery necklace burning along the coast.

'Penny for them.'

Jonas turned to a pretty face, freckles and auburn hair.

'I thought I should say hello.'

He stood back and squinted at her. 'I met you at The Hub, didn't I?'

She smiled. 'You did.'

'You're not going to help me out, are you?'

'A woman could get offended. I mean, if I'm so immediately forgettable – '

He grimaced, but she didn't help him out. 'It's – '

'Mary.'

'*Mary*. I knew it.'

'No, you didn't.'

'You're right. An *akevitt* to make up for it?'

'Well, why not?'

She said a friend had invited her and hoped he didn't mind her being there. Jonas blushed. Couldn't help it. Tried to hide it with a laugh that was too loud, too *loud*. *Gate-crashers have to pay their way*, he managed to say. She had to man the records and the turntable.

'You mean wo-man the records.'

'What?'

'Sorry. Bad joke.'

Now she was blushing and that made him blush again. 'If you don't want to, you don't – '

33

'No, no. That's ok.'

'You sure? You might not like my taste.'

'Try me.'

So he did, and led her through to the living room and the records, where she told him he had *a lot of blues*.

'Don't we all?'

'BB King,' she said. 'I've got this one.'

He looked away quickly. Before the gaze was held too long, glad of a hand on his shoulder. Eggers. When he looked back Mary was talking to someone. He watched her surreptitiously, Eggers babbling on about the fantastic meatloaf and you outdo yourself every year, you'll have us all talking Norwegian next, all that oordy boordy stuff from the Muppets, no, hang on, the chef was Swedish wasn't he, you must have seen the Muppets, did you?

When Mary caught his eye, Jonas again glanced away. He wasn't listening to Eggers anymore, thinking instead about the indifference of memory. As above so below, nothing to be done about the press of guilt that followed the reluctant comparison with another face, another time.

'Why the grump, Mr M?'

'Just feeling old.'

'Well, you *are* old. You should just get used to it and have some fun!'

And off Lacey went, as content now as she would ever be. She came back sometime after midnight to collect her forgotten jacket. He made sure to thank her for cheering him up.

34

Five

First, Fletcher refused the return. Then he deferred it. For years, a spiralling backwards through a series of concentric circles, closer and closer to the village. He'd come closest two years back, taken the National Express from London. But when the local bus turned up he didn't get on.

Nothing was different the next time he took the London bus. The same grey sky and tightness in the gut. Except this time, he did get on the B4 and twenty minutes later was standing by the village green. He had been there - in thought - many times, staring at the invisible crowd of people who knew he was coming or had never stopped waiting for him to return.

Fletcher wandered. He realised that the insistence of certain memories obscured so many others, elusive little hints in the name of a street, a shop sign, the kids spilling out of the school. He decided on a more systematic homecoming and decided to walk each of the village's six access routes, centre to periphery. Today was route five. 8 am and thirty degrees.

He followed the main B-road through the village centre. When the road swung west he turned northeast, following the single-track. Memory was brighter here, out in the open fields.

At the end of the track a building site had replaced the old farm. Back then, it was a spooky place, the residents vanished but the rooms still full of furniture, crockery and chairs, like one of those fake homes at ground-zero of a nuclear test site. But where Fletcher once played hide and seek in the barn or made dens among the straw bales, seven *Aspirational Executive Homes* were emerging.

The seven annoyed him. Six was neater. He should tell this to the show-home salesman, while making clear that he too was aspirational. He aspired to simple things like familiarity. Otherwise the bearing became unsteady, like those precarious, five-high towers of bales, the musty tunnels between them which they knew like moles, the clearings where they sat in an utter, stifling darkness. They thought nothing of collapse, or rats. They were completely fearless.

He turned his back on the houses and faced the yellow patchwork of the rape and wheat fields. The bone-dry earth smelled warm, occasional scuffs of wind lifting and dispersing clouds of dust, making him think of distant explosions on a desert horizon. His hands began to sweat and he wiped them on his new jeans, the pair he'd stolen from a washing line the night before. No more shiny half-masts. He'd wrapped them round a stone and flung them in the river.

A hundred metres or so back down the road he jumped over a fence into a small copse of birch trees, an island in the sea of yellow. He did this a lot as a kid. Sitting and drowsing, dapples behind his eyelids as the sun strobed through the leaves. His aunt called him a *day-waster*.

He opened his eyes when he heard a steady *pad, pad, pad* coming from the road. The runner soon passed and Fletcher hurried to the fence and vaulted over. He'd settled down cross-legged by the roadside just as the man turned at the new houses and ran back the way he'd come. He glanced nervously at Fletcher as he passed, alarmed by the sudden apparition.

36

'Nice day.'

'Nice day,' repeated the runner.

He resisted the urge to run alongside and ambled after him instead, stopping to watch a bright red combine harvester work the wheat. A fog of dust lifted into the hazing blue and a buzzard turned elegantly on a thermal. He followed the hawk down through its spirals, closer and larger, pointing it out to a young couple with a pram who were just passing.

'A lot of them about these days,' he said.

'More and more.'

'Better keep an eye on that baby.'

'Eh?'

'They take small animals, you know.'

The man frowned and Fletcher wanted to apologise but didn't. Instead, he smiled. His aunt would be furious. She was the mistress of politeness and cuffed him round the ear if he forgot to say Mr this or Mrs that. She was also the most slanderous bitch he'd ever met. Fletcher watched the couple walking away. Their baby had started screaming and they looked back a few times. He wondered if they were going to Mortensen's party that evening.

* * *

The front door of End Point was wide open. Fletcher walked past at eight and eight thirty. By nine he estimated about twenty people inside. Not enough for decent cover but he decided to go for it. A quick ten minutes, in and out. When he crossed the street and stepped inside it was for the first time in twenty-three years. He stood in the hall, waiting for an emotion that didn't come.

The partygoers were mostly around his age but belonged to a different species. There was no way into their conversations: the bobo-chic housewife,

37

whinnying like a pony about *the unshakeable integrity of Bono*; the technocrat in deck shoes with his *jolly little escape pad in Provence…*

He let himself into only one conversation, with a fat man stuffing his face at the *smorgasbord*.

'Quite a spread, eh?'

'Free food. He lays it on.'

'That's Jonas. A generous guy.'

'He thinks he's some kind of eccentric.'

'How long's he lived here again?'

'Dunno. He just appeared.'

'Interesting guy though.'

'Yeah? Tries a bit hard.'

Fletcher went from room to room. Mortensen was a bushcraft nut, his living room filled with books on tracking, plants and foraging. A delicately carved set of wooden cutlery and a deep bowl edged in neat Celtic loops told him the Norwegian was pretty skilled with a crook knife.

He knew people with similar skills. They all veered to paranoia. Like Spooky Anderson. Anderson ran Ultra Marathons and once on a winter survival exercise sheltered inside a deer carcass. As he watched a pretty, red-haired woman flicking through a box of records Fletcher wondered if, come the End of Days, he'd rather join forces with Spooky or Mortensen.

A few minutes later, he slipped upstairs. The smaller bedroom he used to sleep in was empty, the larger one used by Mortensen. He went into the bathroom and splashed water on his face, listening to the voices drifting up from the back garden through the open window.

The mistake came downstairs. Passing the living room on his way out, he glanced inside. The red-haired woman who'd been flicking through the records was talking to Mortensen. Fletcher hesitated, now wondering

38

if he recognised her. In that moment, Mortensen looked across, a hint of a smile that promised an introduction if Fletcher hung around any longer. As he turned away he bumped into a teenage girl in a blue jacket, a black bow in her hair.

She smiled, such a familiar smile. The party noise became suddenly muddy. That quick-sense of being underwater, sinking deeper. He walked carefully towards the door, an aperture receding the closer he got.

You're running. I watch you. Your family walks behind you. Mother, father and little brother. You let go the hand of your father to run with the kite. The red kite you have pestered him about for so long. Down by the Sangin bazaar is space enough to fly a new kite. Like the little girl with the blue jacket, who also flew a kite, a yellow diamond, soaring above a brown river under a troubled sky, the fabric whipping and twine singing and her own father holding her tight in case she flew up, up and away, into and gone on the winter wind but happy, so happy, it was all so thrilling, like the Wizard of Oz, looking down on the patchwork landscape and all was innocence and wonder and let the wind take her, up and across green fields and grey seas to sink on cooling thermals closer to that other land, the shattered mountains with their ice-cream peaks, sinking to meet you, another little girl, a little girl with a red kite, who watches her drift down to the jigsaw blocks of the desert town, to the bazaar, and even as the noise becomes louder, troubling, all that matters is the kite. You must suspect something, why else are your eyes dropping from sky to earth? You must suspect but still that smile as you absent-mindedly walk towards me, your father shouting as I am too but how can you possibly understand my language, shouting as a black Toyota exits an alleyway in a white flash, spitting gunfire. Still you haven't run and I don't know why, everything is happening too quickly and I have to return fire, I must, and then I notice your kite, a kite just like another's.

Six

Fixation, it was different from obsession. Jonas was obsessed with plants and animals, tracking. It happened over years, the ongoing delight and surprise of a universe still coming into focus. Obsession was just across a hazy psychological line. So although Jonas could recognise badger scat he'd never spent hours staring at it, as Eggers did with Petra from *Eurocamgirls*.

Every lunchtime for weeks, Eggers 4G-logged onto his iPad. The same Russian blonde with a chest as vast as Siberia, toying herself for the skulking voyeurs. Her slack-jawed expression spoke of day to day banalities: what's for dinner, the itch between her sweaty toes.

Eggers didn't seem to mind and Jonas doubted any imminent bombshell awareness of the weirdness of watching live streaming of a Vladivostok sex-show in the middle of an English dual-carriageway at one in the afternoon, a ham sandwich in one hand and pickle on his chin.

'I don't want to listen to this,' said Jonas.

'Then don't.'

'Can you not turn it down?'

'S'not the same.'

'Do you think this is normal behaviour?'

'They say over half of internet traffic is porn. Do you watch porn?'

'No.'

'Then you're the one who's not normal.' He clicked onto another profile. 'What about this one then?'

Jonas sighed and looked. An immediate sizing-up that surprised him with its *insistence*.'Nah.'

'Suit yourself.'

You get used to things. That was the problem. In time, you could get used to anything, as Jonas was now used to Eggers and his lunchtime show. That was different from liking something. Still, on balance, looking at all the different points that Eggers had occupied on Jonas's love-hate spectrum, there were probably more moments of like than dislike.

For a while, Jonas even tried to let Eggers remind him of Kiev Dimitri, sad Dimi of the bottle, whom he met back in 1999 on the Braunfels museum build in Munich. But all Eggers shared with Dimi was functioning alco-holism. Eggers didn't have Dimi's *soul*, a hinterland ever-stretching like the steppes that Jonas learned about on those long beer-garden evenings.

But Eggers did get him the job, kind of. They'd met in the *Lion*, talked a few times, Eggers telling him one evening that the council was hiring. And he trusted Eggers, a man who'd back you up. Like Dimi, that fight with the NPD skinheads when the Ukrainian broke his wrist.

Jonas got out of the truck. They were here to set the site for the night crew. The traffic was restricted to one lane and thirty mph, but everyone flew past at sixty or crawled by at twenty. One extreme or the other, fixation or indif-ference, speed or slowness. The entire world was bipolar. There had once been a more measured time in his life. Back then the intervention of a man he *kind of liked* to defuse a *Jonsok* party incident would never have happened.

It was Dave. Jonas's new friend Dave from *The Hand and Shears*. Dave went from sober to stagger-drunk without passing go. By ten o'clock he had poured a can of Ringnes on the bonfire because it *tastes like piss*, by eleven he was shouting about *fuckin fish*, and by midnight he had pinned the Good Host against the kitchen wall for reasons no one could interpret.

Jonas brushed it off as the price of party success. More people filled with booze meant more chance of a gibbering maniac.

Enter the Eggers, an intervention as decisive as Jonas's goodwill was naive. He dragged Dave off, who left without a word after a final stare-down. Smiling Jonas watched him go, ignorant of the relief of those onlookers who knew that Dave was a feral swine who'd done time for ABH a few years back. All Jonas saw reflected in that savage face was his own good nature. Here was another Big Haakon, he'd be round to apologise soon enough.

Like after the Garden Incident. Jonas closed his eyes, the beat of traffic becoming memory's pulse.

He was thirteen, coming back from football practice one evening, the whole team straggling along. They reached his house to find Haakon and his father in the front garden. Big Haakon was laughing, holding his father by the head at arm's length, his father's arms frantically windmilling. As bizarre as it was humiliating, a devastating moment in young Jonas's life.

For the week he needed to bunk off school to brace for the taunts, Jonas wondered how an accountant and street-sweeper had become entangled. He never found out. Maybe there was no reason. Sometimes the world just happened. Like his hard-on when he saw Anja Petterson.

Two days after the Garden Incident Haakon had apologised. Came round with a side of smoked salmon for his father and flowers for his mother. Later, when Jonas got to know him properly, Haakon would regularly apologise to Jonas too, no matter how many times he told him to stop going on about it. Yep, Big Haakon alienated most people at one time or another but always apologised. Maybe it was inevitable that when Jonas saw him that last time, years later, Haakon of the Never-Empty Bottle had been *Born Again*, Haakon of the Cross.

And as with Haakon so with Psycho Dave from *The Hand and Shears*. Eggers begged to differ with disbelief verging on slapstick when Jonas assured him that Dave would be round soon enough to say sorry.

'Jonas!' Eggers was leaning out of the cab.

'What?'

'You gotta see this.'

'No I don't.'

'She's gonna knock herself out with all this jiggling!'

'Amazing.'

'It *is* amazing. A marvel of engineering. You should appreciate the skill.'

He left behind Eggers's grinning face and walked down the central reservation into petrol fug.

The patterns of place, once established they were locked in. Pervy Eggers, Psycho Dave, Haakon of the Never-Empty Bottle. And Jonas the Viking. If no one wants you to be someone different then let what you are be *good*. Redemption was the prerogative of the sceptic.

Big Haakon knew all about it. The man who every year got butt-naked and danced round the bursting barrels of the midsummer bonfires. It would suddenly come over him, a wild look in the puffy eyes and off with the clothes. Perhaps it was resignation to the role that made him do it, the realisation that no one would ever accept what Jonas came to know.

He and Axel were twelve. They'd been given permission to get the bus to Stavern and walk the coast, two nights camped out then home. Little parental persuasion was required, it being a more innocent time, perhaps, before we all became potential mugshots in a tabloid newspaper. They bought ice cream, made a

43

den in the woods and fished around on the shore. That first afternoon they drowsed to the sea, Jonas twirling a long-stemmed plant with a pinkish head.

'Armeria,' said a booming voice.

'*Jesus!*'

They turned to see Big Haakon and scrambled to their feet, ready to run. Haakon was a nutter. Always on the booze. He'd beat up Jonas's dad and they'd *watched it happen*.

'A herbaceous perennial. Also known as Sea Pink.'

Thirty plus years later Jonas was still certain this is what Big Haakon said, the memory so vivid for being so unexpected. No need for any embellishment. Haakon took the flower, holding it up to the sun with an almost mawkish look of unfiltered delight. 'You shouldn't pick wild flowers boys, everything has a place and you should let well alone. You listening?'

Vigorous nods.

'You want to know about flowers?'

More nods.

Big Haakon didn't just tell them about the plants. He introduced them to wild food: sea moss and kelp, cockles and limpets. He yelped with glee when he came across a huge colony of winkles, big scary Haakon, the village idiot, Haakon of the Five-Times Broken Nose, yelping like an excited little girl. He sent them for fresh water so he could soak the grit from the shellfish.

'Well, boys, are you ready to learn man's fundamental skill, the skill that made society possible?'

Jonas had never seen a fire-drill in action. It was like coming across an ancient secret. As Haakon made them a dinner of dulse and mussels, Jonas and Axel tried and failed to even keep the spindle in the hearth, never mind catch an ember.

'You'll get it, boys. Nothing special, in the end.'

Those days in Stavern were an epiphany. A vast

44

landscape had opened up and Jonas came home flushed with the excitement of a new knowledge of which his parents were utterly dismissive. They had no idea about Haakon's skills. Didn't trust them. Didn't *believe* them.

He and Axel would go round to Big Haakon's ramshackle house on the edge of town in secret. They listened to him talk about stepping back and tuning in, to the turns of seasons, the weather, all the other myriad details of your particular place in space. They went on plant walks. They learned how to use a crook knife and how to tie a dozen different knots.

They also knew when not to go. When the fairground-lit windows were dark Haakon would be inaccessible, on a bender, roaming his rooms like a big cat. And they discovered Haakon's heartbreak, the girlfriend who drowned one sunny afternoon, waved and drowned. So Jonas learned that everyone had a hinterland, places others could not enter and explanations they would not offer.

A horn suddenly blasted. Jonas became aware of the traffic again. Two thirty in the afternoon and already nose to tail. He scanned the line of cars, back down the road, towards the big intersection where he'd already spent lifetimes, stuck in the rush hour. Always that hopelessness, the world burning as we stare at the flames from our air-conditioned boxes, buy a couple of eco bulbs and re-use a plastic bag. Maybe the kids from The Hub would figure it out.

And maybe to them he would be more than *the Viking*. How about Jonas of the Plants? Haakon would approve. He put out the *Men at Work* sign and watched the drivers watching him.

Seven

Fletcher's mind was a dilapidated place. He thought of it like a ruined old house, ill-lit and full of randomly ripped-up floorboards to fall through. But if you knew you were going to plunge into a hole then you were always braced for the fall. You became skilled at climbing out again.

And you got better, as he had, at managing anomalies. Like this Norwegian, Jonas Mortensen.

Among the theories of the counsellors, their favourite was cognitive dissonance. They went on and on about it. *It's the discomfort experienced when simultaneously holding two or more conflicting ideas or emotions.* He'd dumbly nodded, squirming in the leather chair in the hot consulting room. Later that day he looked the theory up on *Wikipedia* and read the same phrase almost word for word. That was when he stopped taking the counsellors seriously and started giving some extremely dissonant answers to some of their questions.

This morning's anomaly chittered in with a helicopter. It was too high for him to be sure but possibly a Merlin, heading to the nearby RAF base. Even before his heartbeat quickened and the sweat prickled he was back there, hanging out of a Lynx, sweeping low over the plains.

Helmand, when the sunset flared it was red as Mars, so devoid of life that the farmers and mud huts flashing beneath the chopper might be a mirage. Other times the sudden and vivid swathes of colour were breathtaking, as if a painter had tired of grey-browns and slipped in some trees and fields, poppies of course, the Lynx causing waves in the chest-high blooms of white and pink, the stream of Marines moving cautiously, SA80s drawn.

The images faded as the rotor-noise passed. Helmand grew fainter and Fletcher heard again the river boats, the crickets. Afghanistan could not be more insanely different than this ruined crazy golf course. The near absolute contrast briefly threatened to overwhelm him, the ripped green Astroturf of the fairways, the paint-peeling windmills and the mini medieval castle so disconcerting that Fletcher had to close his eyes and start the count-back.

He held his equilibrium, as he had been told. *Work on your equilibrium*, the same patient voice that told him his free sessions were over and he would now have to pay for anymore.

A few moments later Fletcher returned fully to the present. He was sitting inside the big fibreglass Skull. Through an eye socket he could see the beer-can-strewn fairway. Hole thirteen was a challenge. You had to navigate the ball between the tombstones of a mini cemetery then up a steep incline into the mouth of The Skull. Inside, there was room for his bed roll.

In some ways Fletcher liked it here. There was no chance of some drunken bastard waking him up by pissing on his face. Still, he'd come home to sleep in a bed, not a bizarre, giant skull in an abandoned crazy golf course. He remembered it being built just before he had to leave, part of the grand stoner folly of some Home Counties trustafarian to create a seaside-type attraction by the river. There would be camping and kayaking, slot machines and burgers, as well as *Britain's biggest, FUNNEST Crazy Golf Course!* Fletcher had found the sign lying face down in the dried-up moat around hole six, as the entire project had fallen flat.

Beyond the sagging security fence thirty metres away someone walked a dog along the river path. It was just after seven, the kids wouldn't be streaming past to the river pools for hours. When the dog walker disappeared from sight Fletcher slipped out of The Skull. The Norwegian would be away from End Point from seven thirty until four thirty. Fletcher knew this from the shift rota on the fridge which he'd read at Mortensen's party the other night.

The Norwegian was clearly the welcoming sort. It was inevitable that the side gate to the back garden would be unlocked. Fletcher walked through. He was wearing a high-vis jacket and high-vis jackets made people invisible. He was slightly surprised that the sun room was locked. This wasn't a problem. It took less than a minute to pick the lock. Inside, he made a coffee and a cheese sandwich, wandering the rooms with a reaction that swiftly replaced any maudlin sentiment about *the return* with the purely functional: how to get the Norwegian out of this fuckin house. He flicked through Mortensen's books and records then sat on the sun room steps, looking out on the lawn, the bonfire scar that reminded him of ordnance scorch.

Later, he decided to have a bath. As it was running he looked in the bathroom cabinet and found some little bottles of oils. Never in his life had he used bath oils. The idea amused him. He chose one at random, sprinkled a few drops and lay in the water sniffing, trying to decide if he liked the smell. Later, stepping out the back door as Jonas stepped in the front, he decided he didn't.

Eight

'Darling, I'm home!'

The one-eyed doll looked up at Jonas from the hallway table and said nothing. It looked quite serene. Yesterday so angry and today so calm. The doll was clearly a bit high-maintenance.

'Had a good day then, my –?'

Jasmine?

An unmistakeable hint. Jonas put the mail down on the table and listened intently. Then he walked through to the kitchen and saw a half-eaten cheese sandwich on a plate beside the kettle. And an empty mug. Coffee. The mug was still warm. Wake up and smell the coffee.

He hesitated at the foot of the stairs then took them at a run. A second towel was draped over the landing banister, the airing cupboard door open. The jasmine smell was stronger in the bathroom. Water spray in the bath. He backed out, hesitating again as he considered his bedroom door before cutting off the cascade of possibilities by flinging it open. But there was no one sleeping in his bed. And no one hiding under it either. Jonas checked.

Insidious. Jonas rolled the word round his tongue. *In-sid-ee-us*. He sat on a deckchair in the back garden, facing the house. The drink in his hand was hefty, a big Highland Park. End Point gawked back and a crow scrawked. He looked around but couldn't see it, suddenly wondering if anyone was watching him from all these black-eyed windows overlooking the garden.

Maybe just one of The Hub boys, messing with him. Jonas had done it himself. He and Axel once broke into Siggi's house when he was on holiday. Siggi claimed his father had a great collection of girly mags but they turned that house upside down looking for them and found nada, settling for a video of *National Lampoon's Animal House* and handfuls of corn flakes thrown around the living room, their contribution to the food fight started by John Belushi.

Or maybe Spencer P, Lacey's boyfriend. Jonas didn't like the way that little shit looked at him. He could have put Lacey up to it, she and her friend Carly, messing about all soapy and bubbly. It was cheeky but almost proprietorial; you break in, make a snack and have a bath.

The whisky did its job. The second had him laughing, the third leaping behind every door and opening every cupboard with a Miss-Piggy-like *high-YAH*, chopping his hand down like Inspector Clouseau going after Cato. *I am a very philosophical man,* he told the one-eyed doll. Just one of those things, a kink in the space-time fabric, as if some poor bugger in a parallel universe made himself a sandwich, walked out of his kitchen and found himself in End Point.

It was a possibility, certainly, however unlikely and infinitesimally small. Quantum scientists would back him up. In an infinity of universes everything possible was happening. Somewhere light years away, right at this very moment, Jonas wasn't sitting down in the back garden with a bag of foraged elderflowers and beginning the job of separating them from their stems but was instead watching a hamster in a top hat and tails do a merry little dance.

50

Jasmine, though. Why out of all the oils did the mystery bather have to choose that one?

★ ★ ★

'What would *you* do about it?'

Eggers narrowed his eyes. 'You're serious?'

'Yes!'

'You haven't been drinking?'

'Well, I have been drinking but I wasn't been drinking then.'

'Hadn't been.'

'What?'

'You *hadn't* been drinking.'

'I know.'

'I mean the sentence, you don't say it like... oh never – '

'Gentlemen, *would* you be so kind?'

Jonas raised a placatory hand. No one did sanctimony like Granny Hawthorne. She chaired the Village Hall Committee like a Nuremberg judge. Jonas and Eggers had been at the meeting for half an hour, waiting to present the annual reports of the Sports Club and The Hub.

'She should crack her face, make her arse jealous,' whispered Eggers. 'You better change the locks?'

'Too expensive.'

'Get a baseball bat then. You don't want to wake up and find some psycho in a hockey mask standing over you. You don't read the papers but I do. Bad shit has to happen to someone.'

'Would a maniac put jasmine oil in his bath?'

'Jasmine?'

'Jasmine.'

'You some kind of bufty?'

'A what?'

'Never mind. Hey, maybe it was a *woman*.'

'Gentlemen!' Mrs Hawthorne peered over her glasses. 'Given that the two of you have something terribly important to discuss, shall I suggest we move your items up the agenda?'

Eggers galloped through his report. A quick clap on Jonas's shoulder and *I'll see you in The Lion.*

Then Jonas. He reported on auto-pilot. The whisky had left his mouth dry. The committee made him think of zombies and he tried not to look at them, wondering if any of them had recently bathed. He watched himself, his hands with a life of their own, oddly flailing, thoughts taking him here, there and finally settling on the first time he smelled jasmine. Eva's perfume. *Some people don't like it,* she said. Jonas did. It was a scent that would tell him she was here and tell him she had gone: a wet Bergen night, the sharp smell of petrol, and jasmine.

'Any questions for Mr Mortensen?'

Jonas sank into the silence of the unasked questions. As if he was actually melting, the day's sun having super-heated the hall. This is what it would feel like to be baked alive, swelling fingers, a rising whine in your ears as the blood boils, your face reddening, *reddening,* eyes popping out one by one, plop, plop. His watch said eight twenty. Only agenda item eleven out of twenty-four. The meeting would go on for at least another hour. He could stay.

Killing time.

He didn't fancy a night in *The Black Lion's* beer garden and didn't want to go back to the scent of jasmine. The five whiskies had finally counted back to zero and the outriders of his hangover were closing fast, a sickly promise of desolation that Jonas refused. He'd face the house. Maybe drag his bed across to block the bedroom door. Buy a couple of bolts in the morning.

The chair scraped as he got up to leave. Mrs Hawthorne scowled. If she said anything he might just burst into tears. But despondency made no sense on an evening like this, the summer air too soft and scent-heady with honeysuckle, primrose, gardenia... There may be someone in the village who was a lover of jasmine, whose eyes would light up if Jonas happened to mention it, perhaps the woman who had just turned the corner at the bottom of Faraday Street and was walking slowly towards him. For a moment Jonas thought he recognised Mary, she of the auburn hair, the LPs and the *blues*. But it wasn't her. He felt a quick rising disappointment and closed his eyes, briefly, to the sad, enigmatic smile of his dead wife.

Nine

Mary leaned against the door, drinking coffee and watching her husband. He'd given her the mug. *Keep Calm and Conquer On.* Of the billions of *Keep Calm* messages out there he chose that one. In the utility room directly underneath, the terminally ill washing machine moved up a gear.

She wondered if the choice of mug had been a random choice, or if her husband was making some obliquely sarcastic point. There was something about that underline, something to fret about as he lay naked on the bed like a broken starfish, arc-lit by the morning sun.

But he was as straightforward as he was naked. She relaxed the longer she stared, the belly heaving, slowly up and down. Straining, even, like it might suddenly burst. She imagined what it would be like to watch him explode. Right in front of her. Right now. Her feelings were mixed, she decided. Not that she wished her husband any harm. That would be going too far.

He was still ok to look at. The belly might have got him and the bugle long-sounded the hairline retreat but enough remained of the man she'd married. And hallelujah, the cock was still holding up. When the flames died down a big cock was the log that kept on burning. Briefly, she considered going over there and waking it up. But waking it meant waking him.

All of this begged the question of what she was doing staring at him. This was WMT, Weekend Mary

Time, she actually called it that, even if it sounded like a coping mechanism you'd read about in one of those lifestyle magazines. *Whatever you do, always find... time... for... YOU.*

She liked WMT. Saturday and Sunday, six till about ten, when her husband got up, a quiet space she'd filled over time with things he knew nothing about. The space was quite full now. She saw it as a cluttered old attic, dust angling through sunlight. Not so much physical entities as thoughts and considerations, dialogues she had only with herself. While he would understand some things, most he wouldn't, like her decision to volunteer at The Hub.

He rolled over and revealed a big hairy arse. Mary took the cue to leave and, as so often, found herself in her daughter Andrea's old bedroom. These visits were something else he laughed at, although an amused impatience was closer to the mark. *She's not gonna appear out of thin air!* Mary knew that, of course she did. But that was what daydreams were for.

The dressing gown fell open as she walked down the stairs. She did yoga twice a week and started running three years ago, when Andrea was competing in schools' championships. It was a decent body, she reckoned, not bad at all. The challenge would be maintaining what she could for as long as she could. She wondered what her husband would think if he could see her, standing in front of the hallway mirror, stroking her breasts, her pussy.

Pussy. She hated the word and pulled the dressing gown tightly back round her. In any case, she was getting old. There were a few grey hairs down there. *Look at that saggy old minge*, that's what her husband would say. Her irritation was sudden and physical, a prickle down the back, tightness in the stomach. She hurried back up to Andrea's room and sat on the bed. He wouldn't say another word if their daughter *did* suddenly appear, rising from the whine of the washing machine and the dazzling sun: nine years old, mousy blonde hair down to her waist, those delicate few months when she hovered so perfectly between innocence and precocious sophistication.

Then came the banging on the wall from next door. Old Mrs Cole with her walking stick. Mary fell back, eyes tight shut and fists gripping the duvet. If half her life was steeped in cliché then the other half seemed lost to irrelevance. She listened to the decrepit washing machine get louder and louder until she could be screaming and screaming but no one listening.

Ten

Spencer P.

Jonas really didn't like that kid. A few words were all it took for Spencer P to switch back on the break-in speculation that Jonas had finally managed to switch off. A draughtsman with no confidence, that was him, drawing a line, rubbing it out, drawing another...

He'd been standing in the Post Office queue, staring into empty space after a day on the potholes.

'You shouldn't do that, bro.'

Spencer P was suddenly beside him. Mocking eyes and a vague leer. He had a soul patch and three diamond studs in his left ear. A wannabe pimp but the accent more Sloane than South Central.

'Sorry?'

'The *magazines*, Mr M.'

He followed his gaze to the newspaper racks.

'All that trauma. All those poor people. Those victims. You never know when it's going to be you, eh?'

Spencer P picked up a magazine, *Break Time*. Beside it were several others, similar titles, smiling, pretty women but jarring, make-you-frown headlines. *Blind girl kept as sex slave... I changed the locks but was stabbed again... Stiletto psycho...* 'You shouldn't read that rubbish.'

'I wasn't.'

'It's well screwed up. Get this, right.' And Spencer P began telling a graphic story of a home invasion he said was true but must be made up and if made up then

Spencer P was messed up. 'It went on for *three days, man,* they must have been enjoying it, the husband made to watch everything and the kids tied up. They were never caught, Mr M. Can you imagine that happening to you? What do they say at the end of *Crimewatch?* "Don't have nightmares".'

With that Spencer P was gone. Had the kid just happened to glance in and see Jonas or had he followed him there? Was that story *rehearsed?* Jonas looked back at the magazines. As the queue shuffled he found himself picking up copies of *True Life* and *Sensational.*

Killed for thrills…

Home is where the death is…

Sensationalised tears in the fabric of normality. Off-kilter incidents, one of which had now happened to Jonas. *The Jasmine-Scented Intruder.* Hardly a howitzer of weirdness but strange enough to crank the heart rate as he opened the front door of End Point. This time three whiskies made it seem unnerving rather than amusing. That night he read the magazines from cover to cover and checked the windows and doors twice before going to bed. He fell asleep to images of Spencer P, wallowing in a steaming bath. That smug little smile.

His mental state improved with sleep and regressed with breakfast. He was drinking green tea in the sun room, taking in the day, the peace, the new addition to the collection of pot pants and herbs on the window sill. A straggly shrub with lots of six-petalled flowers, like little white starfish.

Jasmine.

Know the plants, it's what he told the kids.

On Tuesday afternoon, he got back from work and found an Amazon package waiting with the mail. A DVD of *Aladdin.* The back cover told him that Aladdin's girlfriend was called Jasmine. Again, he saw Spencer

P's smug face, spluttering now as he throttled the little bastard.

Then Eggers appeared earlier than usual on Thursday to pick him up. He left him in the kitchen and went for a shower, a sudden suspicion making him creep downstairs. A cupboard door was open. Behind it was Eggers, rubbing a particularly scented hand cream around the rims of his mugs.

'You swine. I've been freaking out! I thought it was Spencer P.'

'Spencer? Why would it be him? And why do you call him Spencer P? He's not a fuckin *rapper*.'

Thursday they finished early, Boss Hogg with a mysterious *appointment* that Eggers knew all about, damn straight, a girl named Sue and a husband far away. They stayed in town, a few beers in the park. It was Jonas's idea to hire a boat at the lake, working the oars as Eggers worked the Stella: six cans in forty-five minutes. He fell asleep with his head on the stern.

Jonas paddled quietly to shore, removed the oars and gently pushed the boat back out.

'You fucker!'

'Swim for it.'

'Sod off!'

'Nice day for a swim.'

'*Jonas.*'

'Did you break into my house and have a bath?'

'You on about that again?'

'I can leave or I can come and tow you in. Easy is.'

'Easy AS, you knob!'

'That's hardly the attitude.'

'Look. I didn't break into your house and have a *bath*. Are you insane? Why would *anyone* do that?'

That night Jonas dreamt of boats. These dreams that came in cycles, a psychic turning every six months or so. Tonight there was no rabbit and no child. But still blood. There was always blood.

He was crouched on the shore of a vast sea, scrubbing his sticky red hands. Eggers rowed back and forth, shouting *come and join me, Jonas*. Big Haakon appeared in a deerskin coracle. Then Axel in a dinghy, someone new each time he looked: family and school friends, teaching colleagues, all in different vessels, canoes and skiffs, tug boats, all shouting *come and join me, Jonas*. He shook his head, shouting that he couldn't, he had to clean his hands.

And then Mary. A gondola parting the throng, beckoning to him. Jonas smiled and the blood was gone. A rowing boat materialised but before he could push it out a storm blew up, obscuring everyone. The last thing he saw was the Hirtshals night ferry, Eva and Anya.

He woke late, just after seven. Outside, Eggers was blasting the horn, shattering the last dream-image. Mary, beckoning him. He felt an old, old sensation and stepped into the day.

'You pulling your pud in there?'

'I did dream about you last night.'

Eggers gunned the van and smirked. 'Wet dream, eh?'

'Wet as your boots.'

The smirk vanished. Eggers slammed the gear into second. He was wearing an old pair of boots. Why he waded to the lakeside without taking off his boots remained a mystery.

Eggers said nothing for the rest of the drive to the ring road. In the silence, Jonas thought about boats; the Skagerrak trawlers and the weekend dinghies, the big boys permitted by parents to cast darrows for the mackerel, far out in their rowing boats and Jonas so envious.

The job pressed. Flashbacks in the heat. Naples. Summer of '02, working the roads for the mafia gangs. A similar

60

clinging dust, jackhammers still ringing as he tried to sleep in that broiling shack. And the Italians were always pissed off about something. The English were much quieter.

Apart from Boss Hogg. A big-bellied cowboy in a white hard hat. *Move your delicate arse and move it now*, back into that hard sun, the ring road a tightening noose and the traffic stunning. In Norway you could drive miles without meeting another car. Here, the busier the road the faster the drivers, hair trigger primed when forced to slow down. Jonas couldn't imagine a Norwegian opening a conversation with an account of the route taken and why, the other options, that swine of a junction twelve bottleneck. All these lives boxed in hot metal.

He stuck to boats. Canal barges on the heat-hazed river that curved under the road bridge, half a mile downhill from the fix site. A rhythm locked on, a shovel of tar and a glance at the river, the hard sun glinting, broken, white mirrors on the black roofs of the moored boats.

He had lunch down there. Slumber-time by the moving stillness, feet in the water and eyes closed. When he opened them years had passed, a rowing boat on the far bank and two kids dangling bow lines. Let's call them Jonas and Axel. Big Haakon keeping a wary eye, a benevolent giant.

Haakon was the first to take them out on the water, Jonas's dad interested only in his golf handicap and Axel's in the ice hockey he excelled at before the booze. They once tried to settle on one word that summed up what their fathers thought of them. It took a while.

Bothersome.

Haakon taught them about fishing with the same easy patience he taught them about plants and trees. Simple things like telling a mackerel from a herring by the patterns on their backs, hookless techniques like worm-blobs for catching eels, more scientific stuff like image refraction. *Always kneel when you're fishing. Remember to keep your shadow off the water.*

Axel chose Big Haakon's rowing boat as the getaway vessel when he ran away. Haakon said nothing but knew he was camping wild on the forested island on the other side of the point.

Aegir's Isle. They named it after the Norse god of the sea. For three nights Jonas sneaked out, Axel rowing across to get him. They sat by the fire, eating tinned sardines and honing the design of the hut that would let them live there permanently. It was easy to believe, back then, that freedom was as simple as choosing it. No one had told them about dreams, all those faces, like a series of last visits and who knows when the Big Black would finally fall.

A coot shrieked. Jonas flinched and watched the moorhen flee. The rowing boat boys pulled up their lines. Two crayfish they smashed on the gunwale. He couldn't hold back the traffic, the noose, tighter and louder. He heard the storm and saw the night ferry again, Larvik to Hirtshals, Eva and Anya and a hollowness in his gut. The sun dimmed and he shivered.

It was unsettling how something which never happened somehow persisted as dark patches on memory's big canvas, so that nothing remembered was certain, not even the jewels hidden away and protected so closely.

'Bergen?'

'Yes,' said Jonas.

'I remember Bergen.'

'It must have been different then.'

'Who knows, I've never been back. Might not have

changed a bit. Those houses by the harbour, ancient they were. Maybe the place hasn't changed in hundreds of years. Certainly seemed like that when the night-lights were on. Reflections on the water. Nothing like it, Jonas.'

'I remember it well.'

'If you remember it then what are you doing here?'

'I could ask the same.'

But Jonas never did. To know the end of the story was to end its telling, and the telling was the reason he sought out old Sam tonight as on so many others. Sam meant Bergen.

Again, Jonas let Sam's story lull and take him, until somehow it could be his own and then was.

'I had a woman there.'

'There's always a woman.'

'Blonde hair. Right down her back. I had two nights there while the boat was loaded, some fleapit up by the cathedral.'

'St. Olav's.'

'That's the one. She worked in a bar.'

Logen's, Jonas remembered.

'She was... passionate, I tell you that.'

'That's Norwegians for you!'

'Yeah. You Norwegians, you're so passionate, eh?'

A slicing voice. Jonas looked up into the red face and buzz-cut hair of someone he didn't know.

'Come again?'

'Exactly! *Sex*, s'all you think about.'

Buzz Cut's fat friend started giggling, an odd nasal snuffle, eyes tight shut with cartoon lines.

'Come on now, John,' said Sam. 'Let Jonas be.'

Buzz Cut put an arm round the old man's shoulders. 'No worries, just having a laugh with the Viking.'

He popped a cigarette into his mouth and grinned. Jonas watched him walk away. He didn't know this person. That licence to condescend to a stranger, where do you apply for it?

Sam too watched Buzz Cut but didn't see him, his gaze stalled somewhere in the middle distance. 'I was going to stay there, you know. Do something or other. But I didn't. You know the damnedest thing? I can't even remember her name. I can't see her face, can't *see* it.'

He *expected*, did Jonas. Likely, he expected too much, but rather expect and be disappointed than doubt and be cynical. But even Jonas did not expect old Sam. The first time he heard this story was in *The Lion*, a few weeks after he moved to the village. Standing at the bar ordering a beer. Sam leaned in and asked in Swedish what his name was. Jonas's mouth did the cartoon drop. In English, he replied that he was Norwegian and nearly fell over when the question was repeated in his own language. Old Sam explained that he'd sailed the Newcastle-Bergen route for over thirty years. Merchant Navy, engineer second class.

The old man knew: the steep cobbles and fussy window boxes of Nordnes; the phosphorescent winter glow of those white-panelled houses; the mist on Mt Fløyen as ethereal as a Japanese landscape. And Jonas knew Sam's lost woman too, the barmaid with the blonde hair and the way she turned and winked and, quick-shifting, became his wife, Eva, and every time a different moment and now that evening of the REM tribute band and afterwards a bottle of wine in Byparken and singing *Man on the Moon* as the man himself looks down from his full whiteness in the east and *yes, I see him, Jonas, I've never noticed him before...*

'You should have got married, Jonas.'

'It never happened for me.'

The old man suspected, of course. He tapped Jonas on the hand. 'There's time for everything.'

It troubled him, the way Eva had retreated to the

edge of the light. Once upon a more fragile time he dreamed of her every night. Yet now it sometimes felt he had to remember to remember. Where there was presence there was still existence. Something like that.

'Are you a dreaming man?'

'Haven't had a dream in years,' said Sam.

'Think they mean anything?'

'They can mean whatever you bloody well please. No point in worrying about the damn things.'

Jonas downed the last of his pint. His mother flashed across his mind; *if you keep worrying like that your head will fall off.* Seven years old, this had, of course, worried him even more.

He ordered two more beers and leaned on the bar. Buzz Cut fixed a stare, OTT and making Jonas *giggle*, a little boy's laugh lost in the shouts from the pool table and the sudden laughter, the undulating rush of the football crowd on the TV. Meaning meant nothing in this hubbub. He liked the word hubbub. And skewed by a booze-marched goodwill, he gave in to the moment and bought a couple of brandies. *Carpe diem* and all that crap.

'Your good health.'

'*Skål*,' said Sam. 'What are we toasting?'

'The present.'

'To the present!'

And Jonas walked again with old Sam through the streets of Bergen, arm in arm with Eva and their daughter in tow. There were boats in the harbour, modern cruisers and dark-wood yachts, the kind they promised themselves when they retired. Cruel whalers too, readying for the north Atlantic. Anya once asked about them and cried when he explained. *Why do they do that, daddy?* Another one who sought meaning, poor thing, another who'd see whatever she wanted in a silly dream about lots of boats, whatever she damn well pleased.

'I meant to ask, Jonas. Did you see that news story about the Norwegian who always takes a ladder to the supermarket?'

'Can't say I did.'

'It's because the food prices are really high.'

Jonas was confused. Then he got it. Sam was laughing, he laughed with his whole body, shoulders shunting up and down, an old locomotive picking up speed. That set Jonas off and people were looking and smiling and all was *good*. When he opened his eyes again, she was there.

Eleven

It was a spur of the moment decision. Mary didn't make these too often and wouldn't be making another anytime soon. Jonas started laughing just as she reached the table and for a paranoid moment she thought he was laughing at her. She stood awkwardly, there for the world to see in her supermarket uniform with the misspelt name badge (Marie). She smiled nervously when he finally noticed her, a smile becoming a rictus as the look in his eyes veered from surprise to panic. Somebody else laughed then. And this time it probably was directed at her.

That morning Mary ran her standard 10k. Down the old main road to the small industrial estate by the dual carriageway, turning and retracing her steps, back through the village and out west.

She liked the quiet of the single-track, the view of rooftops and church spire when she turned again at the new housing development. Another kilometre and she upped the pace, driving the arms. She needed to properly sweat, feel it running down her neck and back, soaking her Lycra top. Again she stepped up the pace and felt like she could run all day, day into night and why not, far into the blue-black distance, smooth as a stone across a lake.

The Post Office marked the 10k. Forty-six minutes. Not too shabby but a minute off her best. She'd kicked too soon and paid the price. She stretched as she caught her breath, held the back of each foot and stretched the thighs, reading the small ads in the Post Office window.

Cleaner wanted. Call Jonas on 07871 399747.

Mary remembered and cringed. *You've got a lot of blues, Jonas.* An overt flirt if ever there was. Bad Mary, it couldn't have been more obvious if she'd stuck her bum out and peered over her shoulder, finger to her pouting mouth. She blamed the wine. And it wasn't as if she even fancied him. He was just a nice, generous man, a bit eccentric but genuinely *nice*.

These basic traits extracted, Mary had filed him away under *like*. She'd done this forever, with everyone she met, long before Facebook made a fetish out of arbitrary judgement.

The lack of consistency in her criteria didn't bother her. Facebook was right, it was a gut thing. It had been the same at the supermarket. In three months of working there she'd got to know Daisy, Meg and Debbie. Daisy and Meg she didn't like, for no particular reason, she just didn't. So they only got small-talk. Lucky Debbie, on the other hand, she did like, which meant Mary occasionally shared more personal confidences, little hints, but only hints.

She laughed and a passing group of school-kids sniggered. Over-analysing, it was a bloody illness. Mary jogged home and made an omelette (whites only) while her husband assembled his own breakfast (big and fried). He and his big belly held court, telling her that he didn't need to flap around the streets like Paula bloody Radcliffe because the doctor had told him his BP was normal, cholesterol fine and if he had his liver checked that'd be just fine too.

'When did you go to the doctor?'

'I had that mole.'

'That was years ago!'

'Yeah, well.'

'Well, what?'

'Well, I'm just the *same*.'

She rolled her eyes, knew she was doing it but kept on. Her husband, in turn, rolled his.

As she stared into space, she found herself wondering what Jonas ate for breakfast. If he too had just carefully constructed a sandwich of bacon, sausage and egg, slathered in brown sauce, then any comparison with her husband edged towards one of like with like and a disappointed anti-climax. If, on the other hand, he was eating something different, like a grapefruit, or porridge, then she was looking at a different kind of comparison altogether.

That got her thinking about the advert. Her husband was wiping brown sauce from his chin.

And so, hours later, Mary was standing in front of Jonas in *The Black Lion* in her supermarket uniform. He seemed nervous and that made her even more self-conscious. The awkwardness continued as they silently watched Old Sam shuffle across to the toilets. Jonas invited her to sit down and for a moment she thought about asking him what he ate for breakfast.

'Do you have any... experience,' he said.

'Of cleaning?'

'Yes.'

'My own or others?'

'Eh?'

'Twenty-two years a wife.' She blushed when she said it. *Wife*, as if she had to make that fact clear.

'I see. And what... attracts you to the job?'

'Are you *serious*?'

Jonas visibly relaxed, shaking his head and smiling. 'You're right. I don't have a clue about all this.'

Twelve

Fletcher sat in the over-hot confessional. An unusual tang clung to the air, old sweat mixed with something else, sour yet floral. Is this the smell of sin? He should ask the priest on the other side of the mesh. The man was irritating him, a reedy wheedle of a voice that set his teeth on edge. But the irritation was more than offset by the thought of his aunt's abject horror at him sitting where he was. She said Catholics had *killed God*. Quite the claim, but that was his aunt.

The priest droned on, the head bowed, now and then a question, a full-face glimpse as he turned to wait for the response. The grave, over-studied demeanour jarred with the spouted inanities and Fletcher's anger was sudden, familiar. He wondered what it would be like to stab the priest in the eye, through the mesh.

'Thank you, Father.'

'There's no need to call me Father.'

'Why not?'

'There's just no need.'

Fletcher left the confessional and crossed to the main door of the church. He let it squeak open and shut but stayed inside. The confessional opened a few moments later. The priest appeared, stretching his arms and yawning, a shake of the head and a vague little smile. Then he noticed Fletcher and froze, arms still outstretched. Fletcher stared at him then left.

During one session the shrink asked about religion. If

Fletcher believed, it might help, they said. A crutch they called it, emotional or spiritual. He wanted to laugh, tell them they were a bunch of fuckin dilettantes if they thought belief was auxiliary to self. He'd been on tour in Iraq and Afghanistan and had seen the astonishing absolutism of faith inhabited, not worn.

Faith was dead, he told the counsellor. It was lying in the dirt of Sangin beside the dying Afghan girl, his dead sister's doppelganger. Only morons and liars had faith, hoodwinked kids yet to realise. He'd seen them streaming into church on Sunday mornings, poor buggers. The village was full of kids, more than Fletcher remembered from his own childhood. Youths, as they were now called. *Youths hanging around. Youths with no respect. Not like it was in my day.*

Somewhere among all these kids was the girl in the blue jacket from Jonas's party. There had been nothing in her face. But the jacket: his sister had been wearing one just like it. He had to find her, see her again, remove these irrational anxieties about ghosts and retribution.

On cue, a group of children passed him. He watched them head down Mandeville Alley then followed. Three girls and a boy, twelve years old or so, the boy in a hooded top and baseball cap, the girls in long tops and cute leggings. They turned into the park, dawdled for a bit then sat on the grass. Only then did Fletcher come to a fuller awareness of what he was doing. But no one does oblivious quite like kids, not even a glance as he walked past and stared.

The girl in the blue jacket wasn't there. There were other options. Fletcher had seen a notice-board poster about a youth club, The Hub.

His aunt never let him go to the village youth club when he was a boy. *I don't want you hanging around with all those uncouth boys*. But Fletcher didn't know what uncouth meant and the only activity he was allowed was Reverend Jenkins's Bible Study, Tuesday night. They held it in the church where it was always freezing. A coldness to complement the reverend's character.

When Fletcher said he was afraid he might kill someone and sometimes even wanted to the priest had just sighed, sighed then chuckled, a world-weary optimist in his fool's paradise. *Relax and have a conversation with God,* he told Fletcher, *thank him for everything in your life.* Scary Jenkins would have insisted on a very different penance, a grip on the throat and the denunciation of an evil that only prayer could banish. Fletcher wondered if the priest would have reacted the same way if he'd told him that he once killed a child. Everyone behaved differently when a child was involved, the Catholic Church could vouch for that.

He'd reached *The Black Lion.* Without thinking about it he went inside. The pub was almost deserted, just an old man on a stool at the bar whom the over-dressed barmaid called Sam.

Fletcher sat in the far corner, over by the jukebox. They'd listened to a lot of music in FOB Jackson. He'd seen hard men completely lose it. Booze-free but somehow eight-pints drunk, stripped to the waist and shouting. *Do you looove me, do you love me, do you looove me...* Utterly lost and so very far away until the end of the song and a sudden, disorientating return.

He took out the envelope from his inside pocket and laid the contents on the table, tapping along to the rest of the silent song, *nooow that ahhh can daaance.* He had the papers sent to him just before his discharge, read them a hundred times through eighteen months of drift, a patience that astounded him. It was time to *step it up,* as he used to say, then off to the bar for shots, usually tequila. Maybe Fletcher should line a few up for Mortensen.

72

Thirteen

Li Po stared back. What a man for staring. Jonas knew the little figure in the scroll painting would know what to do, even if he would never have got himself into this situation in the first place.

He shook his head and turned away. What the hell was it with him and Li Po? 'I'm ridiculous.'

The one-eyed doll sitting very primly on the floor beside the scatter of records said nothing.

'I have no sense of my own absurdity.'

He sat down beside the doll. He had no answers to the questions it posed either. Who did it belong to? Had the same person put it in the shoebox? How long had it been in the loft?

It was frustrating. Imagine listing every question you'd ever asked and never had answered. How would the list compare to those which had been answered? Was ignorance or illumination the better measure of a life? Jonas's life sometimes felt like a series of unanswered questions, pouring down faster and faster like the aliens in an old space invader game. What if the final realisation, the heavenly bells tolling closer and louder, was that he'd been asking the wrong questions all along? Worse, he'd been *answering* the wrong ones.

Truly a conundrum, likely irresolvable but still worth pondering on the drive to the ring road, especially if it stopped him thinking about what had happened the night before, which it didn't.

73

Jonas had smiled at Mary. That was ok. And he'd told her that her hair smelled nice. That wasn't. Li Po would have conjured a sonnet from the depths of its auburn glow and all he could say was it smelled nice. As he sighed and closed his eyes a little voice said *the man who knows the way does not say*, which if profound on one level was deeply irritating on another.

It took thirty minutes to get going. Thirty minutes in which *your hair smells nice your hair smells nice* spun round and round like the concrete mixer and Jonas wanted to just *work*, hard labour to stun the brain like a steel-headed hammer so he didn't need to think about Mary anymore.

But Eggers had a rule: no work before three fags. *Gonna work till we drop, no doffing to the Man.* He smoked all three while sitting in the digger, yellow high-vis vest open to the waist. He was well-muscled and liked to show it off. Only seven fifty and already a horn blast from a young woman in a passing Merc. But when he got a cat call from a topless young guy with mirrored sunglasses, leaning out of a very gay, lime-green BMW, he quickly put his t-shirt back on.

'Primary colours!' shouted Jonas.

Eggers looked confused. He opened his mouth to say something but chose instead to raise a middle finger. A man without nuance, sometimes Jonas envied it. He suspected the only complications in the Mary situation were ones he was creating. It was simple. Mary Jackson wanted a job. He had one to offer.

The interview had gone well. At least Jonas thought it had. Most things probably would if they involved two bottles of red, several whiskies, Captain Beefheart, Moby Grape, Nick Cave... and cheese toasties. Yes, a sudden memory flash told him cheese toasties were also involved.

It had been so restrained to begin with, in *The Black Lion*. Over-proper, Jonas thought. He almost laughed. All this formality… for a *cleaning* job? But what if Mary Jackson heard cleaning job as *dead-end job*, why take it seriously, it's not like you're being considered for Prime Minister. This might be the range of her ambition and who was Jonas to judge? She might be limited, which was actually a judgement on you, you snob, so shut up.

Amazingly, Mary passed up her first chance to flee, on the grand tour of End Point. Jonas had a fine boozy buzz, taking the edge off his embarrassment at showing a stranger the messy devastation of his rooms. His *rooms*, he even called them that. *I'll show you my rooms*, as if he was some deluded aristocrat. As he showed her round he wondered, in passing, what the mystery bather had also made of his messy rooms, not that it had put the fucker off.

'I see why you need some help.'

'I know. Totally understand if you're not interested.'

'I'll take it.'

'Well, ok then!'

'What about the rate?'

'Ten pounds an hour, six hours a week. Cash in hand.'

'Then I accept your offer.'

She smiled and Jonas smiled and he thought of Eva. He escaped by saying he was going to get a bottle of Pinot Noir to toast the deal, embarrassed as soon as he said it. Pinot Noir, what a tool, why didn't he just say wine? It all got a bit skewed after that. He blamed Beefheart.

'I saw this at your party,' she said. '*Trout Mask Replica*. Never heard it before.'

'Fast and bulbous!'

'Eh?'

'Fast and bulbous!'

In fact, he repeated the surreal Beefheart line five

times, victim to a sudden, panicky Tourette's. And Mary missed her second chance to flee. She smiled vaguely, considering this babbling oddity, then prowled the living room, glass in hand, picking things up and putting them down: a pebble from the mantelpiece; a soapstone knight from his replica Lewis chess-set; the elegantly tapered, rune-carved wooden spoon that Haakon made him as a going-away present.

All very deliberate, Jonas decided, a space being established. He watched her circle back to the record shelves and sit down cross-legged beside him, hands cupped round her glass.

'How about this one,' she asked. '*Clear Spot?*'

'One of my favourites. I was playing it last night.'

'Then play it again!'

By the time the needle hit *Golden Birdies*, Red One was dead and they were kneeling at the records, heads angled, peering at the titles. Jonas could smell her hair, it smelled *nice*, which was when he decided to tell her, unable to stop himself, already appalled by the potential aftermath, Mary recoiling from the weirdo sniffing her hair, who was now reaching out to touch...

'Your hairs smells nice.'

'Hairs?'

'I mean hair.'

'Thanks.' The smile was quick, gone.

'What I meant – '

'What else have you got?'

And as the lights in his gibbering mind fused one by one, Jonas started pulling out records, anything to talk about other than Mary's *nice-smelling hair*, and so embarked on a long, near-frenzied explanation about how he didn't employ a standard A-Z listing system for the 200-odd albums, oh no, not Jonas, he arranged them thematically, an idiosyncrasy instigated at university which drove everyone he knew crazy because they couldn't find anything or if they did it took far too long because the themes themselves are not alphabetic, you see, there's French chansons beside post-punk and electronica beside that and –

'Is there any logic at all?' she asked, holding up *Pebbles, Volume 4* with a quizzical look.

'Surf rock, I keep that with '60s Garage. There's an internal logic. I like to think of it as organic.'

'You mean annoying.'

'Some have said that.'

Eva, for one.

He tried not to think of his wife as he took the album from Mary. This was also the first time he touched her, a light brush of the fingers, *soft warm fingers*, which he also tried not to think about as he put on *Pebbles* and a trebly Rickenbacker jangle jumped out of the speakers.

Was that when Mary started dancing? Or did that come later, after the whisky? The fragmentation of time and image usually followed the unleashing of the Big Spirit but who knows, he was drunk, drunk with a pretty woman he'd dreamed about, nothing dirty in the slightest but a dream is still a dream because it meant she was in there, in his *head,* and now dancing in his living room, a quite alluring sashay to boot, regardless of the supermarket uniform (complete with misspelled name tag) and the cheese and ham toastie in her left hand.

They made the toasties after she'd told him her favourite soup was pea and ham, and while he couldn't remember how they'd veered on to soup he did remember that the conversation had made them hungry. Cue a kitchen diversion, where she opened every cupboard and drawer and he tried not to slice his fingers off with the knife, listening to her saying something that his hung-over mind interpreted as *I must impose order or he must pass muster...*

77

At 6 am he stood with a pounding head beside the record player, praying that Eggers would be late again and trying to establish when the night had ended from the scatter of twenty-odd LPs.

If they'd played three songs from each record that would make about 300 minutes of music, or five hours. They hadn't got in from the pub until ten thirty. Had she really stayed until three in the morning? On top of *Rubber Soul* the one-eyed doll was looking at him. A vague memory surfaced of Mary asking about it. Please no, he hadn't started on about the *doll*, had he?

'Hey, Thor. You doin any work today?'

Boss Hogg at his shoulder.

And back Jonas went to scooping the hot tar, breathing the fumes that ever evoked childhood, those ancient steamrollers and hard men in caps. In the river distance the same sun glinted off the same boats under same shifting skies, marking time and all that had passed, all that was yet to come. Like Mary, perhaps, his thoughts still revolving like a stop-go lollipop.

★ ★ ★

If anything it got hotter. Came in waves, edging the mercury up and down but always over thirty. Jonas's speed of work slowed to an Italian crawl, a buzzing in his head like a fretting generator.

He felt jumpy. A press of nervous energy. They should write him into the parish emergency plan. *In the event of power outage, plug in the Viking.* To charge him up just place him in front of Mary. Three days would do it, the three days that had passed since the 'interview'. Jonas walked into the village hall for the talent show like a dry-mouthed teenager.

But no sign of Mary front of house. So just chill,

enjoy yourself, and surely Jonas did enjoy *The Hub's Got Talent.* He liked it because he made sure he had nothing to do with it. Helping out meant taking part and taking part meant the enjoyment just drained away. It was the same when he was a teacher in Bergen. He had to be crafty to have nothing to do with organising the end of year show. But Front Row Jo was always there when the curtain went up.

The kids were wary of HGT to begin with. It took a while, one or two voices becoming three and four and more until critical mass was finally reached, that enigmatic process whereby the cheesy became cool. Tonight was HGT III and the hall was buzzing.

Black curtains had been draped across the walls, hiding the vaguely threatening, dauby paintings created by the Golden Oldies Lunch Club and the wooden boards listing the darts, snooker and draughts champions from decade to decade and maybe century to century. Multicolour spotlights shifted randomly across the lines of chairs, catching several glitter-balls hanging low from the roof beams. The R&B was loud, keeping time with the slow flashing Orwellian messages on the 20x20 projection screen pulled down across the stage.

The Hub is YOUR Hub
It's YOUR Time to SHINE
The Hub's Got Talent III
What about YOU?

Half an hour until showtime. Jonas lingered stage-front, watching the auditorium fill. And then Lacey, running up in a black bodysuit, black tights and high heels. She jabbed a hand over her shoulder, the other clutching the bodysuit at her chest, Jonas bemused until she spun round.

'Right, wardrobe malfunction.'

He pinched the fabric together above her bra strap

and pulled the zip up. A little smile as she walked away. He wanted to touch her again. There was so much he missed, so much no one knew and so many who thought they *did*, like the men exchanging glances in the second row. They reminded him of the Three Amigos, Spaniards on the Copenhagen building site whose macho discussions of women were inversely proportionate to any ability to talk to one.

Backstage, he saw Mary. Three days of nervous energy evaporated like tropical rain, her wave and smile cautious proof that nothing too excruciating skulked behind the blank patches in his memory.

The Cheerios were down to open the show and Mary was putting them through a last rehearsal.

Ten nine-year-olds in two lines of four, two stars out front, busting moves to *One Way Street*. The concentration was intense, this was serious! Star Two burst into tears, couldn't get a step right, a simple left foot over right that Mary showed her again and again. Star One was Star One for a reason, displaying a hands-on-hips mix of concern and contempt.

'Divas,' Mary said.

'I know how they feel.'

'Oh you do, do you?'

'I once had to mime along to that Sinitta song *So Macho* at a school show. There were four of us, thirteen years old, stripped to our Speedos, oiled up and prancing around, flexing our muscles.'

'Oiled up?'

'I tell no lie.'

'Wow. Can you imagine the reaction if we started oiling up young boys these days?'

'Outrage.'

'*Daily Mail* style.'

'How was your hangover anyway?'

80

'Nothing that a few hours in bed wouldn't have fixed,' she said.

Jonas blushed. Like an ambush. He watched Mary's eyes catch up with his thoughts. The suggestion hung there in space and neither knew what to say, drawing only more attention to it.

The audience spilled over the hundred. A light, buzzy mood and Jonas jumped in, honest in his sheer delight and who cares about the heat and the sweat. He circulated with glasses of lemonade, greeting people who greeted him. Smiles just happening, both his and theirs. Spontaneity. He forced the thought away. Soon as you think you're being spontaneous you're not.

The Cheerios nailed it, leaving the stage to rapturous applause. Star One's eyes glittered, arena gig vistas opening up, as if her life had just made a significant key change and why not.

After the interval he sat beside Eggers in the front row. His nine-year-old daughter Eloise was next up in a quartet doing a *Girl Power (!) Song and Dance Medley*. The first car crash of the evening.

Each of the girls got their solo moment, outdoing the others in enthusiasm and woefulness. Eggers stiffened, Jonas could *hear* his tension humming, Eloise reaching for a high note and falling horribly short. He avoided Jonas's eyes and clapped enthusiastically as the girls sashayed off. They loved it, beaming and waving, totally oblivious to these cheers of relief.

'Well you've got to give them – '

'Piss off, Jonas.'

The stage went dark, hiding Jonas's grin.

A trumpet kicked in, slow and steady then fast and loose, a spotlight suddenly picking out the player on a raised platform towards the back of the stage. *Danny.*

Zoot-suit and pork pie hat. He built up and up to a final note, slowly lifting the trumpet from stage to roof.

All That Jazz kicked in, Danny playing along, his spotlight dimming as two others snapped on; Lacey and Carly, stage right and left in matching black bodysuits, stockings and high heels. They held their pose, left leg straight and right leg bent, top hat at a coquettish angle.

Jonas clapped wildly as Eggers stared and tried not to stare. The girls, trying to maintain but so embarrassed, stifling the giggles but the confidence slowly building as the *Chicago* routine went on. Now awkward with mistimed kick-steps, now strutting and soft-shoe confident, all pouting lips and jerking hips, arms raising into the last of *all that jaaaaaazz!*

And a moment of pin-drop silence before the applause detonated. Lacey flicked up her hat and winked, the girls strutting off-stage as Danny burst into another solo that he gave up halfway through, holding his trumpet by his side as the music played on. A mime all along.

Jonas glanced at Eggers, who wouldn't hold his eye. The man who wanted to look some more.

Lacey and Carly won by a landslide. The girls worked the room, the boys buzzing like flies, Spencer P more and more furious with Lacey. Ah, the boys, it wouldn't have been Jonas, zero courage to approach the pretty girls, too proud to do an Axel and hook up with anyone. He watched. The laughter would fade. They'd turn around one day and it would be all gone, their childhood.

Fourteen

Jonas's melancholy lingered all weekend. On Sunday
he tried to walk it away, down by the silvery glitter of
the morning river. When he stopped the world stopped
with him, a poise in the ticking morning heat, something unseen and long forgotten that would never again
reveal itself.

'Sycamore,' he said out loud. 'Hawthorn.'

As if familiarity might flush away a nausea never
grown out of because he had never truly grown beyond
himself. He could just imagine Big Haakon's belly
laugh. A lot of crap right enough, the kind of nonsense
some post-rehab celebrity says in a Sunday supplement.
The most pretentious thing about Big Haakon was a
Japanese *yukata* he'd picked up somewhere. Yet even
that was so threadbare and stained, so *inhabited*, that it
made perfect sense.

Jonas gave a silent apology. Made a deep bow to the
memory of Big Haakon, whose *yukata* was undoubt-
edly long consigned to the bin with all his other pre-
conversion foibles and errors.

Roll it all back and it was Haakon's doing that Jonas
was here today. *Know the plants*, he told Jonas, time and
again. So it was a habit, every few weeks a walking tour,
spokes on the wheel of the surrounding area, along the
farm tracks or riverbanks, across the fields, studying
wild flowers, trees. Today, he sought the pea family.
Lilac-funnelling milk-vetch and downy black medick,

the green-grasping reptile fingers of bird's-foot. Simple, utilitarian gorse.

It fascinated him, he sometimes saw it like a time-lapse sequence in a nature programme, the jerky movements of budding plants now a carpet of bluebells, lightening and darkening as clouds came and went and day became night became day. He didn't mind the falling petals or the rotting back. Because all returned, no finality in this ever-turning circle.

The melancholy began to waver. Jonas walked home, reassured that all was still happening as it should, a hesitant hope that shattered in the face of the bearded stranger he found on his couch.

'What the… ' Jonas took two steps forward and then hesitated. 'Who the hell are you?' He was furious more than frightened. Until he noticed the one-eyed doll sitting on the stranger's lap.

'Hello Mr Mortensen.'

'Who –'

'Can I call you Jonas?'

'No. *Get out!*'

'A bit dramatic, I know. I mean, in your shoes I'd have probably shit myself. You haven't, have you?'

'Eh?' Jonas realised he'd seen the man before, briefly, at his party.

'Shit yourself?'

'No.' And an immediate wish he hadn't said anything. Denying he'd shit himself? It was ridiculous.

'That's good.'

'What are you doing –'

'Yeah, yeah, I know. What are you doing here, who are you, all the rest. Should I not be asking you the same thing?'

'This is my house.'

'Is it now?'

84

'Of course it is.'

'Do you know anything about relativity?'

'What? Now look, you just – '

'I know, I can't be coming in here like this, breaking in, sitting here on your couch. It's a comfy couch by the way. But I *can* just be doing that. And yes I did have a bath but that doesn't matter. I needed a wash. I was talking about relativity. Quantum physics. Far as I can see it's a question of perspective. The reality of a situation is determined by the perspective of the observer in relation to it. Yeah?'

' – '

'No?'

' – '

'Fair enough, takes a bit of thinking about. Take your time. Where did you find this doll by the way?'

'In the loft.' And no idea again why he said this, why he was even having this conversation.

'You don't seem the sort.'

'Eh?'

'To play with dolls.'

'I'm going to call the police.'

'No you're not.'

'You're trespassing. This is my house.'

'No it isn't.'

Jonas felt suddenly lightheaded. 'Is that right?' He noticed a brown envelope on the couch.

'That's right. People probably think you bought this house. Why wouldn't they? It's that perspective thing again. If you've never come across a squatter, why would the idea cross your mind? Know what I mean?'

'No.'

'I think you do.'

'I'm going to ask you one more time.'

'To leave?'

'Yes. Leave.'

85

'But you haven't asked me once. How can you ask again?'

'For crying out – '

'Go on then. *Ask* me.'

'Get the *fuck* out of here!'

The stranger picked up the envelope and tossed it across the floor. 'Have a read of that.'

Jonas stared at him. 'Who the hell are you?'

'Read it.'

Jonas picked up the envelope and hurried to the kitchen, trying to leave the stranger behind. But he followed, watching him read. Halfway through the last will and testament of Archibald Hackett, just after the section *leaving the property known as End Point to my grandson, Adam Fletcher*, Jonas sat down at the table. The name on the title deed was the same.

'What now?'

'Well, Jonas. Now *you* leave.'

On the table, his mobile began to ring. Jonas looked from Fletcher to the phone, staring dumbly, as if trying to remember what it was. When he picked it up the caller began gabbling. He told the voice to slow down and realised that it was Eggers. Eggers never phoned. He was asking if Jonas had seen the news, if he'd switched on his TV, because she's disappeared.

'I don't have a TV. Who's disappeared?'

When he put the phone down Fletcher had turned to face him. His gaze was intent, interested.

Jonas had to speak. It was what you did in situations like this, even with a stranger appeared in your home. 'A girl from the youth club has disappeared. Lacey. Hasn't been seen since Friday.'

'How old is she?'

'What does that matter?'

'It matters.'

This wasn't happening. This was another day, a

better day, any day before a crumpled Saab in the pouring rain. Jonas thought of Lacey, the end of another world, feeling vertigo in a place he'd come to call home. He was the dream-man, falling into a beautiful morning from which everything had vanished but this inevitable, silent stranger and all that he brought.

'How *old* is she?'

'Fourteen.'

The stranger blinked a few times. A troubling in the eyes that looked away before Jonas's imagination could spark, a swift exit from the kitchen that just held back from a hurrying.

She as old as you were. Perhaps you had similar toys. A doll, a one-eyed doll as she had, left behind that day you stained Sangin red. Splayed like an x, a cliché of death, bang, bang you're dead, fifty bullets in your head. Except it wasn't fifty bullets, just five, a short burst before my trigger finger lifted into the death both yours and mine, the death that will be called collateral damage, of course. I lie beside you in the dust while the firefight goes on and bullets nick my helmet, my left boot, your eyes locked on mine, a horizontal gaze along the ground, your throat bobbing once, twice and then you are gone and there will be no more memories of childhood and no woman to be, no more winks from that older boy in the bazaar, your mother's hand instinctively tighter on your shoulder even though she has not seen him. Because somehow she knows, as mothers always do, as your mother will grow old with the despair of this perfect morning and the perfection of your death as all deaths are. In dreams I search for you, as I search for my little sister in another landscape untouched by war, a rural arcadia of scudding cloud and drowsy summer so perfect and so empty, no one in it but me, searching hedgerow and cool riverside and not even the sound of an animal, just the

87

selfless wind and a world that is ever empty without you and now without her, who was at least gathered up, who was at least carried that blue morning with arm dangling and her father's distraught face, a man become suddenly old, old as the dark woods where I still look for you.

Fifteen

Mary switched on her mobile just after 8 am. The phone immediately started buzzing and vibrating, the screen an insistent blue-blinking of texts and voicemail reminders from her husband.

As Mary had avoided all thoughts of him since yesterday, so she avoided the messages. But as she laced her Asics she decided she wasn't avoiding him. Avoiding was too deliberate, you had to make an active choice to avoid something. She had simply forgotten about him.

Sunday night was poker night. She waited all week for it. Her husband's best friend Baz started them when he moved into a tiny flat after his divorce. He was frightened, forty-five years old and scared of his own company. So he started a poker night. *Get the boys round.* Not that they knew much about poker, but American movies told them that's what men did.

Her husband always spent the night on Baz's white leather couch, took his hangover straight to work on Monday. That suited Mary just fine. She'd switch off the phone and have a long bath. Sometimes she'd indulge herself with a little silver toy she called The Bullet and feel a bit melancholy afterwards. Last night she'd thought about Jonas and hadn't felt sad at all.

The talent show was the first time she'd seen him since 'the interview'. Yet she hadn't been apprehensive about seeing him. Maybe it was because Jonas Mortensen was her boss now, a functional relationship that put the kibosh on anything else. She blushed a bit as she tied her hair back, spending the next few minutes choosing the most suitable soundtrack for the morning's run. Her iPod playlist was mostly Andrea's. It pleased her no end that she actually liked some of her daughter's albums. She settled on Florence and the Machine.

And ran, eyes moving from road to sky to field. She thought of seasons, which one she'd choose if she could only have one for evermore. Summer seemed an indulgence today, morning pinks edging the tops of the full-leafed hawthorns lining the single-track. Her happiness was immediate but also intangible, a childhood memory that couldn't quite be placed. Her pace had slackened. She was daydreaming. On another day she would have upped the pace, re-set the discipline of the run. Today she'd chill, maybe even take a little detour.

Mary knew what she was doing, but you can know and not admit it. This was one of those situations where she *was* deliberately ignoring something. But she decided it was a freedom in the morning air that led her on a happy-go-lucky wander off the usual route. And if her route was random then she may, of course, just happen to run down Jonas's street.

Crossing back over the road bridge, she didn't really think about the Sky TV van stuck at red. When she saw the BBC outside broadcast van a few vehicles along she wondered about it a bit more. As the vans passed when the lights changed she expected them to take a right at the roundabout, towards town. Instead, they took the second exit, to the village. She caught up with them by the village green that was never this busy, the vans edging into a swarm of people that a policeman in a Day-Glo bib was failing to control. Other outlets were already there, ITV and Channel 4, techno-roadies unravelling cables, a man with a TV camera filming teenage girls tying bouquets of flowers to the railings outside the church.

A child had disappeared, she knew it, the media descent instantly familiar from TV coverage of other places. These things didn't happen *here*, that was the cliché. She felt a quickening sensation, a deep, alienated strangeness, wondering if others did too, all those clustered on the green, adults baffled as kids and even the colours warped, the sky and the trees too vibrant. Everyone looked over-dressed, as if they'd made an effort, watched with tired interest by men with cameras eating bacon rolls from a fast food van parked by the war memorial.

She thought of her daughter, a sudden dread churning her guts hollow. But Andrea was hundreds of miles away. Some other poor mother would be catatonic on a morning couch.

A few people were staring. Looking her up and down. The running kit seemed wildly inappropriate and Mary wished she'd read her husband's texts before now. She started running again, legs gone to jelly and Florence in her ears, building to a spectacular crescendo.

Sixteen

Again, Jonas looked down at his basket as the queue shuffled along. A loaf of brown bread, half a dozen free-range eggs and a packet of breaded ham. And three bags of beef Space Raiders.

The Space Raiders jarred. He wondered if people were staring at his corn snacks. They might be disgusted, I mean, *Space Raiders*? And was beef a more appropriate flavour than pickled onion? Then again, it was the Space Raiders themselves that were the issue. This was a time for *gravity* and they were too whimsical a crisp. They didn't know he didn't even have a TV, they just saw happy-go-lucky snack-munching as he watched the 24 hour news.

There was a commotion behind him. A tubby woman in a blue jumpsuit with a large sunflower motif had knocked over a display of chocolate digestives. She tittered and very loudly said *no use crying over broken biscuits!* People turned away again but all were listening. She started a conversation with the old man behind her, saying it was *such a beautiful day, a good day for the race.* When the old man asked *what race* she said *the human race.*

The queue collectively tensed. No one was interested in Jonas's Space Raiders anymore. Someone tutted and the woman in front of him turned and looked back at Jumpsuit Joker.

'Have a bit of respect.'

The smile froze on the woman's face. 'I beg your pardon.'

'For Lacey.'

'I'm sorry but I don't – '

'The girl that's disappeared.' She held up a copy of *The Sun*, a front-page picture of a smiling Lacey.

'Oh. Oh no. I didn't know!'

The old man beside her looked dumbfounded, *did you not see the TV appeal yesterday? Lacey Lewis. Her poor mum was in pieces, no sign of the dad but what do you expect?* As Jumpsuit Joker apologised profusely the floodgates opened. *You just never, never know,* said someone. *I moved from London to get away from all this,* said another. Jonas listened, caught a couple of eyes and mumbled something for the sake of *taking part,* in case they turned on him too. He was unsettled by a gleam in the eyes, like a restrained thrill at being in the centre of a sensation. When he left the shop the queue was still speculating, refreshed by new arrivals. *Her mother was a mess to begin with… Did you hear about the police briefing… I hope they string the bastard up… they found her purse in the park, it looks bad…*

That was the one that stuck. *They found her purse in the park…* Jonas saw her. Running in the darkness. Dropping her purse. He closed the door and leaned back, eyes closed. Upstairs he could hear the shower. The mail dropping through the letter box made him jump.

Just the mail.

Nothing unusual was happening in the world.

Just a stranger having a shower.

After a while the shower stopped. Jonas tensed, remembering Fletcher's hands on his throat that morning. He took a few steps towards the stairs, listening intently, like the night before.

It was way past midnight. Jonas had been standing outside the door of the spare room for a long time, sure that the stranger was on the other side in mirrored pose, listening to Jonas listening to him.

93

It was ludicrous. To be crouched in his boxers in the pitch dark with his ear to a closed door. He crept back to bed with the same uncertainty as when he first stood in End Point, a tense waiting for something that faded with each day it never came. Except now it had.

After one, the stranger began to snore, belly-deep snores of the contented sleeper. It took a long time but Jonas managed to force him away. As soon as he did Lacey came. He lay in the darkness, thinking of the tabloids about to explode, all that *read between the lines* voyeurism. What had gone through her mind? Maybe, somehow, it had all been quite peaceful.

He realised the stranger had stopped snoring and sat up quickly, braced for bedroom invasion. Or maybe he'd left the house and gone to the police. But Lacey was priority one, they'd just ignore the guy babbling on about a squatter. Fletcher would have to give up and leave.

Lacey put her hands on her hips, she wasn't happy with this switch of the subject. Jonas made himself think of her mother. Susan, he remembered, or maybe Sue: sad eyes, hair dried to straw by too much peroxide. He pictured the TV appeal. Susan overly made-up or completely plain, stripped to her black-heads. Either way, she'd have got it wrong, judgement following, the viewers scouring her words and behaviour for explanation, as if culpability could be gleaned from an ill-considered decision to wear red lipstick for the cameras.

No one could get that right. You could understand it. Too many cynical memories of tearful parental appeals followed by an arrest three days later. He imagined his own parents. His father dignified but strained. And his mother silent, there but not there, as when Jonas would creep downstairs to watch her sitting in the dark, tiny in her big fluffy dressing gown, wondering why she did this, stared into space, something out there only she could see.

At least Jonas could picture his parents turning up to *make* the damn appeal. When Axel ran away to Aegir's Isle his parents didn't bother. No press conference in an over-lit room. Perhaps the police realised that the furious face of Axel's father was unlikely to bring the lost lad a-running. He came round to Jonas's house, stagger-drunk at midday, moaning about *missing shifts to look for that little bastard and when I find him I'll put him through the wall.*

Axel lasted four nights before his tinned food ran out and his uselessness with a rod caught up. He went home and Jonas didn't see him for weeks, the bruises still visible when he did.

Poor Axel. His bruised face slowly pixillated, Jonas falling into a jumpy half-sleep full of faces and voices he couldn't make out. Then a gunshot. He sat bolt upright but realised it was the slam of a door. It was just after five. For a long moment there was silence and he was sure Fletcher was just outside his room. Then footsteps, going down the stairs. Jonas let himself breathe but still tiptoed to the bathroom. A sound from the garden made him peer out the window.

Fletcher was standing in the middle of the lawn with his back to the house. Over and over he slowly pulled his outstretched arms towards himself with steady, noisy breaths, through the teeth like a hissing animal. He was wearing nothing but a pair of white briefs, which disappeared into the crack of his arse when he dropped into a series of rapid press-ups.

Jonas sat down on the toilet. He watched the bright morning sun glinting off the bath taps, the stranger's hiss-hissing drifting in with the birdsong. Here it was, another day in paradise.

Then anger, up like a flare, replacing the incredulity. In a few moments Jonas was across the landing and in Fletcher's room, except it wasn't *his* room, it was Jonas's

95

and these belongings had no place in this space. A sand-coloured rucksack had been propped against the wall, stitched-on battalion patches he had seen on news reports; soldiers with sunglasses, soldiers kicking down doors, soldiers on alert in dusty, God-forsaken desert villages.

Although God was surely with Fletcher. Beside the neatly rolled sleeping mat and folded trousers was a leather-bound Bible. The marker was at Deuteronomy: 22 and Jonas scanned the page until *if a man is found lying with the wife of another man then they both shall die.* He thought about Mary, the stranger some Old Testament absolutist come to warn and –

'It's a lot of nonsense, eh?'

Jonas spun round. Fletcher stood in the doorway sweating. He was holding the one-eyed doll.

'The *Bible*. It's not mine, by the way. My aunt's. This is what she left me when she died. How about that, the last action of a true psychopath. What about you? You a believer?'

'No.'

'Maybe it'll come.' He moved past Jonas and put the doll beside his rucksack.

'I take it you're leaving today.'

Fletcher scratched his beard and smiled. 'What did you do back in Norway? Stand-up comedy?'

Jonas felt suddenly un-tethered, a kite, further and further away, now a speck in the distance.

'Comes a time, amigo,' the stranger continued.

'I want them checked.' And aware of the slight edge of panic in his voice, a breathlessness.

'Say what?'

'Those papers. How do I know you are who you say you are? Adam Fletcher. You could be anyone. You could have made it all up. How do I know you didn't steal them? Or forge them?'

96

'Forge them? Seriously?'

'Seriously.'

'This isn't your house! You want me to drag you round to the police station?'

'No.'

'Then why don't –'

'I've been here for seven years, this is my home!'

'No. It's my home.' Fletcher rummaged in the rucksack and brought out the envelope. 'You saw that. You want to read it again? I mean, you're Norwegian, can you not read English?'

'Just do it then.' Out it popped. Unbidden, but the feeling of defeat was so sudden.

'Do what?'

'Get the police.'

'You really want that?'

'Of course I don't.'

Fletcher stared at him, wild-eyed. *Fuck's* sake!'

And Jonas suddenly wondered about the police, decided to say it. 'Why haven't you gone to them already?'

Fletcher looked to the ceiling and shook his head.

'Don't you want to? What's your story?'

Then Fletcher's hand was on his throat. 'Why the hell did you have to be here? Un... bel... *ievable*.' The grip tightened momentarily before he dropped his hand and Jonas staggered back.

'You're crazy!'

'You don't know the half, mate.' Fletcher walked to the window and leaned on the sill, head bowed. 'No cops. But you're going to leave.' A semi-detached voice, completely sure of itself.

Downstairs, Jonas sat in the sun room. Tightly clasped hands but still the trembling. The house has always been full of him, he thought. The ghost-presence sensed but never seen.

97

A few minutes later Mark phoned. All breathless *can't believe it, can't believe it* and the police are holding a briefing at eleven and can you help, make some phone calls, get as many people to the hall as possible? Jonas said sure and immediately left the house, wandering the streets and then the shop, buying things he didn't really need, anything to put it off.

The stranger was still moving around upstairs. Jonas stopped listening and took the bag of groceries through to the kitchen. He stared at his mobile, thinking about the people he had to call and made toast instead. When he finished he made some more. And then another two slices.

Eventually, he made the calls, shared speculation he really didn't want to, the same gabbled disbelief over and again, as dream-like as watching the stranger appear in the kitchen, make a cafetière of coffee and then lie sunbathing in the back garden. Red shorts and Ray-Bans.

Twelve calls later Jonas was done. He stared at the screen until the screensaver went black and moved his gaze back to the garden. After a while Fletcher came in and started opening cupboards. Eventually, he found a glass which he filled with water and slowly drank. Both stared. Neither spoke. When Fletcher had drained the glass he went back outside.

Jonas watched him. He thought about the one-eyed doll and why the stranger took it to his room.

And felt sick.

* * *

The Hub's Got Talent decorations were still up, black drapes and unmoving mirror-balls, a yawning stage and expectant ghost-light, like a mid-afternoon theatre echoing with the last performance.

Over sixty people milled around, subdued as the dimness in the hall. They watched the police and media set up, little clusters with low voices, turning to the rasp of the runners as someone opened the curtains. Some were angry and some disbelieving but most were simply tense, not knowing what reaction was most appropriate and not wanting to get it wrong.

Jonas felt for them. He wasn't a leader, never had been. But a doer, that was different. So he circulated, offering a hand on the shoulder, for comfort, the *Viking*, whom some knew and most didn't, smiling a smile that sought to be reassuring and ignoring the puzzled looks that said *we'll talk about you later* and *did you see that, the way he looked me right in the eye?*

The police briefed the hall, two detectives behind a table on the stage, a cluster of microphones and three TV cameras tripod-mounted stage left and right, cameramen bent to the lens.

The detectives seemed edgy. Nothing like the tired cops in a TV show. No hint of hangover or existential despair, just two fifty-odd, bank manager-ish men with flat voices that would talk with reassuring mundanity about fixed-term mortgages and self-assessment tax returns. Except it was the finding of Lacey's purse which made this a high-risk enquiry, the ongoing search in the nature park and an appeal for information, however unimportant it may seem.

'We're very grateful for the community's cooperation,' they said. People glanced around and frowned, like why do you think it would be any different? But maybe it was, in other places.

The detectives finished. Not much to say and little to go on. They seemed apprehensive as they asked for any questions, as if nervous about what odd pose a thousand photographs would catch them in as they bounced from one shouted question to the next.

A thump on Jonas's shoulder. He turned to Eggers and Eggers was smug, smugly intense.

'I know how this works, they're gonna make a list of people and talk to them one by one at their homes, not here, imagine that, traipsing off one by one to be asked questions, fuck me that'd be *full-on*, what if everyone got exactly fifteen minutes then someone else, say you, Jonas, were in there for twenty-five? People would notice, they'd think you'd *done* something.'

The media ran out of different ways to ask the same questions that still had no answers. They turned their attention to the locals, absent-mindedly scribbling down the same comments, eyes seeking the next person, the next, that elusive bombshell quote. Apart from the police, hardly anyone had left the hall. People wanted to talk and speculate, as if to do so was to make very clear, very publically, that they, personally, had nothing to hide.

But Jonas of the *bushcraft eye*. He could see the moorings straining hard. Just beyond the communality and camaraderie everyone was looking at each other that little bit more closely. Because how can we all be in it together when only *I* can have certainty about having nothing to do with Lacey Lewis's disappearance? *You*, my friend, you I know nothing about.

So Jonas left the hall and headed down the street to the supermarket. He loaded up with beer, wine, and lemonade, wheeling the trolley back to circulate with drinks that some took and some refused, the lemonade going first and only slowly the beer and wine, as if to be the first to start boozing was to undermine the gravity of the situation but hey, it's a stressful time, take off that edge, as at a wake, that mysterious watershed when it is realised by everyone *at exactly the same time* that they can now crack a relieved smile and get safely drunk.

Mary spoke to him, setting butterflies dancing in his

stomach that he tried not to think about. She said he was doing a *good thing*. Eggers too gave a grim, appreciative smile. He downed a Staropramen and opened another. Two more and he shouted for quiet, raising his bottle. *Here's to you, Lacey, we'll see you soon enough.*

Ah Jack, Jackie Eggers. The immersive man. Li Po would approve. If you're going to watch naked women on your laptop, do it shamelessly. If you believe that a disappeared teenager will return, then shout that certainty to the whole world. For a while the volume level increased, the alcohol loosening the tension. The afternoon teetered on the edge of enjoyment until a tremor of discomfort travelled round the hall and reminded everyone of the context.

People started looking at Jonas's tray with distaste. But he was only trying to help, doing his *good thing*. That was the thing about misjudgement, nobody liked to admit it. Much better to pin it on some sap, who couldn't read the situation, who kept on circulating, an OCD waiter with a goofy grin, Mary now with a gentle hand and a look that said *that's enough now*.

He watched her wander round the hall. Pats on the shoulder, a few cuddles. She'd lived here all her life. Liked because she was known. Maybe under all the fuss that blows through our days like skeleton leaves that's all we need. To be known. No one wants to be the headstone name disappearing under lichen. Even Jonas, the cultivator of non-attachment.

It was after three. Jonas thought of Lacey and the stranger and if you could ever decide you truly knew someone. He did not want to leave this village. He saw his possessions piled on the street and a squad car pulled up because of course there would be police, whatever the stranger said, police looking for details, asking questions Jonas didn't hear.

101

Seventeen

Fletcher studied the girl's picture in *The Sun* then put the paper down on the grass. It was a pity she had to disappear.

It was simpler to see the world as a film, a series of more or less believable set-pieces but all of them still fabrications. If everything was made up then there was no need to get involved. A mind-frenzy may still arise, it depended on the actual absurdity you were facing. Like finding a Norwegian hippy in your house and realising he had no intention of leaving.

He took off his sunglasses and rubbed his eyes. For five hours he'd been lying on a sun lounger found in the shed. The hot sun had stunned him like forty mg of paroxetine, the anger he woke with now broken up. Fletcher liked the heat, even the furnace of Iraq and Afghanistan. He didn't mind the rash, the hot prickle in the crotch and armpits. All that viscous junk, oozing out like oil. It made him want to abuse himself, just so he could feel the purge.

He'd positioned the sun lounger very carefully. Given the height of the fence, it was impossible for anyone on the ground floor of the two houses adjacent to End Point and the one facing it to see into the garden. The first floors offered the only vantages. He could do little about the view of the immediate neighbour but the line of sight from the top windows of the next house along could be cut off by moving the sun lounger closer to the fence. Doing so had the disadvantage of opening a view from the house facing End Point, although the rhododendrons and cypresses at the bottom of the garden partially obscured it. He could obscure it slightly more by moving the lounger away from the fence, though not too far to re-open the view from the upper floor of the second house along. It was all a satisfying question of geometry. When Fletcher finished, he was sure that the only eyes that could spy on him were those of the young family next door. He'd already seen a young woman at the bedroom window. She stared at him after shouting at her kids, playing in the garden below.

They were still splashing and yelping. As he pictured the paddling pool the sun suddenly swelled, bringing a surge of connection that made every detail of that moment in time simultaneously ultra-clear.

'What a great day! I get it from my grandfather, this sun-worshipping. First ray of sun it was off with the t-shirt. Know what he died of...? Heart attack. On the bog. You were expecting me to say skin cancer, yeah? You shouldn't jump to conclusions, always better to wait.'

Fletcher turned. Mortensen was staring at him from the sun room. 'Am I burning? I kinda drift away and forget. Maybe I'll be the one to get skin cancer but I doubt it. Do you ever get the feeling you know what you're going to die from? I reckon it's going to be something – '

'You're still here.'

'Seriously, bro, who's writing your dialogue? Hard to find the words though. Maybe the goodie should get angry, I take it you're the goodie? A fight scene's good for drama. You want a fight?'

'Whatever you say.'

'How'd it go at the hall? You work with kids, Jonas. Think the cops will come knocking?'

'Fuck you.'

Fletcher stood up very quickly. 'This should be easy. Don't make it difficult.'

'You want me out? Then go get the police.'

'What, you still think I'm lying?'

'Why not?'

'You're a parasite.'

'Then go to the police.'

Fletcher raised his face to the sun, looking for another shot of tranquillity. He let his fists unclench. If he wasn't going to the police, then he didn't want GBH to make it an option for the Norwegian either.

'*Jonas?*'

Fletcher recognised Mary's voice inside the house. Jonas had almost winced.

'*Jonas?*'

'Looks like your girlfriend's here.'

'She's not – '

He smirked, watching Jonas try to settle a calmer look on his face as Mary appeared behind him.

'Oh sorry, I didn't know you had company. I knocked at the door but no one answered so I just...'

'That's ok,' said Jonas.

Fletcher watched their smiles become uncomfortable. Mary's eyebrows raised a questioning centimetre.

'This is... *Adam*,' said Jonas, and another pause. 'My cousin. My aunt married an Englishman.'

'It's why you came here,' said Fletcher. 'Isn't it, Jonas, why you came to End Point? Family connections and all that. The pleasure's all mine, Mary. Get her a beer, cuz, one for me too.'

Jonas stared dumbly. While he was getting the beer, Fletcher got two camping chairs from the shed.

'Cheers.' He took a bottle from Jonas and sat down on the lounger, legs spread. He'd positioned the camp chairs to face him. If she wanted, Mary could reach out and touch his thigh.

They sat in silence, Jonas picking at the label on his bottle and Mary looking round at the houses. When she caught his eye Fletcher smiled. 'Hot eh?' He loved the sun, fuckin loved it.

'Certainly is.'

'How do you know my cousin then? He's never mentioned you but he's always been a secretive bastard.'

'C'mon, *Adam* – '

'I'm the cleaner.'

'The cleaner?'

'Well. A friend too, I mean – '

'You've got a *cleaner*?'

'It's nothing you – '

'Helluva house to keep clean, isn't it, Mary? I mean, if it was my house I'd take better care of it. Some people have no domestic sense. Know what I mean, Jonas, some people don't have any – '

'I thought you were leaving?'

Fletcher wrinkled his nose. 'You're absolutely right. Stay out here any longer and I'll fry like a sardine. Hey, that's a pretty good idea. We should have a barbecue. I could go some sardines, something nice and fishy. Fancy it, Jonas? Let's get something *fishy* on the barbie.'

'You've been in the sun too long, you're starting to gibber.'

'You're right.' He stood up. 'Who knows what I'll say next, eh Jonas?' And smiled, the rising awkwardness mirrored by the growing panic in Mortensen's eyes as he waited for him to tell Mary that *she was being lied to*. He gave it several more strung-out moments then walked away.

Jonas watched Fletcher go. *For why*, his mother used to say when he was pestering her. *For why do you ask all*

105

these questions, little Jonas? He heard her voice again as the stranger disappeared inside the house. *For why has this beardy man appeared in your life, little Jonas?*

Who knows? Not Jonas and not his mother, she a presence not quite as inexplicable as Fletcher's but not far off, mostly forgotten if randomly remembered, like a synaptic twitch, caused today by alcohol, no food, and the unsettling after-trails of Fletcher's departure.

For why is this happening, little Jonas?

But nothing as yet *was* happening, no pile of possessions on the street, nothing as yet but a stranger whose face was becoming familiar, a man sunbathing in his garden, *settling in.*

He pictured Fletcher's grinning face. He'd be back, of course, unreal as it all was, as unreal, he supposed, as Fletcher turning up at his grandfather's house and finding a Norwegian living there.

Meanwhile, Mary Jackson cleaned. She'd insisted. Said she wanted to avoid sitting at home staring at the news because it's disgusting how an entertainment is being built from this.

'So, I'm sorry, Jonas, it'll have to be you.'

It'll have to be you. The words revolved as he glanced at her, sweat on her neck and the top buttons of her shirt undone, now and then a glimpse of her breasts. It was exciting, a bit pervy, but what was one without the other? She was staying for dinner. It was so normal, like all the other sounds of the evening, shouting children and clattering dishes, music drifting from an opened window. It almost made him forget about Fletcher, but not Lacey.

Her parents might be sitting in their own back garden, the same chairs, the usual colours and sounds. Everything was everything apart from her. Jonas had tried, he had only tried to help, but teenage girls never listened. He smiled again and Mary smiled back, a sudden lawnmower and Lacey was shimmering, then a shriek from next door's kids and she was gone.

So set the table and welcome Mary's delight at his *puttanesca* chicken, a rare outing for the only dish he could cook well and yes, it *was* a triumph, she was quite right, he accepted the compliments and basked in the glow, maintaining his self-satisfaction until midway down the second bottle of Sauvignon Blanc when he looked at her and suddenly saw another smile.

Estrangement was an express train, still accelerating. I exist at great distances, he thought. From my wife. From this evening.

'How long do you think it'll last?' Mary asked.

'What's that?'

'The weather.'

'Careful, you'll jinx it.'

'I'd be happy with sun like this every day for the rest of my life.'

The weather?

Yes, the weather, they were actually talking about the weather. But so what, Jonas having decided to *enter the narrative space* as Eva would have said, a movie obsessive who chided Jonas for the way he scoffed at terrible films *because there's always something to see, you just have to learn how to look,* leaning towards him the way Mary just had, an evening like this in another life, the two of them babbling on, probably laughing because the sentimentality of memory insisted on it, turning to see Anya waddling across the garden, the first time she'd walked, big green eyes and hands a-clapping, one, two, three steps before falling over and quick as it opened up that space was closing and what remained was only complication.

'Penny for them?' Mary asked.

Jonas had slipped into silence but hadn't noticed, as

he only now registered Mary's smile, which wavered the longer he didn't smile back. 'Do you like films?'

A slight frown but still the smile. 'Sure. Why?'

'Me too.'

'O-*kay*!' And looked away, perhaps wondering where he'd suddenly gone, her smile finally disappeared. In a moment she stood up from the table, crossed to the lawn and lay down.

He watched. A *moment*, he decided, one of those moments. So what to do, what to do?

Ah Jonas, the master of over-projection. But each day was connected to all previous, was it not, now to then to Eva to Mary? So he got up and joined her on the lawn, warm with the day's stored heat, both looking up to the swifts, darting and soaring as if conducting their thoughts, a scroll of detail but not too fast for Jonas to keep up, high but not too high, he could still hear the old wandering song line that hadn't yet been lost among all the other chatter.

'Fast little things,' she said.

Jonas turned to her. Mary's hair had fanned onto the grass, a cascade of red on green. She was smiling again.

'It's like they're writing something,' she added. 'Maybe with the right eyes we'd be able to read it.'

'If we could read... bird.'

'Bird?'

'Bird language,' he said. 'I know bird.'

'You know bird.'

'I know bird.' And he started making odd tweets and chirrups, noises through his teeth and little pursed lip whistles because she was trying and he would too, drawn by that smile.

She was laughing. 'But what does it *mean*, Jonas?'

'It means the wine's empty and I'm going to get some more.'

'Birds drink wine?'

'Yes, they drink wine. Everyone knows that.'

'Mal-beak, I suppose,' and Mary rolled over on the lawn, cackling with laughter. 'I want to hear some music,' she said, sitting up with grass in her hair, suddenly serious. 'Let's get out of the village. It's been a really awful day, I'm a bit drunk and I feel like getting plastered.'

'Sounds like a plan.'

They looked up as if choreographed into Fletcher's beaming face. He wore shades, and had changed into black cotton trousers and a tight black t-shirt, a silver chain around the neck.

'I could do with getting out of Dodge too,' he added.

Eighteen

A strange and kaleidoscopic evening Mary would decide, much later, with the reassurance of hindsight.

It was the symmetries that stuck: Fletcher in the middle of the back seat of the bus, directly in line with the aisle; Mary and Jonas six rows ahead, facing each other across the aisle; the bands of burgundy, orange and flame red, thinning on the horizon as the evening became deep blue then lavender dark; the village green that could have been arranged just so, a TV crew in a corner, floodlit dazzle and a group of watching locals, side-lined in the shadows.

Lacey's boyfriend added another strange kink. As they were waiting for the bus Spencer P cycled past and circled back, staring at Jonas before cycling away. When the bus stopped at the lights outside the village the kid was back, staring up at Jonas who stared back, launching into a monologue about Spencer P that was way over the top, a hostility Mary didn't understand. It took a while to steer the conversation back to where they were going to go.

'Where's the best place for music?' he asked.

And sly Mary sat back in her seat and pretended to think, because she'd done her research before going round to Jonas's. She counted down, five to zero and the eureka moment.

'My daughter used to go to somewhere called *The Underground*. They've got live music every night.

Fancy that?' Jonas did and when she shouted back to Adam he gave a gleeful double thumbs-up that was both enthusiastic and sarcastic. Then he looked at Jonas and winked.

Jonas tensed. He was about to say something then didn't, glancing at Mary, as if remembering she was there. The tension between the two men was palpable. For a quick moment dismissed even quicker she wondered if Jonas was jealous. The Norwegian did make sure to stand in the middle as the three of them walked to *The Underground*, and seemed to flinch when Adam removed his shades inside the venue and asked *do you want a drink... Mary?* her name slowly emphasised, a bit creepy. All through *Pierre and the Pirates'* set Jonas stared at Adam, who danced with odd spastic jerks, a scarecrow plugged into the mains.

Jonas's distraction made her self-conscious. She danced too, half-hearted middle-aged wiggling, hoping no one caught her eye, looking around at first dates and estrangements, glittery-eyed love and disillusion's slow-burn. Awkward, under-age girls crowded the front, conspicuous in the effort to be inconspicuous. She wondered if Lacey came here.

'They don't seem to know much,' Jonas shouted in her ear.

'Who?'

'The police. About Lacey.'

The pounding music, hearing the name, it was startling – a warp in space. 'No. No, they don't.'

'Think they've interviewed Spencer P yet?'

'C'mon, he's just a kid.'

'Lacey was just a kid too.'

And then it didn't seem right to Mary, this entertainment. She stared at the too-skinny lead guitarist with the milk-white skin and an image flashed: a dead body, a teenage girl in a field. The lump in her throat was sudden but still she swayed her hips, the image revolving.

When the song ended she was crying. Jonas put a hand on her arm and looked at her carefully, as if for the first time, then back to Adam, twisting and jerking and no music, oblivious to the amused onlookers, furious moves with his eyes shut, mouth opening and closing.

* * *

Jonas was first off the bus. The real-time screen told him it was 01.21. They stepped into soft-focus streetlights and a purple sky, walking in silence past the green, the TV vans. He had a sudden image flash, the three of them with linked arms, skipping along the street like the Yellow Brick Road. No singing, though, just the scuff of their feet and three perplexed frowns.

At the cross-roads, he and Mary said a gawky goodbye, a hug thought about but avoided. She walked down the street to the left, Jonas watching. Fletcher stood beside him, also watching.

When Mary disappeared he headed right. Jonas looked left, right, and went straight on. Anywhere apart from End Point, Fletcher's face a half-lit cipher, a smirk and a frown, what he knows and doesn't know but no one knows anything, all these houses Jonas was walking past, cottages to outskirt new-builds, all these sleeping people and their untold stories.

So bury the one-eyed doll in the loft, cram the genie back in the lamp and lock it in the garage until the laughing ghost of your past taps you on the shoulder and would you look at that, he's got a *black beard*. Jonas made sure he hadn't left Fletcher alone with Mary long enough to tell her about this lying Norwegian. The problem was the stream of days yet to come.

He stopped, realising he was on Panama Lane. The hole in the fence midway along the lane was still there. He squeezed through, into the woods. The sound of the dual carriageway was startling, still busy even now, the road twenty metres away through the trees and how could he have ever put up with noise like this?

The clearing and the windblown tree took a while to find. Sycamore Camp, his first home in the village. Picking strawberries in Kent for a pittance a punnet had finally sickened him. Three months was three months was too long so leave, Jonas, seek the promise of the western lands...

It was almost unreal now, that urge to keep moving. When you stop you put down roots. But to stop you have to want to. This village was the first place in a long time he'd felt that. End Point was the final proof, the obviously abandoned house a sign and God-dammit Jonas sure liked a sign, even more he liked an open door, and if End Point's door had actually been locked then the locked door of an empty, run-down house was also an invitation.

He sat on the trunk and watched the passing cars. He remembered the compulsion, back then, counting the headlamp beams that crossed his face. Tonight they strobed like searchlights, an unsettling. He thought of Mary but Eva insisted, as overwhelmingly present now as then.

So he let it all stream, a mashed-up cine-reel of dream-memory and reflection, tropical evenings, lonely campsites under Fannaraken's ancient glare, teeming festival Lisbon, barrio alto hip hop and the heavy fug of sex, the stars in the sky here for all those yesterdays but maybe gone tomorrow, gone already, like the conceit that his eyes were the only ones to have looked at someone this way, to have been looked at this way, Eva laughing at their reflections on the window, Caribbean palms twisting like secrets in the dusk and the light of day become a purpling sky and the silhouettes now too dim to be certain about.

A twig snapped. It might be Eva. He waited for the hands over his eyes, the voice saying *guess who?* Or Lacey. He sat in the dark for a long time, picturing the fear in her pretty face.

Nineteen

Jonas endured another day of circlings. He'd stayed up all night, watching the sun rise into blue scarred by wisped whorls, like the after-trails of air-show stunt planes. The stranger appeared soon after, a wordless walk onto the lawn to again go through his stylised exercise ritual, a staccato formality to the choreography that made Jonas wonder if it was less a morning habit than a psychic necessity. As he glanced at Fletcher so the stranger looked at Jonas.

Later, when he came home and sank a beer, head buzzing from traffic, tar fumes and Eggers's gaudy true-crime speculations, Fletcher was still in the garden, star-splayed on the sun lounger. He was unmoving, as if asleep although Jonas knew he was awake, as aware of Jonas as he was of him. When Jonas finished the beer he didn't care anymore, going upstairs to crash out fully clothed. The last images before sleep were stunt planes, looping the loop, over and over again.

He forgot to close the curtains and woke with a new day pouring in. A dead man's slumber, no dreams. For a moment all was clear, understandable. A passing car. Birdsong. Then Mary, her face quick-rising. He'd barely thought about her since the gig but as he grabbed his mobile to send a text her face was suddenly replaced by Fletcher's leer. He put the phone down.

There were no more passing cars or birdsong, just a

Niagara of thoughts. A blast of ECT was needed. What was it the docs said? *Four hundred volts a day keeps the world at bay.*

Outside the bedroom the landing creaked. Jonas was up, the J-Man was *superhero fast,* opening the door but no one there. Downstairs, Fletcher sneezed and Jonas immediately felt as if he was falling, such a long, long way but if you don't hit bottom then you can't shatter into a million pieces. The stranger, would he be looking up, waiting for impact?

He was. Jonas made green tea in his little cast-iron Japanese kettle and sat on the other side of the kitchen table. Fletcher looked back and they stayed that way for a long time, like a stand-off in a crappy Western. Fletcher broke first and looked away with a shrug. This annoyed Jonas, especially the shrug. Because it wasn't as if he'd won, it was more like Fletcher had given up. Jonas wanted to say something but didn't know what, something that made clear that he too knew that this whole staring thing was ridiculous. But to bring attention to it was to show his annoyance at having to explain himself, which annoyed him even more.

When the doorbell rang they looked at each other again. *It's your house,* Jonas wanted to say, *you answer it.* But he didn't because it wasn't. It was Jonas's house so he got up, opening the front door to the two detectives from the briefing in the village hall. When he showed them into the kitchen Fletcher had disappeared. You'd think he would have stayed, a gleeful witness to the squatter bust, a finger-pointing 'fuck you Mortensen, get thee gone'.

But the way they scrutinised him as they sat down, before they spoke. They were the Lacey cops, after all, they were here about her, nothing else. He had known as soon as he opened the door.

The sad-eyed detective told him three copies of a porno-graphic magazine called *Barely Legal* had been found

116

in a locked desk drawer in the office where Jonas did administration for The Hub.

A phone number was written on one of the covers, which they had called. It turned out to be an outdoor activity centre in north Wales called *Black Raven Adventures*. A booking had been made by Jonas Mortensen for the weekend of October 25th. The centre hadn't spoken to anyone else from The Hub and the presumption could only be, *don't you agree, Mr Mortensen?* that he had written the phone number himself and the magazines were his.

Jonas answered. The detectives looked at him the same way he'd been looked at in Bergen years back, a shifting mix of suspicion, pity and contempt. He wondered if it was something they practised in the bathroom mirror, channelling all those American cop shows.

He wasn't a suspect, they stressed. It was unnecessary to take him to the police station. Too many media. *Like Doberman dogs*, said Sad Eyes. *Chasing bones. We try to be discreet.*

But when Jonas let them out he saw Gladstone emerge from his café across the street. He stared at the two detectives as they got in their car then back at Jonas, who waved a hello he hoped wasn't too friendly, *exaggerated*, because that wouldn't be normal at all.

★ ★ ★

Eggers was four coffees down. Wired. Full of the same speculation and bullshit as the day before. He babbled about motives, suspects and then, later on, discovered the word *perpetrators, they're always using it in those Scandy crime dramas, you should know about them, Jonas*. He kept repeating it, *perpetrator*, savouring the sound as he libelled a range of people whose possible guilt was shaped by how much and for how long Eggers had disliked them.

No sign of Jonas on that list. He wondered how long it would take for word to get round.

'I knew this day would come,' Eggers insisted.

'Did you really?'

'Did you see the reconstruction on the telly?'

'What reconstruction?'

'Lacey. Her last movements.'

'I don't have a TV.'

'There's darkness in the best of places and the best of places have the worst of shadows.'

'Where did you read that?'

'I didn't. I made it up.'

'Really?'

'Nah.'

And on and on with the speculation. He only shut up when the jack hammer was going.

'Nowhere is innocent,' he stated in the van at lunchtime.

'Shut up, for Christ's sake!'

'Telling you.'

But Eggers seemed genuinely affected. Didn't even open the laptop and watch the usual lunchtime show. Just picked at his tuna and mayo sandwich and stared at the passing traffic.

'It's happened before, you know.'

'Here we go again.'

'It has!'

Jonas left him to it. The obsession was typical Eggers. Here was an all-purpose addict of roving compulsions. Alongside the booze and the porn were the food fads. Like the pickled eggs a couple of years back, so strange that Jonas gave it an historical title: the Time of the Eggs. Every day for weeks they had to stop at a chip shop for a pickled egg. Eggers only weaned himself off with mini pork pies and yes, Jonas, they have to be *mini*. The Lacey mania would go on and on until Jonas

118

seriously considered ending it with a clatter of the tar shovel.

Instead of murder he fired up the jack hammer. No ear protectors. Pounding his thoughts to dust: Eggers; the detectives and the magazines; the stop-motion memories of Mary at the gig; Fletcher's grin. But Eggers sought him out. When he switched off to a startling quiet there he was, hurrying towards him and waving a mobile which Jonas saw was his own.

'I answered your phone. It was Mark and I figured Mark from The Hub and he might have some info.'

'Does he?'

'Yeah.'

'What is it?'

'We have to get back.'

'What for?'

'What's with the demon hammering, you on commission?'

Twenty, thirty cars crammed into the village hall car park. Eggers pulled up beside a Sky TV van. He lit a cigarette, settled the shades and swaggered towards the hall, Eastwood in a high-vis jerkin.

Jonas watched him go. He leaned against the van and thought about the magazines and who might know. A paranoia flash saw it happen, the TV crew by the door swinging the camera his way, the microphone in his face and *what do you have to say to these allegations?*

Inside, the hall was sweltering, much more male than the police briefing two days ago. He felt it, an excitement, all the more obvious for the attempts to hide it behind over-played frowns.

People remembered the Viking with the drinks tray. Some nodded, some looked away and some stared, as if daring him to say something. Jonas thought about the guy in Vigeland Park, Oslo, who said he recognised him

119

from the front page of *Verdens Gang,* then punched him in the face.

So let benevolence and camaraderie light the sweaty face but hit the dimmer switch, keep the mouth shut. Jonas smiled a small smile he hoped was low-key but suddenly worried was too enigmatic. Or too jovial? Or just really irritating? He decided to stop smiling.

'Jonas!'

He flinched at the tap on his shoulder. Mark. Electric-pink Bermuda shorts and an anxious babble.

'They want me to speak. I'm a *community leader,* apparently. The police want to stick with specialist search teams but they want to broaden it. I don't agree, what do you think, the police know what they're doing, don't they?'

Gone before Jonas could reply. He watched Mark climb the stairs to the stage, wondering why he chose *those shorts.*

The same table had been set up on stage. Mark was sitting alongside several other local luminaries: district councillor Bacon; the chairman of the parish council; the high school headmaster; the chair of the Rotary Club... A consensus would have taken a minute but they each got three, *the community should organise a parallel search... the police aren't making use of local knowledge and almost five days have passed... why are they still focusing on the park..?*

And then Mark. He gulped. He was bold. He made the absent counter-argument, *the police were the experts... they know their job... do we want to risk hampering the investigation?*

But as the disquiet rose, the more beet-faced Mark bumbled on. His voice took on a wavering shrillness and Jonas willed him to shut up and sit *down.* He reminded him of those out of place teachers back in

120

Bergen. No gravitas. The kids were merciless, like the crowd in the hall. Jonas picked out an underlying edge to the hostility, the same he had felt in Gladstone's look when the detectives left End Point that morning, an as yet unstated suspicion directed at someone who works with children and hasn't a child just gone missing?

Councillor Bacon brought the judo chop. The octogenarian Cabinet Member for Communities, ten times elected and a man of unswerving patrician certainty, silenced Mark with one line.

'As elected district councillor, I am the authority, Mr Stephens, and I call for a show of hands.'

'No' was called first. Mark's arm went up, along with a dozen others. The mutters rose, people turning to see who'd voted no. Some arms came down but Mark seemed to enter a state of stasis. His arm stayed up, palm out like a fascist salute, fingers strangely waggling.

Jonas couldn't help it. He watched his own arm rise up. Instinctive, an eccentric reaction from an eccentric man. Mark and Old Sam knew he was like this, Eggers too but Eggers had caught his eye and looked genuinely appalled. Jonas lowered his arm, down into the murmurs.

'Yes' won in a landslide.

Councillor Bacon went full Churchill. *Time is of the essence... community frustration will become community determination...* The TV crew arranged people behind him, kids and adults, older people, the visual will of the community reflected in the councillor's shiny bald head.

Suck it up. That's what the kids in The Hub said when someone screwed up. That's what Lacey would say. *Suck it up, Mr M,* he could hear her, if only he could hear her now. So Jonas could do nothing but suffer the stabbing looks on his treacherous back as he headed to the toilet to splash cold water on his face that was scarlet for a reason and everyone surely knew why.

He crossed to the urinals and chose the one furthest from the door, wondering if most men would do the same, even if no one was standing at any other. He directed his piss onto the blue disinfectant cube, which set him thinking about how long it would take to dissolve.

Imagine it was your job, Lacey, that you're a boffin working for Unilever? Would you wake at night, heartsick at the degeneration of your cancer-curing idealism? Or would you be excited by building the ultimate, long-lasting disinfectant cube? And why blue or yellow? What's the reason, Lacey? Why, in all the urinals of all the world, are they only blue or yellow?

Lacey had started laughing now, a great sense of humour that girl. Jonas watched her laughing until she cried, he'd seen her cry a few times but that's what hugs were for. He hoped she wasn't disappointed with him. The no vote meant nothing. Don't read anything into it.

The door banged. He turned to two men, one he didn't recognise but the other he did.

Psycho Dave from the *Jonsok* party. 'Well, look who we've got here, Dr No himself.'

The other man laughed.

'Heard the police said a little hello.'

Despite the sense of threat, the words were actually a relief. The visit from the detectives was known about but not the reason, yet. On the outrage spectrum Dr No was infinitely better than something magazine-associated like *look who we've got here, Mr Paedo himself.*

Jonas walked to the hand dryer and Dave stepped in front it. He turned to the paper towels but the unknown man moved towards him. He braced himself and Munich flashed, the three skinheads who jumped Kiev Dimitri when he went to the bar in Laimer's beer garden. Dimi was big. He'd taken out two by the time Jonas reached him, just in time to get his nose burst.

Then the door opened again and there was Eggers. *Let it go, lads* and the two men backed off.

Eggers stared at Jonas as he crossed to the urinal and when Jonas tried to speak he said *shut it* so Jonas did. Psycho Dave laughed, ushering him towards the door with a deferential flourish. Jonas took the invite, listening to their raised voices all along the corridor until the door closed, how Pete and Jake saw him fiddling with Lacey's zip at the talent show... doesn't take Stephen fuckin Fry to figure out what the cops wanted... weird Viking cunt.

Eggers, though. Jonas had disappointed him. This was actually upsetting. He leaned against the corridor and noticed he was shaking, shaking as he stared at the opposite wall, the knit-and-natter and playgroup posters, health and safety notices, small ads. Normality always re-asserted. Jonas had learned long ago how to outlast judgement. The first step? Fall in line.

Suck it up, Mr M.

Nothing to be done.

The only thing to do with fate was accept the damn thing. It was probably a deep genetic thing, evolved over hundreds of centuries. Think of the first people in Norway, stepping ashore from warmer climes. Now imagine that first Arctic winter, huddled and dying, horrified by the disappearance of the sun and screaming into the bone-cold. Then, over *looong* time, they figured out how to survive. They learned how to live with it. Nothing to be done.

So let them stare when Jonas came back into the hall. Let them frown when he joined a group mapping out a search of the woods. All aboard the Atonement Train, Jonas and Mark and all the others who'd voted no, now helping out, each with their own reasons to consent.

Even Fletcher, it seemed. Jonas hadn't noticed him until now. He was with another group, down by the stage. Then Mary appeared. She stood with her arms folded as Fletcher walked over. He spoke to her for several seconds, a frown creasing her forehead. When Fletcher straightened up and looked right at Jonas, Mary did too. She *scoured* him with that gaze.

His first thought was of a school assembly. Singled out by the head and made to stand.

The next was just as random.

His mother.

The incessant post-divorce questions when he came back from the fortnightly father weekend, a cross-examination of his dad's behaviour, movements and *does he talk about me, son, does he ask about me, Jonas, does he?*, her sad desire for information as overwhelming as Jonas's was to know what Fletcher had said to Mary. She was still staring, then someone was asking him something and when he looked back Mary and Fletcher were gone.

The need to know, it could push you close to the edge, close and then over, down like a stone.

And when you finally did know, how did you know you did? How many times had you been truly sure you had all the information needed to be utterly certain? Never, it never happened. As with Eva and Anya, the hospital and the trial. Jonas had to know every medical and legal fact, poring over them obsessively because he was convinced that in knowledge there was comfort. There wasn't. But it didn't stop him looking for it in those details.

A few people were staring again. The Atonement Train was a relic, the engine rusted and seized. He thought about the magazines. Someone breaking in to The Hub and picking the lock on the drawer. Then a phone call. He saw a bearded man whispering in the half-light.

Twenty

Jonas closed the front door. *A bearded man whispering in the half-light?* Where did he get all this nonsense?

They weren't waiting for him. No Fletcher sneer. No disappointed Mary shaking her head. He waited a bit longer then went up to the spare room and knocked on the door without thinking.

As if he was intruding.

Fletcher. He was settling deeper. The sleeping mat and bag had been left out instead of rolled up, clothes taken from the rucksack and folded into a neat pile under the window. The one-eyed doll seemed happy enough, peering back at him from the sleeping mat with strange and unknown significance. It had been carefully placed there, no casual pick-up-and-throw.

As Jonas had again been cast off. Big Haakon once told him *you're nothing without roots, son, just a leaf drifting on the stream.* You took those roots for granted until one day you noticed they'd come loose and *whoa,* you've drifted a long way, these surroundings sure are strange…

He found the will and the title deeds in a rucksack pocket. He could burn them but Fletcher would simply produce others. Those magician-like gifts should be appreciated. Despite Jonas now locking every door and window, Fletcher still found a way in. Changing the locks would make no difference, he was sure of it.

Archibald Hackett… leaving the property known as End Point to my grandson, Adam Fletcher.

Something in the different names. Jonas went downstairs and cracked a beer. Sat in the glooming kitchen and wondered. Something in the names, stopping him going to the cops and getting him evicted. 'Something *fishy*, Holmes.' A terrible English accent that made him laugh.

'What's fishy?'

He looked up, startled. 'Where did you come from?' Mary was standing in the sun room doorway.

'I was in the garden.'

'How did you get in?'

'You gave me a key. So I could do the cleaning?'

'You were there all along?'

'Sometimes you can't see what's right underneath your nose.' Her smile wavered.

Jonas set aside for later any thought about what that might mean. 'You want a drink?'

'Sure. In a minute.'

First of all she cleaned. A point being made. Jonas watched her hoovering until she waved him away and he went outside, into a poised emptiness, fans of cypress on a coal blue sky. Now and then a dipping bat.

Five minutes later she joined him. The dozen or so tea-lights he'd put on the grass between the deck chairs flickered in the shadows like questions. She sipped at her glass of wine and glanced at him, observing without catching his eye while Jonas did exactly the same.

'I can't remember the last time I hoovered.'

'Tell me about it.'

'You were in there for five minutes!'

'You can get a lot done in five minutes!'

'I have allergies.'

'And?'

'That's why I don't use it, the hoover. Makes me sneeze.'

126

'Right, *sure.*'

And still the surveillance. These interactions, where no one acknowledged there were two dialogues happening; the actual conversation with the other person and the hidden, underlying considerations. Maybe schizophrenia is our natural state, echoes of an old paranoia, one eye on the foraged berries, the other on the drooling neighbours a few caves along.

'I love the summer sky,' he said. 'It gets so much darker here than Norway.'

'What's that like?'

'Endless dusk.'

'I don't know if I'd like that, it seems sad in a way. Like you're waiting for something that never comes.'

'The darkness?'

'Yes, the night. I like the night. Well, nights like this.'

'You haven't seen the winters!'

A disguised formality to the conversation, he thought, a dance with awkward steps. He took her as she him, modest hands and cautious twirls, waiting for the right moment for a letting go, a calypso spin away from *nothing truly said* and revealing, for a moment, what lay beneath.

She glanced up, up and away, a smile coming to her face. 'The trees look like waves on a beach.'

He followed her gaze, up to the cypress fronds, lazy undulations against the light grey sky. 'You know what? I never remember in motion, it's just snapshots, like photographs.'

'How do you mean?'

'There's no movement. I want to remember like a Chinese painting.'

A little smile now.

'I'll show you.' He took her hand and she tensed, briefly, but let him lead her to the living room.

He pointed at the scroll painting above the fireplace. 'Li Po. He was China's greatest poet. Well, I don't

127

know if it's really him but I'm sure it is, I like to think it is. *Lifting my head I watch the bright moon, lowering my head I dream that I'm home.* Look at the brushstrokes. Everything's moving, you can *see* the wind blowing in the trees. I want to *remember* like that.'

She looked at him, carefully holding his gaze this time. Those underlying considerations, bubbling up.

'How did you end up here?' she asked.

'The village?'

'Yes.'

'I worked construction. Few years back I was living in Bergen and signed up for an oil rig job in Scotland. I decided to stay.'

'Simple as that.'

'Not much to say. A few jobs here and there and then I came here. Eggers told me about the council job.'

'What about your family? Don't you miss them?'

'My mother's dead. I was never really close to my father. He lives in Larvik, south coast.'

'No children?'

'No.'

'You like them though, don't you?'

'Of course. I used to teach, once upon a time. In Norway. It's why I volunteer at The Hub.'

She looked at him. Away and back again, that way she *looked*. 'Fancy going for a walk?'

Jonas said ok but wasn't sure. The world was ever impending, always something coming but who knows exactly what, a confetti of endings to this night falling from Mary's gaze.

They headed along the street, past Gladstone's café and then right, towards the village centre. By *The Jade Dragon* their steps came into unison, a beat they noticed at the same time a few moments later, a quick look enough to break the rhythm, one again become two.

'Disgusting.'

128

For a moment Jonas thought she was talking about him. The *magazines*, Fletcher, that's what he'd said to her.

'Look at it.'

She was looking directly ahead and shaking her head.

The village square. Like a location film shoot. The residential cars parked beside the green had gone, replaced by Winnebago-style broadcast wagons that shouted *we are the TV, we are the NEWS!*

Thick wires trailed to throbbing generators and floodlights. Even now, way past midnight, people milled around, half-cut drinkers from *The Mucky Duck*, a few teenagers and a gaggle of media types in white shirts and skewed ties, sitting on a bench, drinking Corona beer with chunks of limes stuffed in the neck. Some of them were eating fast food from the vans parked haphazardly on the green itself, retail initiative on the sacrosanct *green*. Mrs Hawthorne would be appalled at the *Gourmet Chef* dishing up *authentic Turk-shish kebabs*, *Rockin Rocco* his *Pizza the Action*. Scowling over all was the church, aloof in its floodlights, the steeple following its Alpha course into the sky, reaching, as ever, for the universal.

'It's all a show,' Mary said. 'Look at them, stuffing their faces like they're at the pictures. Lacey's disappeared and it's all a big laugh. Like Saturday night TV, a bloody blockbuster.'

She stalked across the square, right up to the group of journalists. Jonas listened to her harangue as he followed. They turned to him, plaintively, he thought. He smiled and shrugged.

'Do you have children?'

No reply.

'Do you have *children*?'

Again the glances at Jonas, puzzled, like, *what's with your crazy woman, control her*. One of the men stood up

129

and Mary pushed him back onto the bench. He held up his hands, backing off.

'You're a bunch of parasites!'

Someone whooped, over by the kebab van, someone else said *course we are* but hey, dontcha know, the public wants what the public gets, so why not a few cold beers, a doner and chips to fuel the energy to find the fresh angle, we're on the other the side of the arc people, slippety-sliding from *breaking news* to *our top story* to the three-day interest peak to *in other news* and remember, there's lotsa competition out there, a new series of that God-awful talent show has just started so c'mon, its bread and circuses, raise the game. And one journalist did, stepping back to a safer distance and filming the incident on his mobile phone and there, *there's* the development to take the story back to the top of the news!

Mary's rant ended abruptly. She looked around as if she wasn't sure what to do then hurried away at a near run. Jonas followed. She was still furious, arms wrapped around herself and only slowing down when the streetlights ended and the darkness began. She stopped altogether midway along the river bridge, the traffic lights casting wan shimmers on the water.

'I wouldn't mind at all,' she said. 'If I thought for one minute it would help find her.'

'Maybe it will.'

'Yeah, right.'

And she turned quickly. Flint in the eye. He saw Fletcher again, whispering in her ear. She knew about End Point. She was going to ask what the *fuck* are you doing here? What's your *game*?

'You seemed to know her.'

'Lacey?' The night tilted a little.

'That night at the talent show. I watched you. At your party as well. You seemed very close.'

The traffic lights changed to green, a colour to match

his sudden nausea. Whatever Fletcher told her had nothing to do with End Point. This was something much more troubling.

'I liked her a lot.'

'Liked?'

'I mean *like*. I think she sees me as a father-figure. Have you met her parents?'

'They're not exactly... present.'

'I've known people like that all my life, they shouldn't be allowed to have children.'

'Shouldn't be allowed?'

'No. They shouldn't. All they do is pass on pain and trauma, and the whole cycle repeats.'

'We've all got the right to have kids!'

'The right to inflict pain? They need to be protected from their parents, and kids like Spencer.'

'Spencer? He's ok, he's just – '

'He's a little pervert and he doesn't deserve her!'

'And you do?'

He stared at her. 'What does that mean?'

'Something Adam said. Forget it.'

Jonas didn't speak. He was thinking of Big Haakon, and how if everything was interconnected then there was no way of knowing when something long buried might re-surface.

'I'm going to tell you something,' he said. Very carefully, a voice he wasn't sure he recognised.

'Do it then.'

And he was about to. And then he wasn't. *Do it then.* It sounded harsh, a bit too greedy.

'Come round tomorrow night. After the search.'

At that exact moment, Fletcher was studying Mary's face in close-up, 14x zoom. For a second she seemed to look right at him. He held his breath, a familiar, animal response, feeling a dissonant prickle of vulnerability

131

and security caused by clarity of the night-vision binoculars and the dark night. They called it *black light* in the Marines. It should be *green light*.

The Yukon Ranger binoculars were the best kit he'd used outside Marine-issue. The counsellor wouldn't be happy. He'd told him to avoid associative triggers: war films; news reports from warzones; anything military-related that *might take you back to that place you don't want to be.*

Later, long afterwards, middle of the day in some overheated shopping mall, middle of the night on the hostel sheets, Fletcher would want to track the counsellor down, scream at him that there was nowhere to go other than *back to that place.* It was at least normalising in its nightmares and its flashbacks, *that place* made so much more sense than here.

He focused on Mary's eyes. He knew who she was now. He'd probably known since he saw her at Mortensen's party. He looked away from the eyes and studied the mouth, the elegant curve of the chin and jawline, trying to remember, wondering what it would feel like to touch her the way Mortensen now did, a hand on top of hers and Mary now turning to face him.

He'd followed them from End Point. He'd been in the trees. He watched Mary's outburst in the square then lost interest, heading to The Skull and setting up the tripod, facing the binoculars out the left eye, east across the golf course. No particular reason other than why not, he liked the Black Light. Then Mary and Mortensen appeared on the road bridge. He had to force himself to stop staring. It felt too much like his aunt behind the net curtains. The counsellor said he was obsessive but that every compulsion was a symptom of something deeper and once those depths were uncovered the compulsion would fade, *like morning mist.*

The counsellor was a liar or a fool. Those images were

going nowhere, no matter all those conversations and all the milligrams of the drugs that made muddy shapes of the dying and a mumble of their animal screams, but the images all the more unsettling for being not quite visible and not quite audible. The counsellor was captivated, he wanted more.

So after telling him how he killed the Afghan girl Fletcher told him about his little sister.

The counsellor had flushed, trying to hide his exhilaration but obviously thinking conditions, *syndromes*. Fletcher helped him down the diagnostic path, gave him detail, easy-flow nonsense about searching for pictures of young girls in magazines which he would rip into pieces and bury in parks and woods, roadside verges. It was priceless, the way the counsellor's concern mingled with his professional pleasure and touched on such hilarious self-importance.

It wasn't too often the counsellor came across a Corporal Fletcher. He could see the bland consulting room now, sitting again in that chair, not a couch like in a film, just a hard black plastic chair and nowhere to put your elbows. Hands held up in front of his face, Fletcher was demonstrating how he ripped the pictures. *The shreds fall like confetti*, he told the counsellor.

The village teams were going to search this area tomorrow. He imagined the excitement of coming across a patch of disturbed ground, digging down to a pile of ripped up paper, obviously a picture of a girl, a teenage girl like Lacey. They would cluster round, thinking about a dark figure, stooped in the middle of the night, dirt under the fingernails. And the longer he thought about that crouching, digging figure the more familiar became his doubt.

Two hours later he finished the sweep. No paper shreds in the blackberry bushes, no tell-tale disturbances on

133

the ground. He climbed back inside The Skull and checked the binoculars. Mary and Mortensen were gone. The only movement was the shifting colours of the traffic lights on the river. He swept east to west and back again, searching for a similar monochromatic certainty about something that might or might not have happened here. The edgy panic had gone. It was bizarre to think he could do something as unsettling as rip up pictures of young girls. And then bury them? No one passing him on the street would suspect this of him, as he wouldn't think it of them. That's the thing, we're all so normal until we aren't.

Twenty-one

Jonas was in Big Haakon's kitchen. Dirty dishes and his fat dog Freki. A howling wind drove hailstones against the window. Axel was standing beside him, shouting *duck and dive, duck and dive* as Haakon danced round him, boxing-gloved hands hanging loose then suddenly jabbing, Jonas always a moment late to protect himself. Mary appeared at the window. She was laughing.

'You getting up today?'

'Go *away*, Axel.'

'Who the hell is Axel? You're not in Viking land now, boy.'

Jonas flailed, surfacing from sleep and trying to re-root himself in space. Big Haakon kept on pummelling but the voice wasn't his. He opened his eyes to Eggers's grinning face, appearing and disappearing behind the white pillow that he was beating him on the head with.

'What's the deal, man, stop doing that!'

'I'll stop doing it when you get up. Or maybe I won't.'

'Christ sakes!'

'Blas-*phemer*!'

And Eggers whacked him savagely, full on the face, forcing Jonas to roll over and get up.

'You made it. Well done. I thought you were dead to begin with. First few thumps you barely moved.'

'Is this punishment then?'

'Eh?'

'For voting no.'

135

Eggers threw the pillow at him. 'If you like.'

'Could have been worse.'

'You saw Dave and his friend.'

'Thanks for that.'

'Don't thank me, Jonas. I could've slapped you too.'

'What are you doing here anyway?'

'You still half asleep? You told me to pick you up.'

Jonas nodded vaguely. He looked behind Eggers at the open door. The chair he'd jammed under the handle the night before to prevent Fletcher getting in was over by the window. It had a pile of clean underwear on it, the pile he put on the floor when he moved the chair.

'How'd you get in?'

'Eh? The key, dumbass, the one you leave under the plant pot. That's another dumbass thing to – '

'Not the front door. The bedroom.'

Eggers looked at him carefully. 'Get the pills, will I dear? How did I get in? Through... the... *fuckin*... door.'

When Eggers went downstairs, Jonas pulled it open and shut a few times, making sure it still fulfilled its function as a normal and not a magic door. He moved the chair back under the door handle and pulled it down. The handle got stuck under the back-board and the door wouldn't open. So how had Fletcher got inside? Had he come in the bloody *window*?

Across the landing the spare room door was closed. Maybe he was in there and maybe not.

'You coming then?'

'On my way.'

Jonas already hurrying down the stairs. No way he was hanging around for the bearded ninja in the red shorts to come swinging out of the loft and kick him in the throat. No sign of Fletcher downstairs either. Just his coffee mug on the table beside Eggers and an open sun room door. Eggers might have looked at him strangely, or maybe it was just Eggers being Eggers. He nodded at the open door. 'Thought you were paranoid about another break-in?'

Councillor Bacon preened on the green. A tweed-jacketed peacock of grave demeanour. But the strap of his megaphone was rainbow coloured, a dash of Gay Pride which gave a fruitier counter-impression, the venerable councillor as a ripe old queen. He was helped onto a bench and waved his arms for quiet. The whole village seemed to have turned out, briefed by Bacon in the fizzing rain.

Jonas scanned the crowd, clusters of families and friends under a hundred umbrellas. A police officer in a yellow bib stared at him, the gaze locked on every time Jonas glanced up. He looked round but not too closely. Told himself no one else was staring, no other hints that the magazine story was out.

It would, of course, just like he remembered. Right now someone, maybe that staring cop, was firming up the cartoon snowball, ready to roll it down the hill and swallow him up.

His thoughts drifted to Lacey, Bacon just a buzz on the edge of his consciousness, avoidable, unlike the girl. His stomach turned when he thought of last night's conversation with Mary. Heat in his cheeks now, hotter the more he turned it over. He kept his head low but when he looked up again there she was, twenty feet away and frowning, probably wondering about his big red face.

That British comedy show from the 1970s, his dad loved it. Jonas couldn't remember the name. The one with the big finger that would come down from the sky. That's what Mary's appraising glance felt like. A comedy finger, pointing right at him. All it needed was a sudden klaxon and the crowd scattering, Jonas caught in the spotlight from a police helicopter.

The Day-Glo search teams straggled out of the village towards Ragley Woods, spilling like the rain onto the road. Jonas was in Group One, the western team. When they veered onto the muddy river path, Group Two kept on the road, heading for the 4x4 access, coming in from the east. Both groups would rendezvous at Smitty's Leap in the dead centre of the woods.

At 9 am precisely a whistle blew sharply, spooking a flock of river ducks to flight. Left and right of Jonas at ten metre intervals were people he didn't know. Team West headed into the trees to look for Lacey, who wouldn't be found because when did that ever happen?

At least Jonas liked the woods. They were imperturbable. Made him think of druids in the cool dawn. He'd thought about bivvying down with them when he arrived in the village. But a car park notice-board told him Ragley Woods were used for academic research. The metal cages in the trees were for analysis of bird behaviour, the staked-off areas around badger sets to investigate territorial patterns. Chances are there were cameras. He didn't want to be filmed building a shelter, a white-skinned Bigfoot with darting eyes. So he headed instead for the sickly copse of car-stained white-beam down by the dual carriageway.

Team West found nothing. Closest they got was a boiler suit. An excited shout after lunch brought everyone running to a stagnant pool. A piece of dark fabric was just visible under the murky water, a quick hook and grab with a hazel switch and.... Jonas chuckled, nudged the man beside him. *Imagine what his wife said when he came home in just his boots.* The man just stared. *C'mon.*

138

Lacey had a great sense of humour! He decided it best not to tell him this.

The ghost men appeared soon after. He'd left the line for a piss and was zipping up when there they suddenly were. It wasn't until they hurried closer that he noticed the black balaclavas.

Then Jonas was running and they were running and sometimes you slip and sometimes in the worst of places, like now, foot on a wet root and *thaaar he goes,* Jonas tumbling down a bank but savvy enough when he hit bottom to curl into a ball, brace for the kicks.

'Watch your step there, Thor.'

He tensed.

Nothing happened.

A long minute later he sat up. Cautious like, but no one around. Beside him, rain pattered a magazine left open at the centrefold. A young woman in a cheer-leader's outfit lay with her legs spread, hands cupped round her breasts. He lay back down and whacked his head off the ground a few times. He should go running after the balaclava men with a Formula One safety flag, make a frantic T with his hands. Time out lads, time *out,* slow this all down!

He remembered the policeman on the village green staring at him. Off-duty down the pub. A few pints, a few loose words. Everyone but Jonas wanted to be the centre of something.

Twenty-two

Mary kicked at a rotten log. White shreds of dead wood spilled onto the wet grass, like maggots. Her thoughts of journalists were automatic, as was the nausea. She was all over the TV.

The morning shows of Sky, BBC and ITV all led with Mary. Each news anchor settled a straight-from-the-box sympathetic frown and delivered variations on the same theme, *local anger... an overspill of frustration...* And over the shoulder of each a similar freeze-frame of Mary's angry face, the mobile phone footage of her outburst on the green repeated again and again.

Turning TV off and radio on she heard a trailer for the morning phone-in, the supercilious presenter – who used to present an '80s game show – intoning about *media prurience... the close-knit rural community,* blah-de-banalities that had her switching off again.

Because of Mary a fourteen-year-old had gone missing all over again, the girl she was now searching the woods for. The rain made it worse, saturating the world in the melancholy reason for being there, her hiking boots leaking as the downpour met warm earth and created a steam-like haze that made vague coloured daubs of the searchers to her left and right.

Her husband had cried off from the search. She'd got in at 1 am the night before but he hadn't appeared until three. He crept around in the dark then fell over. *That's how I must have tweaked my back,* he said in the

140

morning, his breath like something had died in his mouth.

Not that a bad back stopped him shoving a hand between her legs. Mary closed them tightly then opened them. She was thinking about Jonas, the look on his face as he watched her hoovering his living room. She liked it. She wanted that look. She'd been wearing her yoga pants, the ones that showed off her bum, and a loose white shirt. It was hot, natural to leave a couple of buttons open. Like an erotic movie, *Emmanuelle the Maid*. All so very, very English.

Her husband would probably be more appalled by the cleaning than the flirtation. She'd be demeaning herself, or rather him, bringing him way down in the estimation of his poker friends, his *P-Buds*, as he called them. The supermarket was bad enough, but cleaning? He'd hate it, which gave her a sense of satisfaction that was wildly out of proportion. She moved her legs further apart. Maybe he'd even be a bit jealous, his wife bent over in a strange man's living room, lazily running a hoover back and forth, his eyes on her. She pushed her husband's shoulders and he obliged, moved down, did what he was good at.

Then Lacey flashed. She remembered what Fletcher had said and felt repulsed: by Jonas, by her husband's hands, by herself. She curled into a ball and thought about jacking the job, before deciding it depended on what he told her that evening. *I'm going to tell you something*.

Jonas had been at the 7 am search briefing. She saw him briefly. When he chose the western group she joined the eastern. It was his fault she felt so apprehensive. Instead of just telling her, he'd made a big thing of it. *Come round tomorrow night*. All these people looking for Lacey and no one knew what Mary Jackson knew, not that she knew anything. A sudden whistle shattered

141

her thoughts. A man was waving his arms at her and shouting. She was too far ahead of the search line. She had to move more slowly. She stared at the ground and imagined coming across something, a trainer or a t-shirt. Just don't make it a person. Her stomach lurched when a shout brought people running. But the Wellington boot was falling apart and must have been there for years. She wondered who'd left behind a lone green boot, now an adopted part of the mud and beech husks, the grey roots gnarling out of the earth like bones.

The search took a 10 am break. Mary was soaked. Lomax the butcher ambled over, face the colour of a sirloin steak. She cringed inwardly when he said he'd seen her on morning TV.

'You're a legend,' said Lomax.

She wondered if her husband would think the same when he caught up with the news.

When Lomax walked off she noticed Adam. He was standing under a big beech some metres away, talking to Jackie Eggers, Dave from *The Hand and Shears* and someone she didn't recognise. Dave jabbed a finger in Eggers chest and the man she didn't know pulled him back.

Mary had gone to high school with Dave. He was a nutter then and still was, worked the saw-mill and had two vicious kids. He waved at Eggers dismissively and he and the unknown man hurried away. Eggers shook his head and looked to the sky. Adam had disappeared.

Cousin Adam.

Mary had cousins, and didn't know much about them. Yet it seemed odd that cousins from different countries found the opportunity to dislike each other as much as Jonas and Adam. She imagined her daughter, mock-serious. *How very unusual, mother*, then laughing. Mary missed their conversations, Kitchen Confidential they called it. Andrea wanted to come home and help

142

with the search. Mother and child, looking for someone else's daughter. The idea was unbearable. She remembered when Andrea was Lacey's age, boys becoming interested, men.

Men like Jonas? Again, she thought about what Adam had told her and Jonas still had to.

Twenty-three

Jonas left the search and hurried back through the trees, twitching at shadows and sudden birds. He didn't see the balaclava men again. Most of the village was still searching the woods so few people saw his muddy hobble back to End Point. It was something, he supposed, some might call it luck although others would just scream *fuck*, as Jonas did at one point.

He showered. Lay on his bed with the window open. A soft fussing rain, now and then the quick rush of a passing car. He heard a blackbird too, which made him think of The Beatles.

Eva.

She loved The Beatles.

Jonas cried, although he didn't want to. That Lutheran imprint from the old country. Never moan, just *endure*, a fair day's work for a fair day's pay and all the other crap. Well, fuck that. Fuck stoicism. Tonight he'd peer in the mirror at his bruised face and feed his sadness, look again for forgiveness from Eva for what had happened, the story he had to tell once more.

Downstairs, he found Fletcher in the kitchen. In trousers, amazingly, but still bare-chested. He was devouring a bowl of pasta, dribbles of tomato sauce on the table. He said nothing but followed every move Jonas made. When Jonas spun round to tell him to piss off, the table was empty. He went into the sun room and saw Fletcher lying starfish-splayed outside on the wet grass.

'You should try it.'

'Where were you this afternoon?'

'The search.'

'Didn't see you.'

Fletcher sat up and turned round. Grinning. 'Have I done something wrong?'

'Forget it.'

'Suit yourself,' he said and lay back on the grass. 'What happened to your face? Looks *nasty*.'

Jonas closed his eyes. Let it go. Be like Li Po. Keep quietly sweeping the steps of the temple.

'It's cold.' Fletcher was waving his arms back and forth on the grass, like a child making a snow angel.

'You'll *catch* a cold.'

Fletcher stopped moving and turned round. He looked as if he was about to laugh, then frowned.

Jonas looked away. This unbidden concern, he wanted to take it back. But it was said, was it not, by *gurus and wise men*, that compassion should be maintained regardless of circumstance. And if compassion could be sustained in all this weirdness then imagine a month, six months, a year from now; J-Man and the Bearded Ninja, a couple of likely lads, whistling a merry tune, a friendly salute as they pass each other on their way to and from the morning bathroom. The strangeness of today is the normality of tomorrow, Confucius said that.

He looked at Fletcher, who'd gone back to his rainy angel flailings. He was sure Fletcher hadn't been one of the balaclava ghost men. One of them was too squat, the other too tall.

It had to be Psycho Dave.

Or Buzz Cut.

Anger hit him. Not frustrated anger that Jonas

145

remembered from teaching, some little bastard giving him cheek and that sudden urge to slap him. This was different, the kind that spooked you for a long time, uncontrolled, pre-socialised anger like back in primary when he got in a fight with Peter Møller and couldn't stop, whacking Peter's head off the playground concrete until a teacher dragged him away. He would have killed him, he was sure of it.

In a short moment he was in the street, running. Buzz Cut's local, *The Black Lion*, was closer than *The Hand and Shears*, where Psycho Dave worked, so Buzz Cut it would be. Jonas was going to glass him. With his own pint glass. Walk right up, wait for the smirk then *glass him.*

Inevitably, Buzz Cut wasn't there. Jonas stood in the doorway for a few moments, chest heaving. Clara and Old Sam were talking at the end of the bar and turned round to stare.

'Jonas. You ok?'

'Looks like he's run a marathon,' said Clara.

'Get this Norwegian a drink. Jonas, come and join me. I was thinking about Bergen this morning.'

Jonas's shoulders sagged. The anger suddenly drained, a tremble in his hands now, a weakness.

'I tell you again. I have no idea why you're here. Why did you ever leave that fine city?'

Old Sam's eyes were bright. Jonas gave the cue, automatic. 'I ask myself the same thing.'

'The women, eh?'

'Bergen women are the best, Sam. You know they are.'

'I most surely do.'

Old Sam launched again into his story about the barmaid at *Logen's* whose name he could never remember no matter how he tried and I've even looked at books, Jonas, can you believe it, lists of Norwegian and Scandinavian names but none of them were hers but surely one of them must be and how could I forget her, blonde hair to her waist and not a day goes by without me thinking about her and maybe she thinks about me, Jonas, do you think she does?

'I don't care, Sam.'

The old man turned. The light in his eyes seemed to waver. 'Well... She really was beautiful.'

'I don't care, Sam. Every time I come in here you tell me the same story and I just don't care.'

'There's no need to – '

'Shut up, Sam. Shut up!' And Clara was suddenly there, telling him to calm down, calm *down*.

Old Sam was silent. Clara stood at a wary distance. Jonas gulped down his pint but couldn't get rid of the lump in is throat. He looked up at the gantry mirror and in the reflection of the window saw birds in the sky, little birds as carefree as the children whose affection was forbidden. When he got up to leave Sam placed a hand on his arm. A hard squeeze.

'Be careful, son...'

Jonas looked at him but the old man was staring straight ahead.

'... with the friends you have.'

Jonas went home. Sat around. Played Can records. *Vitamin C* over and over until the world shifted so off-kilter that anything would make sense. Fletcher appeared once or twice. Standing in the doorway. A grin like irony defined. The ninja with one motive, *getting him out*, a Zen presence that could wait forever until the *koan* detonated. *Ah, I get it, you want me to leave!*

Mary appeared at 10 pm. A soft but persistent rapping at the front door. When he opened it she pushed past him quickly, a glance backwards but the street was deserted. Her smile was brief. He thought of old Sam, how friendship was so fragile. One, two blinks and it's gone.

'I was worried. I didn't see you at the rendezvous in the woods and I didn't see you back in the square.'

He pointed at his nose.

'What happened?'

'I walked into a tree. Didn't want to sit there bleeding with everyone watching.'

'You walked into a tree?'

'Big beech.'

'Looks like a bitch.'

'What?'

'It looks sore.' She moved her chair round to his side of the table and gently touched her thumb and forefinger to the bridge of his nose. 'A bit swollen. You should go to the doctor.'

'It's fine. Don't fuss.'

'I'm not fussing.'

'It's *fine.*'

'Just let me *look!*'

'*Ok.*'

She touched his nose again. Let her hand brush his cheek as she sat down in the chair.

'I've been thinking about you,' he said.

She blushed.

'I don't know what's happening here and God knows I've never been good at this.'

'Jonas, don't – '

'Sorry. Forget about it.'

'You said you had something to tell me. On the bridge.'

He was silent for a moment. 'What did he say?'

'Adam?'

'Did he say I had something to do with Lacey?'

'Maybe.'

Jonas shook his head and walked out into the garden.

148

The security lamp clicked on and illuminated Fletcher's towel, a dark rectangle on the wet grass. Like the opening to a chasm.

'I get it,' he said. 'You see an older man with a young girl. He's affectionate with her. And the stories you read. Bloody hell, they're enough to strike you blind. What do we really know about people, eh? How fragile is our trust that we can imagine that scenario, *believe* it?'

'Look Jonas, I'm – '

'You're here for my confession, is that it?'

'What do you expect? I ask about Lacey and you're all peculiar and say you've got something to tell me. What am I supposed to think?'

'Oh I don't know. That it might be something else. That your suspicion might just be wrong. That maybe because we seem to like each other I might have something to share with you.'

'Well, share it then.'

He stared at her. She'd stood up, little fists bunched at her sides. She looked ready to burst out crying.

'I came to Britain when my wife and daughter died, Eva and Anya. 22nd September 2005. A drunk driver outside Bergen. My daughter would be the same age as Lacey, fourteen.'

Mary blinked.

Her lips parted slightly and she seemed to empty of air. She sat down heavily on the sun room step. Jonas flung Fletcher's towel aside and sat down on the grass with his knees to his chest.

'Lacey reminds me – '

'*Don't*, Jonas.'

A hand touched his shoulder. He didn't turn until it gently shook him. Mary's hair, outlined in silver by the kitchen light. Her face in shadow but Jonas still able to see the concerned frown, the darker space of a mouth saying such gentle words of apology and sympathy.

149

Eva.

It could be her. Taking him by the hand and leading him back across the garden and into the dark house, up the stairs to his bedroom where she slowly undressed him, gently pushed him back on the bed and straddled him, night becoming breath in silence until all was white light, a voice he couldn't quite make out and again that self-pity he didn't want to think about.

He pretended to be asleep as Mary quietly dressed. He let her slip out without the goodbye that would have been simple but unbelievably complicated. He heard Fletcher leaving or maybe coming back and didn't care. Tonight he wouldn't barricade himself in. Nothing could reach him but remorse.

Twenty-four

Fletcher left End Point sometime after one, not wanting to hear any more of Jonas and Mary's strangulated fucking. He lay in The Skull unable to sleep, annoyed with himself for thinking about them. He kept seeing Mary, head moving against the pillow as Jonas pushed into her.

He hadn't gone out with Mary for long. Two weeks, Fletcher reckoned, hardly any time, even when you're sixteen. There was no logical reason for this jealous niggle, his reaction to the memory disproportionate, as usual, to what he actually remembered, which was little. For much the same reason, it was hard to decide if Mary's tired vulnerability was the effect of the teenage girl she'd been and not let go, or the middle-aged woman she'd become and didn't accept. He'd be sure to ask her when she'd figured out that dreams were the midwife of disappointment and growing up was about losing the ability to delude ourselves. Mary lived in disappointment. He'd seen her in her midnight kitchen, the radio softly on, staring out the window. Teenage Mary would surely be horrified by this clichéd affair with a man who was the *simple inversion of her husband*, as the counsellor might have described it.

Everyone liked absolutes. Fletcher found it reassuring when the counsellor called him *an introverted feeler*. But there was complacency in labels, the black and white got dull without some colour. So he cranked up the trauma-tised veteran role, rolled out lines like *I have seen such horror*, the gratuitous detail unsettling the counsellor but then, more slowly, himself. Because the horror was actually impossible to overplay, like Lieutenant Robinson, who stepped on an IED and it *was* as if a grey-red cloud had stained Fletcher's vision ever since, a burned-on after-image and an ever present echo of the explosion on the edge of his hearing. He wondered about Mortensen. A classic extrovert and connection seeker, he would have played straight with the counsellor. Yet each would have reached the same place, in the end.

The Norwegian must be wondering why he hadn't gone to the police. His contempt may be growing by the day. But Fletcher could handle that. He knew patience, cold winter doorways, hand out with the Styrofoam cup and diesel in his nostrils, waiting for the coins and watching the suspicious eyes, pity like a gemstone among all the indifference. In his mind, Mortensen was already gone, fading like the summer, a barely acknowledged presence and not even an irritation. One morning he'd realise he hadn't seen the Norwegian for days.

As the girl's disappearance would also fade. *The Race for Lacey... The Long, Hot Search for Lacey.* The headlines would move on to other lurid fascinations. Trauma passes, in time, leaving behind the guilt of chance remembrance, driving past Lacey's old house and why do you think of her now when you make this journey so often? Perhaps we remember as one person and forget as another, whoever we might have been at any given time in all the pouring years.

He glimpsed her then, his little sister, beyond The Skull in the shadowed distance by the fairy castle of hole seven, as she was before they made him leave here, before they made him kill. Or perhaps it was the girl in Sangin, it was so difficult to be sure these days. Fletcher had to get closer. He scrambled down out of The Skull and ran across the golf course.

152

As usual, she never let him get close. When he reached the crumbling plaster towers of the fairy castle she was back over by The Skull, which glowed in the light of a quarter moon as if daubed with luminescent paint. His sister was sniggering at him, sniggering as he stared at her.

You ask again. How much do I remember? But you know I remember it all, how you stood that morning on the sunlit path in your blue jacket and red and white polka dot dress as the sun beat down. Such a hot summer, as hot as this year's. I see your hand shade your eyes as you shout back I hate you, I hate you, I hate you because we have fallen out. Or rather it is me who has fallen out with you, once again. What do you expect, you are my little sister, you want me to notice you, always to notice you. If I did not then I do now, I see you everywhere, as there, lying in the Sangin bazaar in that pool of swelling red as every sound retreated, as if I had been plunged under ice water, and in truth I have never surfaced, never felt Molloy's hand on my shoulder, saying something I can't understand as I dip my finger in the sticky puddle the girl has left behind. So red. Red under blue, red as the polka dots on another dress in another place, so far away it is sepia-tinged and yet so immediate. How can I separate you, you two who are one? How can I possibly choose how to remember when you ambush me like this? Two against one, like bullies, like Private Davidson at boot camp before I broke his jaw. Your endless questions, each said with that little smile. Even God could not answer them, he who must let us all down in order that faith can be tested. Be glad you will never know the feeling of waking one morning with the absolute certainty that life has played a terrible trick and you will never figure out the scam. Be glad you will never feel the slow curdling of the spirit and optimism of the little girl who sang as she skipped along the English hedgerows and drew smiles with a kite on the Afghan blue. Be glad of that and leave me alone.

Twenty-five

On Friday morning Jonas phoned Boss Hogg. Told him he was sick. Hogg said *whatever* and hung up. Jonas kept listening, until a voice told him *the person you are calling has hung up*, again and again and now a different phrase: *the person you are calling knows all about the magazines... the person you are calling...* He should call Hogg back, tell him what he told the detectives, that if they were his, would he be stupid enough to leave them in a youth club drawer?

A week since the talent show, the first Hub night since Lacey had disappeared. A few of the parents complained about inappropriateness but Mark went ahead. *It's what she would want,* as people always said, an insistence on normality that was more about their ability or otherwise to deal with a situation than any real sense of what the person might think.

But Jonas. Here was a man who truly did not have a clue. To turn up to The Hub or not? Every time he decided yes he saw two black balaclavas and rain pattering a dirty magazine. By 6.30 he'd worked himself into a state of near stasis, only dragging himself from the house with the thought of needing to appear normal. As he opened the front door he realised that normal had packed up and fled. Trying to be normal might actually seem abnormal. He closed the door again. And opened it. Just breathe and walk, feel that gossamer soft air, Flash Gordon colours streaking the western sky, lilac and violet, blood orange.

154

To watch was to have the world slow. To have the world slow was to *chill out, Mr M.*

He managed it until Spencer P appeared. Suddenly beside him on his bike, a look of amused disgust. Jonas opened his mouth but Spencer P was saying something he didn't quite hear and accelerating across the village hall car park, veering towards the alleyway across by the health centre, Jonas sprinting after him and a twinge in the hamstring, the little bastard had made him pull a muscle and when he got to the alleyway Spencer P was gone.

He could hear his heart hammering, a hammering now becoming a humming, getting louder, maybe the sound of an imminent coronary and a panicked hand to the chest but the sound actually beyond him, he realised, above him on big blue a small plane, circling down, accelerating and throttling back, now melding into the whine of a sudden lawnmower, noise and heat suddenly swelling and when Jonas turned round Pete the village hall caretaker was staring.

It wouldn't do at all.

Li Po and Big Haakon. They'd roll with it. Haakon of the Apologies, the alcoholic who remembered just enough to keep forgetting. If you never learned then it must be a gift to be able to forget. Haakon disappeared after every binge and the idea was immediately appealing, ride it out, hide in the woods once more, Sycamore Camp and those headlight beams, crisscrossing his face like endless wagging fingers and tsk, tsk, Jonas, this is no way to behave and they were right, it was no way to behave, he was Jonas Mortensen. Jonas of the Plants. Mr M would not be cowed. So throw open the door to that hall and stride in. He belonged.

Mark disagreed.

Not straightaway.

His first action was to stare and bite his lip, his second

155

to get a big red embarrassed face as he watched Jonas get a coffee from the kitchen. Jonas waved and sipped, pondered Mark's face. It was alarming how a red that couldn't get any redder actually *got redder*. How long would it take him to crank up to whatever he was going to say? Five minutes, in the end.

'Evening.'

'Evening.'

'What happened to your face?'

'Walked into a door.'

'Look, eh... I think – '

'They aren't mine. Those magazines.'

'This isn't the time or the place, the kids will be here soon.'

'Did the police talk to you?'

'I was mortified. They asked if I'd ever phoned that outdoors centre and I haven't. They'd checked it out. They phoned up the number on the cover. You were the only one who called!'

'Who have you told?'

He looked away. 'I phoned round.'

'Thanks for that.'

'C'mon, Jonas. I didn't know what to do. I was going to call and then I wasn't. I didn't do anything until today. I've got a responsibility.'

'Today?'

'Yeah. Why?'

'You're a liar.'

'What?'

'Because people knew yesterday, Mark. *Yesterday*. So how's that, how did they find out?'

'I don't know. I didn't phone anyone until today.'

Jonas believed him.

'You should go home. It's the first time we've met since Lacey's been gone. The kids are going to be upset and we need to – '

'We need normality. Isn't that why we're here? That means me being here and – '

'Think about it from – '

'We're doing mushrooms.'

'Mushrooms?'

'*Mushrooms.*'

The word hung limp in the air. Jonas's hands shook as he set out the pictures on the table by the stage: fairy-ring champignons and panther caps, Fool's Morel and cep, some actual chanterelles he'd picked in the woods during the search. The idea was to have a quiz, *The Shroom of Doom*: guess the edible among the poisonous, build the knowledge that Jonas would test on a field walk.

The kids began to straggle in, about a dozen, fewer than usual. Most looked at Jonas then looked away.

Mark gathered everyone together, made a heartfelt speech about how *we all need to stay strong for Lacey, she'd want us to carry on as usual*... Eggers's daughters, Eloise and Laura, appeared a few minutes afterwards and made straight for Jonas, giving him a big hug. He held his arms away from them, aware of staring eyes. Typical Eggers, they hadn't been told yet.

'Will we find her, Jonas?'

Before he could think of any answer that wasn't utterly empty there was a loud shout of *Eloise*.

'Dad?' said Eloise.

Jonas looked towards the door of the hall. And the man himself, Eggers, striding towards him.

'What are you *doing*, dad?'

'Why don't you tell her, Jonas?' Eggers stopped a foot away from him.

'Come on, this – '

'Shut up. Tell her why the police talked to you.'

'Mr M?' said Laura.

'Come on then, *Mr M*. Tell her. You gonna?' He

leaned in, his nose almost touching Jonas's. 'We just got Mark's message. You've got some nerve being here. I want you gone. *Now*.'

'You don't really think – '

'Shut it. Just shut it!'

'What about you, *Jackie*? You forgotten your lunchtime shows?'

'What's he talking about,' asked Eloise.

Eggers flushed and stepped forward. 'Keep your mouth *shut*. I don't work with kids.'

'You're such a – '

A violent shove shut Jonas up, his head whipping back. He stumbled into the table and scattered mushrooms, losing his footing and down onto his arse, looking up as they all looked down and he finally realised his mistake. In being here, expecting nuance at a time of absolutes. He stood up, grabbed his back-pack and walked quickly across the hall.

In the lobby he almost knocked Mary over. She looked confused, then almost crestfallen.

'I take it you got a call from Mark?'

'Yes. Look, Jonas, I – '

'Everyone's made up their mind.'

'Can you blame them?'

'Can you meet me tomorrow? In town. Can you do that?'

Mary sighed and looked away.

'Please.'

'You should go home.'

'*Mary*.'

But walking past she reached out, touched his fingers. So lightly, an ambiguity. He thought of that night in his garden, an appraising gaze of this man, Jonas, whom she didn't know at all.

Twenty-six

As ever, the Saltmarket was crowded. Jonas stood in the town's main shopping street and stared up. Forget adverse weather, technical faults, there were no anomalies in the certainty that was a *scheduled flight-path*. SAS 263 perhaps, Oslo to Bergen. Up there in the contrail blues, heading west-north-west. Truly our lives were a search for the most direct flight.

So far he'd counted six smooth then furring white lines made by passing aircraft. Another appeared, north east to south west, bisecting two other, parallel lines and creating a Z. It delighted him, made him think of that black and white *Zorro* serial, he and Axel and swords made from sticks, a delight even the sweaty smell of pasties from the *Cornish Café* couldn't overpower.

People were staring, a few even looked up. *What's up there, what's up there?*, well whatever you want, write your story, white on blue and a gradual vanishing, *as all of us too must pass*. Straight from the Hollywood script, the stereotypical gloomy Scandinavian. Jonas might be long gone from Norway but it's as impossible to wipe off the genetic boot-print as it is to laugh at an Ingmar Bergman movie. All those endless winters, waiting for the silver in the east.

His happiness, it verged on manic. Mary had agreed to meet him. He was down for a Saturday shift but took another day off. Boss Hogg just said *whatever*. Anymore and it would become a pleasing habit, maybe the righteous principles of the old country were losing their grip.

The thought made Jonas wildly content and he returned every furtive glance from the passers-by with a beaming, care-in-the-community smile. Who cares, the sun might be hot, the street crowded with shrieking herds of teenage language students and over-friendly charity volunteers, but he'd escaped from the village, put distance between himself and the night before.

No one had followed him out of The Hub. No one jumped him on the way home, Eggers with a *banzai*, some maniac in a balaclava, not even Mary, running towards him with concern, tear-stained cheeks and throwing her arms round his neck, like a bad melodrama, which it was.

Back at End Point, Fletcher was sitting in the kitchen eating a Chinese takeaway. Rice in his beard and lips shiny with spare rib sauce, opening a can of beer and watching Jonas watch him.

'You packed yet?' Fletcher wiped his mouth on a white dish towel, leaving a browny streak.

'Have you?'

'I can wait. No worries.'

'Have you got a balaclava?'

Fletcher picked at his teeth then studied something on the end of his finger. 'Bit hot for that. Unless you're planning to stalk another little girl. Summer nights, creeping in an open window?'

'Fuck you.'

Fletcher reached into a bag of prawn crackers and started munching, open-mouthed. 'You need to relax, bro. Thought the night with Mary would have helped.'

'What's with the doll eh? You *freak*.'

Fletcher angled his head. 'C'mon, man, you can do better than that.' He got up and left the kitchen.

Jonas stared at the takeaway remnants. He felt the touch of Mary's hand as he left the village hall, saw her back arch in the half-light. And then the instinctive thought: *who would you choose, Jonas, if they were both standing in front of you right now, who would you choose?*

Just before midnight Mary texted to say she would meet him in town the next morning. Five hours after he had seen her at The Hub. Five hours to make a decision. He went to bed and again jammed the chair under the door handle. When he woke it had again moved to the window.

There was less activity on the village green. Marginally less, but noticeably, interest in Lacey faltering, despite the TV vans and the roving bands of hacks, the clusters of police and locals. A military occupation must be similar, that sense of over-exposure, a growing familiarity with the unfamiliar, a normalising that would abruptly end when the editorial interest guillotine came down. How long would it take, ten days, two weeks, longer? A special unit probably monitored ratings in real-time, phone to hand, ready to move the circus on.

Jonas gawped like everyone else. He paused at the war memorial to take it in, refusing the spectacle even as he indulged it. A few people glanced his way, because they all knew now, didn't they, come the day a sharpening of the pitchforks, come the night the mob... Like Big Haakon he'd hold his head high. But not *too* high. Instead of the busy bus stop by the green he chose another which hardly anyone used, a few streets away, round on Tanner Avenue.

There was a film crew midway along the street, directly opposite the bus stop. A small crowd was watching and as Jonas appeared some of them looked across. Maybe they knew him and maybe they didn't and where was the *damn bus when you wanted it*? A camera had been set up at the end of a garden path in front of the third

161

house in a terrace of four. Beside the cameraman was a boom operator and a mini-skirted woman with a clipboard. The woman called for quiet and a moment later a teenage girl in a short blue jacket and a red and white polka-dot dress came out of the front door. She walked down the garden path and turned right at the gate, along the pavement into the distance until a loud shout of *cut*.

He watched the re-enactment. A tightness in the guts. Then another take, forcing him to watch Lacey disappear again. The *details*. It was so obvious it took him a while to notice. They'd got some basic details completely wrong. The red and white polka-dot dress, that wasn't Lacey's. And her hair was blonde, not dark. The only thing right was the blue jacket. Then he remembered that Eggers had told him they'd already done a reconstruction. So why another?

When Jonas finally dragged his eyes from the criss-crossing airplanes he walked to the east end of Saltmarket. Then right, into Brandywine Passage, towards the University Lands, the crowds thinning until he was almost alone among the narrow lanes and the high limestone walls. Spires above him, tall bookcases through leaded windows. A solitary cyclist appeared, a smiling young woman, black flowing college robes as she passed. Jonas smiled back. Beside him, a stretch of scaffolding encased in blue plastic was whipped by a sudden gust of cold wind, rippling the length of the plastic and reaching the end just as the cyclist turned a corner.

Dissonance. It was always there, snapping at the heels. Did you really think this sun-blushed day, with its gentle calligraphy of white contrails on blue, would make it easy, Jonas, *to get away*?

He walked on, up to *The Mayor*, next to the independent

162

cinema he last went to years ago, a Hungarian movie called *Kontroll* with a beautiful woman who rode the Budapest subway dressed as a bear. He often used to go to *The Mayor*, the pub run by a skinny old Irishman with a pinched face and glacier-green eyes. Every space on the walls was covered with posters for classic films: *La Dolce Vita*, *The Asphalt Jungle*, *For a Few Dollars More*. He remembered a rainy winter's day, roll-ups and Jameson's, arguing movies with the Irishman in the near-empty pub, Johnny Cash and Kris Kristofferson on endless loop. *The Mayor* had been given a gastro makeover: tapas and Thai curries, a wine list to *rival the best restaurants*.

Three and a half minutes.

Jonas timed it. Three and a half minutes for the muzak to drive him into the garden, where he found a table beside a purple-flowered clematis filled with bees, and sipped his whisky. He stood up too quickly when Mary appeared, cracking his knee on the table. She didn't smile. Offered no sympathy. He wondered about this as he queued at the bar for her white wine.

'*Skål.*'

'Cheers,' she said.

'Nice day, eh?'

'We're not going to talk about the weather are we?'

'I guess not.'

'There used to be a beer called Skol. There were adverts on the TV with cartoon Vikings. I remember once, my parents were away and my brother was supposed to be looking after me. He came home with a case of Skol. Twenty-four cans. I remember him puking in the fireplace.'

'Sounds like a good night in!'

'You mean out.'

'What?'

'You say "that was a good night out".'

163

'But I mean in.'

'In?'

'Yeah. Back home. A night in with a few beers and *then* we go out because the booze is so expensive. We call it *foreplay*.'

'Foreplay?'

'No joke.'

A smile that started and stopped again. She glanced down at her wine, twirling the glass.

'Thanks for coming,' he said.

The eyes flicked up, bored into his. 'I don't want your thanks, Jonas. I'm not doing you a favour.'

'I didn't mean –'

'Finish that.' She nodded at his whisky. 'I'll get you another.' She knocked back her glass of wine and stood up. He realised she was waiting for him and quickly downed his whisky.

Afternoon drinking. Jonas dug it. He was kinda drunk now so no problem with saying *dug it*. Made him feel like a proper boozer. Young Mr M loved Charles Bukowski and old Jonas got nostalgic, now and then indulged an afternoon buzz and if there was ever a time to indulge it was now.

All this he told her, babbling into a day becoming more over-exposed with each drink. One day he'd be one of the old men sitting at the bar and nursing a two-hour pint. He *wanted* that.

'Really?' she said.

'Why not?'

'They're a bunch of old farts, that's why. Counting the days till death. If I get like that you can put a pillow over my face.'

'Your wish is my command.'

'One of them put his hand on my arm when I was getting the last round. I bet he had a hard-on.'

'Can't blame the man.'

'Pervert.'

'If the hat fits.'

'The cap.'

'What?'

'If the *cap* fits. That's the phrase. You know what you are?'

'Do I want to hear this?'

She didn't return his smile. 'A romantic.'

'What's wrong with that?'

Something flared in her eyes and disappeared. She looked up to the sky for a moment then back at him. 'What is this?' She leaned forward. 'Me and you. What do you want from me?'

'Well I – '

'Am I supposed to feel sorry for you? Is that it? You tell me your wife and daughter were killed and we have sex. Was that the reason you told me? Now they find some dirty magazines at The Hub. What's that all about? What am I supposed to make of that? Why am I even here?'

'They're not mine.'

'Of course you'd say that!'

'They're not.'

'Who *are* you?' she said.

'I'm sorry. I shouldn't have asked you to come – '

'Oh shut up!' And she got up and left.

Two people at the next table glanced over. Jonas stared down at his whisky glass. A fat wasp was creeping round the rim, little feelers stroking the air before it flew off and returned, flew off and returned. For a sudden and perfect moment he felt just like that wasp.

Mary returned. The hair around her face was damp, as if she had splashed herself with water.

'You believe me?' he asked.

'Do I have any reason not to?'

165

'Plenty, I suppose, if you think about it.'

'That's true. But I'm here.'

'I know.'

'What does that tell you?' She leaned back, taking a long slug of her wine and not taking her eyes off his face. Then she carefully placed her glass down and folded her arms. 'What now?'

Jonas shrugged. 'It seems like you want to go home.'

'Does it now?' She smiled briefly. 'What do you know about Pushwagner?'

'Pushwagner?'

'You're Norwegian aren't you?

'Last time I checked.'

She took a flyer from her pocket. 'I saw this in the bar. You heard of this guy?'

'Yeah. But I've never seen any of his stuff.'

'We're going.'

Mary decided she knew what she was doing. She felt guilty that Jonas's revelation about his wife and child had been such a relief. But the magazines unsettled her. She believed they weren't his, probably. It just seemed so unlikely. He was a nice guy, remember, and she was drunk.

They walked down the street, back to the city centre. One of those days when everyone seemed to stare. Another time she might have hurried to the nearest toilet to check herself; any stray loo roll hanging out of her trouser leg, a bogey dangling from her nose?

Today, she felt defiant. She wanted people to stare as she walked down the street with Jonas. She wanted her husband to see her and imagined him coming out of a shop, double-take and incredulous. As incredulous as he'd been when she got home from The Hub to find a You Tube clip of her village green outburst hooked up to the big TV. The video was paused, Mary caught

166

mid-harangue, her husband asking what the hell she was doing there at midnight. It had taken him two days to catch up and Mary was *sooo* impressed, called him *semi-detached* and almost said she had been there with Jonas Mortensen.

Suddenly Mary didn't want to be seen with Jonas. She wanted to run to the nearest toilet and lean on a sink, stare into the mirror and think about this some more. When she grabbed Jonas's hand he looked startled.

The exhibition was at the modern art gallery on the corner of a revamped square. Air-brushed, she thought, or steam-cleaned, no sign of the previous inhabitants, the homeless with their dogs and mysterious bundles. She imagined them bundled into trucks, dumped miles away.

A large, half-open mouth with a row of bright white teeth and rose-pink lips had been painted across the white brick entranceway. The mouth stuck out a lurid, flame red tongue, painted across the wall and doorway and unfurling down onto the paving slabs in front of the entrance. To the top left of the mouth were the words *Soft City* in bold black lettering.

'Check it out!' Mary said, a tone that made her wonder if an impostor had taken over her powers of speech. Jonas seemed a bit wary, as if he didn't know how to react to this new, *relaxed* Mary. She thought how brusque she'd been in *The Mayor* and felt a bit embarrassed.

Forgive me, Jonas, she thought about saying, *for the erratic nature of my behaviour*, stifling a laugh and realising she was more drunk than she thought. Only men in cravats said things like *erratic nature*. Yet she was in a university town which maintained a small but probably statistically significant population of cravatted fogeys, young and old. A cravat shouldn't be able to influence

167

a choice of words but somehow did. Or was it a choice of thoughts?

'Jonas?'

'What?'

'Can you choose your thoughts?'

'Thoughts? I suppose so.'

Mary turned, stuck her tongue out, mirroring the image on the gallery wall. 'I... agree,' she said, as certain as she could be but later wouldn't be certain at all. 'Do you like cravats?'

'Not really, why – '

'Me neither. Not on your nelly.'

'What's a nelly?'

She was pleased that he didn't know what *nelly* meant but realised she didn't have a clue either. So instead of answering she pushed him through the doorway into the gallery vestibule.

They wandered the exhibition for a while before she put a finger on what she thought about it until she realised that *finger* was right on the money. Pushwagner pointed a finger.

Soft City was a dystopian graphic novel written in the 1970s. The original drawings had been laid out in long exhibition cases. Anonymous everymen wake *en masse* at the same time in identically drab, Soviet-style tower blocs, take the same pills and commute with rigid choreography in identical blue suits, hat and briefcase, clocking in to Soft Inc., a corporation-cum-agent of control, bombarding the worker-drones with martial, materialistic images.

In another room, the novel had been animated, sound-tracked by dissonant electronic percussion, *Eraserhead meets Aphex Twin*, said Jonas, and who was she to disagree?

Messages flashed. *If you don't make it you are fired... Who controls the controller? Roll Dollars...*

168

'You Norwegians are a happy bunch.'

'Blame the winters.'

'What, and *we* don't have winters?' Almost spat out, a swift return of harshness that surprised her.

The second floor showcased Pushwagner's paintings, occasional canvases in cavernous space.

Jonas and Mary were the only visitors, the lighting dim and shifting, slow-motion disco spots across the room. Their footsteps clipped, moving through the recurring themes of alienation and paranoia, duped humans as complacent machines, dancing on a building roof in *Apocalypse Frieze* with symmetrical ranks of tanks on either side, the sky crammed with rockets and parachutists, *Self-Portrait* an outline of a lozenge-shaped head but instead of a face it was a cathedral-like building, row on row and level on level of box-like compartments.

She stopped in front of the bending, liquid skyscrapers of *Klaxton*, filled with thousands of windows and the same face peering out of each. It reminded her of windows overlooking Jonas's back garden and she felt a quick unease, the odd one out among the identikit people she'd lived among for decades, years of familiarity and comfort and a horizon accepted as final, who all looked at Jonas in a different way, who all thought differently.

He appeared at her side, looking directly at the painting. After a moment she took his hand.

'What do you think?' he asked.

'That you're a strange man.'

'Not me, the painting.'

'I know what you mean, Jonas.' She still hadn't looked at him. 'You know what? I'm going to believe you.'

He just nodded.

'It just seems too obvious.'

'Thanks for the ringing endorsement.'

'I'm drunk, good as you're going to get.' He pulled his hand away. 'Or maybe I don't believe you.' She grabbed his hand and kissed him, then abruptly turned away. 'So what now?'

Jonas looked perplexed, as if he didn't know if she meant right now, or now in general, as in *them*. 'Do you want to get another drink?' he asked, a tad pathetically, she thought.

'Do you want to fuck me?'

He flinched.

Mary almost flinched too.

It didn't suit her but she persisted, trying not to look embarrassed. 'Well, do you?' She was having an affair. She should be saying things like this. That's what risk was. 'Cat got your tongue?' And she kissed him again, pulling him towards the disabled toilet in the far corner. Inside, she checked the door, quickly discarded her skirt and panties and sat up on the sink unit.

Jonas was very hard very quickly. She braced herself with one hand and put the other on his backside, pulling him in. He'd hardly begun before her eyelids were fluttering and her hips jerking. She let out a strangled moan, keeping her eyes tightly shut until long after he finished and the only sounds were the buzz of the fluorescent light and his slowing breath.

When she opened her eyes he was staring at her. He seemed troubled and she felt self-conscious. She thought of Pushwagner's windows, all those faces staring at disaffected Mary, the odd one out.

Twenty-seven

Fletcher's aunt would disapprove. She disapproved of everything he did while indulging his little sister. As both a bigot and a po-faced obsesser about the correct, he wondered if she'd be more livid with him for being back in the Catholic Church or that he'd just dipped a finger in the font.

Nothing happened, his finger didn't dissolve. He saw his aunt's sour-faced reflection and stirred the water until she fragmented.

Across by the altar, the priest was watching. Fletcher found nothing troubled in the man, no sense of a self-examination made and even one thing found wanting. The Taliban touched the void. They took the Sharia and stepped way back to before the division of the Absolute. You couldn't argue with them and that was the point. You had to respect the Salafi crazies.

He maintained eye contact with the priest as he walked towards the side altar and the portrait of the Virgin.

On a whim, he lit a candle and attempted a prayer that became a memory of End Point. He and his grandfather, all those near-silent meals. The old man was the only one Fletcher kept in touch with after he left, the only one who knew he'd changed his name. It was his grandfather who told him his aunt had moved away. He didn't tell Fletcher where she was and Fletcher never asked. You draw the line and you stay on your side.

Couple of years back he told McQueen about the old man. McQueen was a decent sort, identikit mouthy Scot and ex-Black Watch, two fucked-up tours in Iraq. They'd run into each other down Victoria and bounced around for a while. They were sitting in some God-awful December soup kitchen off Tottenham Court Road, Fletcher flushed with the goodwill that comes of a full belly and going on and on about this *country house* that had been left to him.

McQueen screwed his eyes shut and shook his head, saying *go fuck yourself and your fuckin fairy tales*. And Fletcher laughed again now as he had then, until McQueen was screaming, throwing his tray at him, loud as the priest was silent, standing by the altar and staring.

McQueen was always on about the nine thousand homeless ex-servicemen, lost in the fog of PTSD and whatever cocktail of booze and drugs was closest to hand. Fletcher never felt like he was one of them. He had a place to go to, after all, and felt bad for laughing at McQueen.

But McQueen never got the full story from Fletcher, same as McQueen had his own secrets. He told Fletcher about the Basra detainee one evening when he was drunk, what he did and how he got away with it. As with McQueen so with Fletcher, always the next, crucial detail left unsaid.

It was overcast when Fletcher left the church. He went to the library and watched a sad-looking young woman read a story to a group of screaming toddlers. He left when he tired of the glances from the counter woman, who seemed to be trying to place him. *The Black Lion* was just around the corner but he was getting better at dealing with booze. Instead, he headed for the café.

Andrew Gladstone. Fletcher had finally placed the fat red face a few days back. Gladstone was in the year above him, good at football. This made him popular with the girls, someone to be admired. Now he owned a greasy spoon and had a wife fatter than himself. He didn't admire Gladstone anymore. He made him think of a school reunion on a wet November Tuesday in the back room of a provincial pub, over-loud music and the stale tang of despondency.

He stayed in the café for three hours and drank two Americanos. Gladstone always stared but would never recognise him, lost to any awareness including that of the self. His only other sign of life was to glare at him for picking the black bits from the sugar bowl, a pathetic flaring of pride from a man who'd long since stopped taking an interest in his business.

On April 17th, 1991, seven thirty in the evening, Gladstone had glared at him for a very different reason. The memory didn't upset him, because now had nothing to do with then.

It was a mistake to go down to the Sports Club, a few drinks to relax. He sat in a corner table and drank pint after pint, turning over the questions the police had asked him about his sister's disappearance. She'd been gone thirty-six hours and for twelve of them he'd been sitting in an interview room. He didn't think he'd said anything to contradict himself.

Gladstone came in with a few of his football buddies. They dragged him round the back of the club and kicked the shit out of him. The next morning, when Fletcher looked out of his bedroom window, they were waiting along the street. That's when he moved to End Point, his grandfather a near-recluse who had only recently moved to the village. No one knew him.

Across by the till, fat Gladstone of the present day was staring into space, mouth hanging open. Fletcher took a sip of cold coffee and remembered they didn't have any left in the house.

The thought was almost amusing. *They*, the familiarity of it, Fletcher and Mortensen as housemates. Now that the police had locked on he wondered how the Norwegian would deal with it. Fletcher remembered the trauma of '91. The unravelling.

That morning he'd heard the Norwegian on the phone, taking the day off. Soon after he followed him to the bus stop. Only then did Fletcher realise he was on Tanner Avenue. A film crew had set up outside number nineteen, a small crowd watching. He should have just walked away.

The house had changed. He looked up to his old window, top left. He remembered bright white frames, ever-clean windows that he had to scrub every third Saturday. Now the window frames were peeling and the glass grubby, the neat garden replaced by a sun-parched lawn bisected by a path with weeds between the concrete slabs. Two bright-painted gnomes sat on either side of the front door. It would have appalled his aunt; she didn't do whimsy.

Fletcher stood beside kids who weren't alive back then, parents who told themselves they remembered, moth-drawn to the TV lights as years before they would have flocked to public executions, eager to be part of an event they'd talk about later with the authority of *being there*. Because it was the taking part that mattered, not the authenticity of the experience. And the reconstruction wasn't quite there. The producers had got the clothes right, the blue jacket and the red and white dress, but the girl was a bit too skinny, the hair too dark.

He talked to the cameraman when they were re-setting the scene. The programme was called *Cold Cases* and re-visited unsolved crimes. They were filming in Leeds when they were told to get back south. A teenager had gone missing in the same village where another girl had disappeared twenty-three years ago. They'd bumped the planned episode for this one. *There's never any connection*, the cameraman said. *It's all in the suggestion. We call it Project Fear.*

'We're closing in ten minutes.'

Gladstone's pasty face brought Fletcher back to the present. He was holding out a piece of paper, the bill. In a film, Gladstone's eyes would narrow. He'd say, *don't I know you?* Instead, his eyes moved towards the window. Fletcher followed his gaze across the street.

The rain was heavy. Through the rivulets on the glass he saw Mortensen, the front door of End Point open and the Norwegian throwing things onto the pavement, Fletcher's things.

'What's he doing?' said Gladstone.

'Beats me.'

'He's a funny bugger,' said Gladstone.

'Know much about him?'

'More and more these days.' Gladstone fixed him with a meaningful look.

'That right.'

'A right *funny* bugger.'

Fletcher and Gladstone watched from the covered arcade between the café and the hair salon.

The spectacle was theirs alone, the hairdresser had closed up long ago and the rain swept off every passer-by. Fletcher considered the most effective way of shutting Mortensen up if he noticed him standing there watching him. He felt oddly liberated at watching his possessions being scattered, ready to blow away, no proof at all of his existence.

Gladstone slowly shook his head when Mortensen slammed the front door. With a last drag on his cigarette he flicked it into the street, clapped his new buddy on the shoulder and disappeared into the café. Fletcher flinched. Twenty years a Marine and he still jumped at

175

that fucker's touch. He'd see to that particular issue in time. Or maybe not, it kinda depended.

By the time Fletcher walked down the street and back again the café windows were dark. He gathered up his sleeping bag and roll mat, the only witnesses a couple of passing cars, the rain so heavy he didn't worry about the occupants noticing too much. He took his things round the side of the house and flung them over the fence into the cypresses. When he returned for his rucksack he saw his aunt's Bible face down in the pavement muck. It had landed open at Luke: 15, something tedious about tax collectors. He flicked through the pages in the pouring rain until he found something more fitting. Leviticus: 24. *Punishment of blasphemy.*

Fletcher came at Mortensen from the back garden. The Norwegian was sitting at the kitchen table and didn't notice him until he'd reached the sun room. He barely had time to stand up before Fletcher was on him. He swept Mortensen's left leg and caught him as he fell, one arm tight under his neck and the other free to plunge the knife under the ribcage. As he had been trained.

Instead, he propelled Jonas through the sun room and into the garden. When the Norwegian tried to run past him Fletcher swept his leg again, Mortensen landing heavily on the grass. He did this five more times. He wanted Mortensen to feel the futility of trying again and again to do something he would never succeed at. No yelling and no anger, nothing but distant thunder, timpani rattle on the sun room roof and Mortensen's rasping breath.

The rain let up. The Norwegian lay unmoving on the grass. Fletcher sat on the bottom step of the sun room and looked up to the lightening sky. He'd known the monsoon in Belize, streets turned to mud rivers, white eyes in black doorways. Bangkok too, always a troubling memory, on leave and stripped to the waist, full of Sang Som and Singha, screaming into the deluge. He remembered the sudden easing, the tension draining from his shoulders just as swiftly, leaving behind a vacant vulnerability, the odd sense of a question un-posed.

He leaned back on his hands, watching Mortensen sit up slowly and look cautiously around, bracing for the next kick that wouldn't come. Fletcher let his breathing settle and thought of Mary, a sentimental image of her dabbing at the Norwegian's bruises with a clump of bloodied cotton wool, brushing back the wet hair. That kind of concern, it never lasted.

Twenty-eight

Sometime after five Mary got home. She'd just closed the front door when she heard a car in the driveway. Her husband, back from Saturday afternoon pub football. She rushed upstairs and popped three paracetamol, switched on the shower then stared at herself in the mirror.

It was always other people who had affairs. Mary judged them, as everyone did, from a position of complete ignorance. Some she could understand and others just seemed tragic, a waste of years. Surely the guilty one (there always had to be a guilty one) must realise it and break down, knees hugged to the chest and a primal wailing no one would hear.

We were once so happy...

Mary wasn't fussed about that. She didn't *wonder where it was all going to end up*, as the over-sympathetic sofa matrons of daytime TV would ask the conflicted caller. At the moment she was preoccupied with sex. The Dirty Sex of the Toilet Tramp, as she'd decided to call it.

Leaving the Pushwagner exhibition, she'd insisted they take different buses back to the village. *These are such watchful days*, she told Jonas, then winked. As soon as Jonas got on the waiting bus to buy his ticket she was gone. Waving him off seemed needy, too normal an aftermath of furtive sex. But when Mary got to the corner of the street she stopped to watch the bus drive past. It was only when she noticed people glancing at her that she realised she was smiling. There was a pleasant tingle in her groin. It was like being in a film.

The thrill lasted as long as the buzz of the alcohol. The journey home administered the final blows, the relentless shaking as the bus jolted along the potholed road, slamming the afternoon against her cranial walls until it was a shatter of morose pieces and a headache.

The mirror had steamed up. Mary decided not to have a shower. She wanted to face her husband. A defiant, passive-aggressive reaction that somehow made her feel better about herself.

All this leaning she did, leaning and watching. She noticed it again as she leaned against the frame of the door separating the living room from the kitchen. Her husband was sitting on the sofa watching cricket on the amazingly stupid eighty-inch plasma TV. She heard herself say things like *how was your day, dear, what do you want for dinner?*, listening to his distracted replies.

In reality, she'd said nothing. He hadn't noticed her or maybe he had and was just ignoring her, no sudden fright when she said hello. His grunted reply made her feel equally invisible.

Still invisible when she sat down and rested her shoulder against his. He didn't turn, suspiciously, and ask about the alcohol on her breath or the *smell of sex*. He just edged away until they weren't touching. Mary watched the TV. A man in white kept on carefully hitting a cricket ball nowhere at all. She felt a little bit like that man in white and almost burst into tears.

Her headache had started to fade. She closed her eyes and imagined it was Jonas's hand she was now reaching for, the same cool afternoon breeze and even the endless cricket was enjoyable. Because it was all a question of the lives we choose to inhabit. If we got it right then the

179

details might remain the same but the responses would be so very different.

'You heard about the magazines?' her husband said.

Mary opened her eyes. Her husband had pulled his hand away. There was a cat food advert on the TV.

'The porn mags,' he continued.

'Yeah.'

'What's he like then?'

'Who?'

'The Norwegian. Jonas.'

'I don't know that much about him.'

'You know he just appeared out of nowhere. A few years back.'

'You mean he moved here.'

'Yeah. Out of nowhere.'

'Isn't that what most people do when they move somewhere new?'

'He's an odd bod.'

'An odd bod?'

'Yeah.'

'Says who?'

'People.'

'Who?'

'Just *people*. Why are you defending him?'

'He says they weren't his.'

'Well he's not going to admit it, is he? I wouldn't!'

'Yeah. You wouldn't want the police taking a look at your internet search history.'

'What's that supposed to mean?'

'I'm not an idiot!'

'Have you been drinking?'

'Ten out of ten, Sherlock. Why don't you offer your services to the police and help find Lacey?'

'I told you I hurt my leg and couldn't help out with the –'

'You know I've got another job?'

'Eh?'

'Another job. I clean. I'm a *cleaner*. For the man with the porno mags. Jonas.'

'What the hell are you talking about?'

'You know those two things in your face. Just above the nose. They're eyes. Why don't you try opening them?'

This time she did have a shower, long and very hot. He'd followed her, of course, stood outside the cubicle and rambled on with his questions that she let stream away with the water. In time he got bored and left. After drying herself she chose her best underwear and left by the front door. He appeared again as she closed it, more ramblings cut off by the slam.

She'd primed Jonas about the underwear. Back in the gallery toilets, legs on his shoulders. *I'll come round later, dress up for you.* A strangulated voice that surprised her and made him push harder.

Agent Provocateur, a black lace bra and matching thong with mesh front. She didn't know why she'd bought them and had only ever worn them for herself. Standing in front of the mirror, considering the angles, how it could be better but so much worse. *I'll come round later...* Cringe-worthy, but a relief she hadn't blurted out other embarrassments; *oh you like that, don't you?* and *right there baby, right there*, things they said in the film playing in her head.

She felt ill at ease as she hurried through the village. The heavy rain had emptied the streets but there was still the possibility of bumping into someone she knew, who would study her from under their umbrella and just *know* that under her jeans a pair of £50 panties chafed her bum crack. Then a bird dipped across her path, making her flinch. She followed it into the bruised sky and when she lost sight of it found herself thinking

181

about Jonas and Lacey. A sudden uncertainty settled across her. For a moment she almost turned and went back home. Instead, she considered the best approach to End Point. Not the route to take but the attitude to assume when she got there. She decided on nonchalance, a confident walk right up to the door. She was just the cleaner, doing her job. But she didn't have the key ready in her hand and had to pause, rummaging in her bag looking for the damn thing, trying to keep the umbrella above her head and failing, rain now trickling down her neck.

When she did find the key the door wouldn't open. She panicked, felt a heat in her cheeks, sure that a crowd had appeared on the other side of the road. She waggled the key then realised the door must have been open and she'd just locked it. She finally stepped inside the house just as a car passed. Supermarket Meg stared at her from the passenger window.

Jonas wasn't in. She checked the living room, kitchen and back garden, noticing that the lawn was all churned up and muddy. Sudden inspiration brought a shy smile but when she went up to the bedroom to strip for the naked man waiting on the bed he wasn't there. So she had a pee in the en-suite toilet, expensive knickers at her ankles, wondering what to do next.

'Hello?'

The voice came from the bedroom. Mary smiled. She quickly stood up and stripped to her bra and panties. A quick 360 in the mirror told her to go for it and she threw open the bathroom door.

'Sorry, *sorry!*'

'Christ sake!' Mary slammed the door closed and leaned against it, heart hammering. She quickly dressed and sat on the bed, shaking her head and *fuck it, fuck it, fuck it*. When she had composed herself she went

182

downstairs and found Fletcher sitting at the kitchen table.

'I'm sorry, I didn't know –'

'Don't worry,' she said. 'It's my fault for creeping about.'

'Have something to eat.' He nodded at the plastic bag on the table. 'I always get too much.'

'What's on the menu?'

'Lamb jalfrezi, prawn bhuna and chicken pakora. Keema naan and rice. Pilau.'

'Bloody hell, you got worms?'

'Saturday night take-away.'

'You're not supposed to take it *all* away!'

Adam frowned and looked away. 'I told you. I always order too much. Never seem to get it right.'

Five minutes into the meal Mary knew she'd made a mistake. She should have gone back home. At least the rain gave her something to listen to, because Adam Fletcher certainly didn't want to talk. He destroyed dialogue with monosyllables, looking at Mary as if waiting for her to ask the one question he would answer.

Behind the rain came thunder, the gloom quick-falling. Adam didn't get up and switch on the light and though Mary wanted to she just sat there, thinking about the rain pounding on the sun room roof. *Like voodoo pandemonium,* she wanted to say, *don't you agree?*

But Adam would say nothing. He'd just keep staring and chewing, waiting for that question.

Mary began to eat more quickly. The chicken was dry and greasy at the same time. Sticky clumps in the throat. The underwear she was wearing sickened her, the realisation that the bra and panties had only ever been seen by her and Adam, this shadowed man who was *forcing her to eat*, even if that was ridiculous because she could get up and leave any time. But she kept on eating, avoiding his eye, wondering if to push her plate

183

away would be to have him reach across and slap her, telling her to *sit your arse back down and eat your dinner.*

'Why did you tell me that about Jonas?'

He briefly stopped chewing. 'Don't you believe me?'

'Well I...'

'You heard about the magazines too, right?

'I did but – '

'What's not to believe?'

'It just doesn't seem like him.'

'Why? Because you know him so well. What do you really know about him?'

'Your cousin.'

'That's right. My cousin.'

She looked at her plate, lamb shreds, oil separated from sauce. When she looked up he was smiling.

'You really don't remember me, do you?

And then she did.

As Fletcher told her, he wondered why it didn't make him feel any better. No relief followed the confession. How he had changed his name from John Hackett in 1992, just after turning nineteen. Soon afterwards Adam Fletcher joined the Marines. *Adam* because this was a rebirth, *Fletcher* after the police chaplain, the one who held his hands across an interview table.

'You'd think it would have been difficult, but it was the easiest thing I've done in my whole life.'

He speared a piece of lamb. The curry wasn't bad. He'd had worse, cross-legged on threadbare rugs, sharing meals, fatty mutton stews that left a film on your lips, like the forced friendliness that coated those evenings in mistrust. Hearts and minds was a joke, the punch-line a group of preternaturally calm men with plastic-tied hands, an IED hidden in a turban.

'You had New Kids on the Block posters. All round your bed. I was into the B-52s and used to take the mick.

184

You had a Wilson Phillips tape you played over and over. Remember that?'

'I can't believe – '

'You dumped me for Craig Adamson. He had an American flat-top haircut. Prick thought he was Vanilla Ice!'

She stood up quickly, quick as the image that flashed in his mind. Mary in her posh underwear. He hadn't seen anything like that back then. He wanted to do things but felt guilty. Every time he imagined it he saw his aunt, slapping him on the face and calling him a dirty little boy.

He grabbed her by the arm as she reached the kitchen door. 'I hated you. Not for long though.'

'Let me go, John.'

'*Adam.*'

'Ok. I'm sorry. Adam.'

'You didn't know about this house, did you?'

'What are you talking about?'

Her voice was shrill. He wondered how soon it would become panic and how he would defuse it, as they'd been taught; re-establish control by slowing the situation, deconstruct into manageable pieces. He let her go and she hurried down the hallway. 'No one knew.'

She hesitated at the door. 'Knew what?'

'This was my grandfather's house. A total recluse. Hated people and I'd never visited him. There was no way I was going back home after they let me go and he took me in. I used to watch people from the bedroom and none of them knew I was here. Even my aunt kept her trap shut.'

'Everyone thought you'd left.'

'I did. After a bit. It's not easy when you know you won't be coming back. He died years ago and left me the house. I thought that maybe enough time had passed. But here I am again and I don't think it has. I keep

185

seeing all these faces and none of them has changed. Apart from the way they look at me. They don't see John Hackett. They don't look at me that way.'

'I never thought you did it.'

'For what it's worth.'

'What?'

'That's what you're supposed to say. *For what it's worth I never thought you did it*. It's more poignant.'

Twenty-nine

Jonas, the exhibited man. Let them stare, let them all stare. First the startled bus driver, the same one who'd dropped him in the village less than an hour previously, eyes watching in the rear-view, following him down the slippery aisle. Then the passengers, who clocked him one by one, darting eyes as he slumped down, assessing the limp, the dirty clothes, the threat.

Don't you know he tried to kill me?

But Jonas said nothing. Just a shout for himself, a *scream*, taking away the pain in his side, maybe a broken rib. Pull it out and plant it, grow another Jonas, a better one, one to replace the dying one, dying on his back in the mud and rain, Fletcher's hands tight around his neck.

He smoothed his hair and wiped the mud from his trousers. A stumble in the front door, the realisation Fletcher wasn't home and hey ho, out with his stuff. Big Haakon, he could hear him going on about *the vibes, you gotta listen to the vibes, man.* The other voice chipped in too; *never alienate the unknown.* A biblical aphorism, maybe, the Bible he'd also thrown in the street. Some people reacted poorly to blasphemy. His mother with her hand-at-mouth horror.

Fletcher's violence.

The bus pitched like the Larvik ferry before they got the stabilisers. He folded his arms and closed his eyes, shunted and shoved but somehow falling asleep, opening his eyes to wet city streets, multicolours of umbrellas through rain-dappled, foggy windows, hurrying people going who knows where but likely somewhere warm and homely, an arm around the waist, two lovers and a sweep of rain across their secret garden, all so comforting, *easing through*, like the bus now moving into the bus lane, overtaking all else as he was soon hurrying along King Street, into the shopping arcade and over-heated department store to find a toilet where he wiped away the dirt to reveal the mirror-face which may, just may, pass muster.

Clean-faced, Jonas found a trendy bar called *Axis*, Saturday-night-crowded but a group just leaving and he snagged their table. Four twenty-somethings in identikit ripped denims appeared moments later and asked if they could sit at the other chairs. He watched them, sipping an expensive continental lager and trying to figure out what he was doing there. In the noise of the bar the village seemed reassuringly distant. He could, if he wanted, just disappear.

He was an exile, after all. Get up that gangplank and cast off, ply the route and take the weather, a look to the horizon and the sea a mirror to walk on, back to a gentler time, collecting bonfire wood with Axel, Big Haakon's delight at his first bow-drill ember, the first time he saw Eva's face, looking back at his in *Robinet's* that July night when they first met. Her first face, so different from the last, slashed forehead to chin, head on the Saab's dashboard.

He raised his face, closed his eyes for a long time. When he looked down again, the four people across from him were staring, wondering about this stranger who they sat with but didn't join, despite the *incontrovertible fact* of their collective presence at this sticky table.

Hey folks, we're *one*. A revelation to shout above the MOR techno. *Think about it*. He'd have them all nodding in wonder, the first time they had realised that even the simplest of connections was still a connection and with connection there could never be true exile.

The four people suddenly laughed. He looked across and caught the eye of the brunette with bad skin hidden under thick make-up. A deepening frown as her eyes flickered across his face. Only now had she noticed his swollen eye and cut lip, only *now*, meaning it was the first time she had noticed *him*, Jonas and his burst face being *interchangeable*.

So there was no connection to insist upon after all, Jonas a simple stick-man, without a face, a child's approximation in whom they had no interest other than a means to let them sit down.

'Do you want to know what happened?' he shouted.

She ignored him.

'Do you want to know what happened?'

A raise of the eyebrows and the face now turning to his, impatience trying to be cool. 'What?'

'I was beaten up by a man with no clothes. In the rain. Every time I got up he pushed me down. I got muddy.'

She nodded, slowly, and mouthed *ok*. As if choreographed, the four friends reached for their drinks.

'He's called Adam and he lives there. Adam. *Adam*. Like the first man. Can't argue with that eh?'

'Look mate.' It was the male, on his left. He had an asymmetrical haircut, anvil-shaped. 'We're just out for –'

'I needed to be around people. Connections, you know, like we're all sitting round this table.'

Soon after, Jonas was asked to leave. The bouncer's tight white t-shirt reminded him of Fletcher. Maybe that was why he resisted the hand on his shoulder and pulled his arm back, knocking over a drink and

189

insisting on paying for another, dropping the fiver as he was shoved outside.

The rain poured. He sheltered in a Chinese takeaway until the counter man insisted he order or leave.

Jonas chose a spring roll, dripping with grease that coated the inside of his mouth. It was an ugly taste, he told the man it was the ugliest spring roll he had ever eaten in his life. *Ugly*, said the man. *Yes, ugly*. Jonas wasn't expecting art, not from a cheap takeaway, that would be absurd, but he certainly insisted on plainness. Ugliness was laziness, no care had been taken over this food and the establishment should at least strive for plainness. *Don't you see?*

The counter man didn't see. Jonas stepped out the door and was nearly bowled off the pavement by a skinny, whey-faced man pulling a little cart with a Dalmatian sitting in it. The man zipped into the next street, the Dalmatian leaning into the corner to retain his balance.

This was how the breakdown would happen. In the rain with the after-image of a Dalmatian on a cart. Maybe it had looked around with a goofy little doggy smile as it turned the corner, a Scooby Doo-like guffaw at Jonas Mortensen, the man who lingered, lingered and didn't see. He hurried to the corner and watched man, cart and Dalmatian pass a group of people leaving *The Pickled Shepherd*. Not one turned to look at the strange procession. It might never have been. Yet they all stared at Jonas as he walked past them and into the pub.

Apart from a group of men in a window booth, Jonas was the only customer. He took an adjoining booth and stared at a pint he didn't want. The gantry TV was showing a baseball game and there was nothing as boring as baseball, especially baseball with the sound down. He watched

190

anyway, watched for decades and had a thousand more beers he didn't want, and suddenly baseball made a perfect, solemn sense. Strip the pizzazz and the pose and it was a meditation, a prayer, *religion itself*. There was liturgy in those stats, allegory in the field-positions.

Jonas understood, he got baseball! He'd watch from this holy moment on, take his place in the church. He was so engrossed he only heard the voice the second time it asked the question.

'Can you settle a bet?'

The man peering over the top of the booth had a moustache that made Jonas think of the police. 'What about?'

The man's eyes narrowed. 'Where are you from then?'

'Is that the bet?'

'I said, where are you from?'

Another red face appeared, at the side of the booth. Jonas looked back at the TV. 'Where are you from?'

'Here mate, I'm from here.' The man looked down at his friend and cocked his head at Jonas. 'Another one. They just keep on coming and coming. Telling you, we have sucked Poland *dry*.'

'Leave the bloke alone Mickey.'

'You think I'm Polish?'

'Yeah. I think you're Polish. Must be a right dump. Leaving your home like that. A right... *fuckin*... dump.' There was laughter when Mickey sat back down on his side of the booth.

Fat Xavier!

Jonas almost burst out laughing. He might have been intimidated if Mickey hadn't reminded him of the pompous little owner of the vineyard in the Beaujolais. Fat Xavier didn't like *all you Scandy-men* and sniped at Jonas for weeks. The fear in his pinched little rodent face when Jonas dumped a basket of grapes over his head still brought extreme joy, even now.

191

He looked back at the TV. Baseball had slipped out of focus, once again the tedium of tubby men with bats. What would it be like to be Polish? In fact, he could even be Polish. What did it matter to be Polish, Norwegian, Martian, a funny little green Martian, so far away from home that his sense of identity was sure to be stronger than anything possible on earth?

Only when you stopped moving did it matter. That's when people started asking questions. For a long time after leaving Bergen no one had. He worked construction and picked fruit in half a dozen countries and no questions, as if exile had stripped individuality and explanation, imposing a collective, instead, of stained hands and exhaustion, camp beds in fetid barns that angry men like Mickey flung open in the dawn with a near sexual relish.

The booth men were laughing at him again, Jonas who was every other who had come here and was yet to come: grafter Poles, Baltic nomads and coy Romanians, the dream curdled in the back of a locked lorry and two months at Calais to strangle the last optimism before the indifferent journey to work the fruit and building sites, wash dishes and clean toilets. Maybe they would visit a pub like this, a couple of drinks to chill out awhile, a few quid for themselves instead of being sent home. To listen to a bigotry even more demeaning for being amused rather than angry. Nothing to do but drink up. Drink up and leave.

Along the street Jonas threw up, barely breaking stride and walking on. He wandered the streets and passed the art gallery. It was hard to believe that the afternoon with Mary had happened, that he'd ever been in this city at all, this place of spring rolls and Dalmatians, baseball and bigots, buses to the whispering outposts and Jonas now waiting for his.

Mary wouldn't be there when he got home. Past 10

192

pm now and she said she'd be round at seven. *I'll come round later, dress up for you...* When the B4 appeared he watched it leave.

The old man at the River Hotel's reception desk barely looked at him. When he finally did the pupils dilated, as if his vision was returning to the present from contemplation of a time long since passed. *We've all got ways to go*, the old man might have said and Jonas replying *yes, I just need a night, a night before I go on*. But the old man gave him the key without a word.

The mattress sagged. Too many dream-tossed nights. Jonas put his face to the greying sheet. A faint smell of sweat, stories and old memories. They drifted like dust in sunlight, none of them his. He closed his eyes, opened them. He saw strange faces, heard unknown voices.

Mary hadn't phoned.

He didn't know why he didn't phone her.

He wrote a text message then deleted it. Eva made him. He always listened to his dead wife.

She felt close tonight, the blue drapes reminding him of the *Himalayan Inn*, Kathmandu. It was all in the setting, a lost heyday glimpsed in tired decor, when the carpet was unstained, the grouting china-white and curtains were proud to be *drapes*. Kathmandu, the end of their honeymoon, three weeks of Annapurna dazzle-calm to three days of culture stun in the crowded poor-streets. Diesel fug and smouldering rubbish. Mopeds and street horns, multicolour night-signs of bars and bazaars, restaurants, on and on through tourist Thamel.

Just the leavings: Eva, frozen with a bottle of Everest beer clutched in her hand, face contorted in a shriek, a cockroach on the sheets. How could the world move with all these leavings, all the friction they brought to bear, slowing us down? No wonder we come to feel so jaded.

193

'Drapes.'

He said it out loud, again and again, the word more odd-sounding the more he said it, separating the letters, the flat *dr*, long *apes* and lingering *ess*. *Dr*-appe-ss. Dr-*app-ess*. Eva was laughing but he suddenly felt weak, as weak as Anya on the floor of the Saab, who looked untouched but whose neck lolled horribly when the paramedics lifted her, lifted her so carefully.

Tonight, as then, no strength.

He sighed, and the room too seemed to breathe heavily. Rain pattered the window. He heard Mary knocking softly at the door, trying to get in, but this no man's land was for ghosts only. He felt no guilt about this first woman since Eva. Turn over the stones, peer in each of those dusty cupboards, the only certainty is that there never is any certainty, just an on-going chain of assumptions and who really knows if the crack in the pavement is a smile or a frown.

He only wanted to stop. He came to the village to stop. As he told Lacey, *slow down, stop awhile.*

She was young and beautiful, all the time in the world. Lacey who liked him too. No one would get it. He'd learned what to expect and how there was no way back, no matter the sad siren call of a far-gone wellbeing. He thought of End Point when he first broke in. Standing in the living room, dust angling through watery light, the slow fading light of the life of the unknown former owner, hanging around because it still had no idea where to go next.

Eva was no help.

She was dancing now, over there by the bathroom door that creaked when he opened it. He bent to the hinge for a while, pulling the door back and forth, waiting for the creak, back and forth and Eva still dancing until finally he lay back on the worn carpet and looked up at the crack in the ceiling and waited for sleep that didn't come, the cracks stretching as he stared, spidery zigzaggings always back where they started when he closed and opened his eyes.

He sat up suddenly. Someone else must be doing this, in a world of six billion a Japanese man could be sprawled on the tatami, staring up with eyes that refused to blink until he saw how complicated the web of cracks would become and finally get it, understanding that tracing every connection was impossible and you finally had to just let it all go.

What a relief, just imagine that *incredible relief.*

And they began to cry, Jonas and the Japanese man, as back and forth went the creaking bathroom door, Eva still dancing and a sudden image of the little shrine with photos and a daily candle that he had built to her and Anya in the Christinegård house before he finally had to leave.

★ ★ ★

Jonas woke cold on the hotel room floor. Light leached through the curtains and the room seemed poised, as if someone watching had just left. He had a crick in his neck and an erection that disgusted him as much as the taste in his mouth. He was sick on the carpet, the mess confusing him until he recognised last night's spring roll. Half-remembered remnants, the whole of the previous day felt like that. Eva hovered, quietly faded and there was Lacey.

He felt guilty, the self-pity of a seedy hangover. He thought about her as his guts spasmed again.

Thirty

*You, dead. Dead in the bazaar. Dust and blood on your face
that is becoming Azidullah's, coming closer, bringing me tea.
We sit in a quiet room back at base and talk about aftermaths.
I tell Azidullah how silent our aunt's house was the night you
disappeared, as silent as that other house must be raucous,
your house of mud and clay in the mazy tumble of old Sangin.
There you are lying, you who is she, under a white sheet but
the face revealed, the relatives wailing, wailing as we did
not do in our house, so different in the west, so much more
sophisticated we think, when nothing is more civilised than
screaming at death brought in the name of that so-called
sophistication. You would shy away from them, from the
police and the army, who come in their khaki and their black
and white to poke their noses. Downstairs, I hear the questions again. I listen and I feel guilty. But they are not here
for me. Today is not yesterday. I am not sitting on our aunt's
sofa with the plastic covering to protect it from my dirt, I am
not being asked what I did that day, every hour of that day
and why we were fighting, as if it was abnormal for brother
and sister to fight. I am not watching a policeman study the
cuts on my knuckles but it is just a fall from my bike and
straight away the little glances and why should they believe
me, why should they? Because I am lying, I sit on the sofa
and lie about those cuts as easily as I tell the truth to the two
men from military intelligence; bureaucracy idling, looking
at its watch, just give it straight and simple corporal. And
Azidullah pours me more tea. He places his forehead to mine*

and his hands on my cheeks. His concern is so very genuine.
We drink tea, he and I. And I cry for you both, I cry for you
both...

The one hundred count-back stopped the images at
forty. They told Fletcher to think like a TV, just a matter
of pressing *off* on the remote control. Bring on the black,
the little red standby light.

He blamed the police. Sunday morning at seven am,
it could only be the cops at the front door. He lay in bed
until they stopped knocking, leaping up when he heard
the door being opened half an hour later. Then Jonas's
voice, the Norwegian back from wherever he had disappeared to the night before. He was talking to someone,
several sets of footsteps heading for the kitchen. Fletcher
moved to the top stair. He could just hear the two detectives asking questions about the missing girl, the same
questions in multiple ways, monotonously probing for
the way in. He remembered the technique.

Then Azidullah came.

He was a captain in the Afghan National Army. A
gentle man with three young children, proud pictures
in a wallet. Nine years dead, Azidullah was still an
occasional presence, the last time a winter night in
Liverpool, Fletcher passing a mosque and the sound of
prayer.

Allahu Akbar, Allahu Akbar.

Fletcher had started to repeat the words, to himself at
first and then out loud. Azidullah was suddenly beside
him, smiling, encouraging him, *louder, louder.* They were
thrown out of a café, shouted at in the Toxteth halfway
house. *Allahu Akbar, Allahu Akbar,* the two of them, all
through the night, Fletcher falling asleep to wake with
Azidullah again vanished.

They'd patrolled together, joint ISAF-ANA patrols.
Smiley-faced info operations and sweets for the kids.

197

Schools and food aid. Roll out the big sell to bemused locals, insurgents among them and who's who, who the *fuck* is who? Always that cold fear but smiling Azidullah with the patience of the desert. Fletcher learned that the pat on his arm meant *now we wait.* His gaze would lower, contemplating the distance, waiting for the moment to give Fletcher his cue to continue. *Reconstruction. Democracy.* The next few words in a dialogue endlessly built and torn down. *Enduring Freedom.* The Afghans did just that. They endured until the foreigners took their freedom home.

Fletcher sat on the stairs as Azidullah did, leaning forwards, head angled, flattering the interest of the men in the kitchen who didn't know he was listening. He considered moving further down but couldn't rule out hitting a creaky stair. No reason to be careless, as Azidullah was careless to sit outside that teashop. The man on the moped put thirty-five rounds into him.

Fletcher memorised every question the policemen asked and every response that the Norwegian gave. Fixated concentration, he'd learned from his aunt. The Marines noticed it early. They called it an aptitude, said they needed soldiers who could listen. It was all about intel, like the detail filtering up from the kitchen.

Detective A told Mortensen that they knew Lacey had returned to his house after the midsummer party, an anonymous tip. Why hadn't he told them? The Norwegian couldn't say. He only managed a barely audible *I see* when told that they had checked with their Norwegian colleagues and knew about his conviction back in Bergen. Detective B couldn't hide his derision; if the police knew then Mortensen could be damn sure the media soon would.

The police would get there in the end, thought Fletcher. But they once thought the same about him.

Thirty-one

'I want a week off,' said Jonas.

'That's why you're calling me? It's Sunday *morning,* Jonas.'

'I want a week off.'

'Whatever. In fact, take more. Take two weeks.'

'A week is fine.'

'Take *more.*'

'Why?'

'I want you to.'

'A week's enough.'

'Why don't you think about something more long-term?'

'What's that supposed to mean?'

'Just a piece of advice.'

'I'm taking a week.'

Jonas ended the call, looking at the handset as if Boss Hogg might appear on the screen.

No way he was going to work. *Think of it as a piece of advice.* I hear you, boss, no finger needed to stir the tea-leaves to read how *unusual accidents* happen on a work site. Only forty minutes since the two detectives had left but Hogg already knew, clear as the day was blue.

Jonas sat on the bed. The police had been waiting outside when he got home from the hotel. A casual lean against a black BMW at seven thirty on a Sunday morning. Only cops did that. Someone passing End

Point would notice, then a conversation in the shop, a couple of texts...

A swelling anxiety made him stand up. But standing just made him more anxious, meant he couldn't process. It was completely ridiculous. So he sat down again, deliberately. The trick is to keep breathing. Another surge of adrenaline forced him back to his feet. Fuck it, he *was* anxious, he really was but he still didn't know why he hadn't told the detectives that Lacey had come back to his house after the *Jonsok* party. He just didn't. They didn't believe him.

Really, they said.

Really.

In his pocket, his mobile rang, as it had when he was showing the detectives inside the house. *Don't mind us*, Sad Eyes had said. *Feel free to answer.* Jonas hadn't then and didn't now.

Mary again. Not one phone call the night before and now three since 6 am. She was probably furious at him for standing her up. *Standing her up*, like they were dating. He threw the mobile on the bed and started pacing round the room. He used to do this for hours in prison.

Remember, how spartan that cell was. Others had post-cards, pictures on the walls, odd trinkets. One guy had a collection of miniature Mickey Mouses, neatly lined up on his desk. *My little boy sends me a new one every month.* All Jonas had was a perfectly round pebble, smooth, black dappled with grey. He found it in the recreation yard and took it with him when he was released. It now sat on his bedside table, a totem of reassurance. When Jonas smelled it he smelled the sea and when he put his tongue to it he thought he could taste salt.

The pebble mattered. Like him, it belonged elsewhere. He picked it up and closed his eyes, seeing the churned grass of the back lawn where Fletcher had beaten him up. The detectives had noticed but didn't ask about the divots and muddy ruts. He hefted the pebble, feeling the weight. Fletcher entered the scene. Half naked and lying down, basking like a snake.

Imagine standing in the sun room. Throwing the pebble. Would Fletcher's forehead crack loudly as it landed, like a gunshot, echoing around the houses? Or would it be more of a wet plop, the skull splitting like a watermelon? Maybe, who could tell, maybe this was the unknown future purpose that made him take the pebble with him when he was released. A near miss was more likely, a thud on the grass that had Fletcher looking up and seeing Jonas.

Like that they would remain, two unyielding Samurai, a stand-off in time-lapse, summer accelerating into autumn, winter, the clouds shifting cirrus to cumulus, azure to weaker blue and gunmetal grey, now teeming rain and snow flurries, the two of them unmoved because to move was to give ground and to give ground was to be the one to leave.

He hefted the pebble again, threw it in the air and caught it. You needed poise to make a direct hit. But a hit could kill and a killing meant the return of the detectives, more questions. *Why'd you do it son, why?* Jonas as Cagney, still defiant as they strapped him to the Chair.

How many times in a life did we answer a question? Ten questions a day means seventy a week, 3000 a year, 200,000 in seventy years. Why this need to know? When the last motive is uncovered freedom is dead. The police should be told that all their questions are killing freedom. *Why did Lacey come back after your party?* She just forgot her jacket, that's all.

The bedroom was stifling, heat trapped by closed curtains, closed windows. He put the pebble on the bedside table and sat down on the bed again. Palms on the knees. Sweat on his naked body. The mobile phone on the bed blinked blue. Probably another voice mail from Mary. He wanted to go to her but didn't. Big Haakon was holding him back, that epic miscalculation on the day of his release. No repeats, no do-overs, once was most definitely enough.

10 am, a thin winter drizzle and a small backpack, the cliché of the prison doors banging shut behind him.

He had walked into town, tyres on wet tarmac and the searching eyes of passers-by who knew where he'd come from, he was sure. Then a train to Oslo and on to Larvik, a bee-line for familiarity and Big Haakon – another outcast, who'd *understand*, who'd swing open a welcoming door and then a tear-filled bear hug, an overflowing glass, the sweet stun of oblivion.

But Haakon's garden had been tidied. There was a neat lawn, flowers in little rows. The doorbell actually worked and the stranger who answered had bought the place three years ago.

Tore still had the shop on Haralds gate. Newsagents knew the news and Jonas's conviction had made the nationals. Tore recognised him as soon as he came in. The shop was unchanged, the same mustiness that now smelled like the dusty values of the town itself. Jonas couldn't shake the feeling in Tore's gaze that by leaving he'd rejected those values, a first step on a corruption that had its inevitable full stop in the darkness on the edge of Bergen.

Tore's grudging directions took him to the northern outskirts, a house on a subdued, new-build estate. The woman who answered the door wore an oversized silver crucifix on a chain round her neck. She said nothing for a few moments, leaving him in the downpour, face set with triumphant disdain, as if she'd just won a long-standing bet that he'd turn up one day.

Haakon sat in a high-backed chair in a spartan living room. A tiny TV set. No bookshelves. A coffee table complete with Bible. He must have told the woman all about Jonas Mortensen, a fallen son of Larvik, this town which proved its goodness by welcoming himself, Haakon of the drunken binges, Haakon of the Apologies, back into its forgiving embrace.

'You shouldn't have come back,' said Haakon.

Instead of that blank indifference Jonas saw a smile from another lifetime, Haakon peering over his shoulder at the orange ember Jonas had finally managed to create from the bow-drill.

'There's nothing for you here.'

'This is my home.'

'This hasn't been your home for a long time. You can't come back and pretend it is.'

'I wanted to see you. It's been so long.'

'You wanted to hide.'

'What? Hide where?'

'In the past.'

'What's wrong with that?'

'That little girl. Your daughter. She never got the chance to remember where she came from. You robbed her of the nostalgia you come here to indulge. I suppose you think about me with a little smile. The drunken idiot from your childhood. I'm offended that you've come here.'

'You've no idea how sorry I am.'

'There's a train at four.'

Jonas walked back to the harbour. Stood for a long time with the bobbing yachts, the rigging singing, dark squalls moving on a barely lighter Skagerrak. The sea was viscous, as if time had externally slowed. Inside, it seemed to have sped up, a tumble of memories and somewhere nearby that precious hoard of childhood, he just had to remember where he'd buried it.

The joujouka gulls cackled, and a lurch in the stomach told Jonas, finally, how much time had passed. He saw the arrogance in expecting the same Haakon. We shift, do we not, running waves in a blustery nor'easter, cross the watersheds but still wonder how our feet got so wet.

One continuity was guaranteed, his father's unshakable contempt. The house by Langestrand kirke wasn't too far away. He had written to Jonas in prison to tell him *you are no longer my son*. The usual melodrama, like the way he left in a midnight blizzard to move in with the golf pro he was convinced looked like Gabriela Sabatini and who left him three months later.

It was no day for another terminal visit. Instead, he headed for the station, a watery coffee, hesitation from the teenage girl taking his order, shrewdness in the eyes, blue eyes like Anya, following him onto the train, eight hours in the *exile wagon*, back to Bergen, to Christinegård...

The water pipes suddenly coughed in the bathroom. Jonas's head jerked up. Hypnagogic images shattering. He tensed his body and relaxed. Tensed and relaxed. Then forced himself to get up and get dressed in a pair of shorts and a t-shirt. The memories became shadows, slipping away with an ease that was troubling. He stared at the phone on the bed, ever-blinking with Mary's name, listening to a ringing he gradually realised was coming from the front door.

'There's interest, Jon - , Mr Mortensen. People want to know why the police have been talking to you.'

He'd expected this sooner. A journalist. Pink-faced and too much aftershave. He looked across the street. Gladstone was sweeping the pavement outside the café. He stopped and leaned on the brush. Jonas waved and Gladstone waved back a few moments later, a *significant*

few moments, sizing up the situation and what he made
of it.

'Mr Morten–'

'Go and ask the police.'

'I'll ask them too.'

'So why bother asking me?'

'I'm just interested in your take. Maybe I should come
in?'

Gladstone had been joined by the hairdresser from
the ever-empty salon. She'd dyed her hair green, something to do in the absence of clients. They were talking
as they watched.

'You think I'm embarrassed?'

'No. I think you're terrified and don't have a clue
where this is going to end. I can help you.'

'That right.'

'I can get you 10k for your story. Might come in handy
later.'

'What story?'

'Fifteen at a push. People have a right to know.'

'No they don't.'

'Are you saying that –'

'What I'm saying is that you're getting confused
about rights. People might want to know. Doesn't make
it a right.'

'What are you, the village philosopher?'

'I studied it.'

'And now you fix potholes.'

Jonas made to close the door and the reporter stepped
forward.

'Don't be a prick all your life, I'm only trying to –'

'You're only trying to do what?' Jonas grabbed him
by the shirt. 'What the *fuck* are you only trying to do?'

'Look up the street!'

'Eh?'

'The street. Look.'

205

Jonas held his grip and looked to his right.

'See that blue Ford? That's the police. Red Golf on the other side? That's my photographer. You really want the cops to come running and my buddy to snap it all for the front page?'

'Fuck you.'

'Look Jonas. Cops blab. A few quid here, there, piece of piss, mate. I know about Norway, your wife and kid. 10k. You can get ahead of the game and you better believe that this is a game. I don't care if you really killed Lacey and you know what? No one else does. You're the *guy*. You're the bogeyman. You better tell your story before someone tells it for you.'

Jonas let go of the journalist. Stared right at him. 'Can I tell you something? Off the record?'

The journalist's eyes lit up. 'Course you can.'

'People like you. You'd take a picture of your dying child before you called an ambulance.'

He slammed the door.

Slumped to the floor. Above him the letterbox clacked and the reporter's business card landed in his lap. Jonas immediately crumpled it, then, a few moments later, smoothed it out.

His face grew hot. Gladstone, that pause before he waved, the green-haired girl, Tore the newsagent and Haakon of the Cross before them, Haakon who may at *this exact moment* be holding court after a prayer meeting, telling the whole damn group about this man he once knew, Jonas Mortensen, who'd grown in the repeated telling to become the reporter's demon, the aberration in our midst who reassures us of our own goodness, our normality.

Only then did he register Fletcher at the end of the hall. The sun from the kitchen doorway was dazzling and Jonas couldn't see his face, just a black outline in quivering, silvery light.

'Everyone's got a story,' said Jonas. 'You haven't told me yours.'

'You don't want to know my story.'

'Try me.'

'You know they're going to search this place.'

Jonas closed his eyes.

'They're going to have crime scene vans and flashing lights, police tape everywhere. Maybe even those white boiler suits, you know the ones. That the forensic people wear? It's all gonna get a bit CSI, hope you've cleaned your bedroom. But they'll know if you've done that and they'll want to know why. You're kinda screwed either way. People are going to stand on the street, watching it all happen. For hours, like the circus. Probably be an ice cream van.'

'Just go. Go *away*. GO!'

'What did you really do when she came back? For that blue jacket. It was blue, wasn't it?'

When he opened his eyes Fletcher was gone. He stared into the streaming light until his eyes hurt. Upstairs, his mobile was ringing. This was the hunt. This was what Jonas remembered.

Thirty-two

Lacey disappearance, arrest imminent? Mary listened to Jonas's voicemail message, watching the black on yellow BREAKING NEWS tickering along the TV screen. She shoved the mobile in her pocket, annoyed he was still ignoring her calls. The TV cut to a montage of recent events; yellow-bibbed search teams, flowers outside the church. And Mary herself, shouting at the journalists.

She closed her eyes, opened them to the endless boxes of breakfast cereals and their happy cartoon faces. How long would she have to stare at them before the world regained any sense? Daisy passed. At the end of the aisle she raised her head to the TV and looked back.

Mary's anger was sudden, the *sod it* just as quick. People could think what they liked. She'd lived here all her life. Sometimes the glaringly obvious went under the radar while carefully managed secrets might have been broadcast from the church steeple. 24-7 media speculation and reality TV was made for places like this, gossip and suspicion an antique instinct.

When she went into the store room Daisy was there again, with Meg, whispers that abruptly stopped. They knew she worked with Jonas at The Hub and Meg had seen her going into his house. As deviant by association she had two choices. Go to ground or ignore the gossip. With typical decisiveness she chose the latter and with the same decisiveness changed her mind on the walk home.

The change of mind troubled her. She felt she'd let Jonas down. If we were all in need of some solace, then some needed it more than others. Mary couldn't imagine the awfulness of losing her daughter. As he'd been forced to tell her, so Jonas would tell the police the story he wanted to keep buried. The world was like that, every secret on borrowed time.

From the entrance to the cul-de-sac she could see her husband's Renault parked outside the house. Without thinking, she carried on past, heading for the trees that led round to the nature park.

The picnic area was deserted but she still felt self-conscious. Sitting at a table in her supermarket uniform wasn't normal. Only old people were allowed to sit and stare. Daisy and Meg would somehow find out. She imagined hurrying up to them, an excited whisper like theirs.

John Hackett is back.

Twenty-three years later, just as Lacey disappeared. Mary would be the centre of a sensation. Suspicion would swing lightning fast from Jonas to John. They would remember what John did, supposedly, to his sister who was never found. *No smoke without fire*, they would say again.

As with his little sister, Mary didn't believe John had anything to do with Lacey. Nothing she had ever known suggested the world moved in so neat and obvious a manner. Other people must know this but that was why they ignored it. They wanted certainty, the crowd outside Jonas's house or the tabloid headline from May 1991, John Hackett's haunted teenage face.

What does he know?

She disliked John's assumption that she wouldn't say a word to anyone. But she wouldn't. Except Jonas.

When she phoned again he finally answered. She

209

was brief. They agreed to meet. She decided not to tell him how angry she was about him ignoring her calls. It seemed needy. The sun swelled and she raised her face. There was a heaviness in the air, a storm on its way.

She hoped at this very moment that her daughter was sitting in a pub garden getting completely plastered, full of the certainty that life was a long, straight super-highway through ever-lasting happiness. Mary wanted that certainty too. Perhaps she would finally leave the village and its decrepit stories that were forever etched, like the old initials and I love so-and-sos carved onto the picnic table. She wanted a future, like the one Andrea saw when she looked at the boy she'd told her about on the phone, the one with the *glacier-blue eyes*.

Jonas had green eyes. Mary couldn't believe he'd stood her up in his own house. Or rather, John Hackett's house. What a charade, the cousin thing, all of it. She wanted to know why Jonas was living there and was annoyed for not asking him on the phone. Now she had to wait, again.

★ ★ ★

Axel once told Jonas that girls liked to do this. Lie on their backs in a field and look up into the clouds, making shapes from the wisps and puffs. *You're right in there if you see a bunny or a teddy bear, girls love all that.* Jonas was doubtful, even aged fourteen, when any stratagem, however desperate, was to be considered in the fevered effort to get his hands inside a pair of knickers.

Big Haakon brought more sophistication. Told them about the art of reading portents in the clouds, the shamen who spent lifetimes waiting for the map to reveal. *Just a matter of knowing what to look for, boys.* But lying there and looking up, Jonas didn't want to find a damn thing in the clouds.

210

Now and then he poked his head up above the wheat. Looked across to the road to see if Mary had appeared. She said she'd meet him at the end of the single-track to the west, out by the new housing development. The longer he waited the more likely he'd be seen. Round the village it would flash that the Viking, *Jonas of the Porn*, was hanging about in the middle of nowhere. Hence the field, a wade into chest-high wheat, skulking like an animal.

Getting there had been problematic. The photographer's car was still parked along the street from End Point and another had appeared a few hours ago. Two people inside. Then there was the man in the wraparound shades, who periodically appeared outside Gladstone's café to smoke a cigarette and stare across the street. He made phone calls every fifteen minutes, turning away as he did, as if he knew Jonas was watching and might read his lips.

So reassess, Mr M, no way you're leaving by the front door. He'd seen it. You see it all the time. The stock in trade of the tabloids, a series of photos running across two pages: the *hunted*, peering over his shoulder as he scurries out of his house. The TV equivalent would be a hand shoved in the lens of the camera poked in his face, the inevitable *no comment* followed by a nervous glance back, always that glance back, and in that glance is only ever culpability.

He left via the back garden. Into the cypresses and quickly over the back fence to the side-street, an over-exposed walk-cum-run through the deserted housing estate, into Panama Lane and the woods of Sycamore Camp, the canopy camouflage of white-beam and birch, beech and hazel, counter-clockwise to the westerly fringes of the village, quickly across open ground, a scrubby field mined with sun-dried cow pats, and there was the single-track.

Mary appeared just after eight thirty, a light wind

carrying the pad of her trainers on the road. He peered above the bobbing wheat, watching her run to the entrance of the building site. She looked good in her running gear. Tight Lycra running top and loose, mid-thigh shorts.

She stopped and looked around but Jonas didn't stand up and wave. He wanted to observe, just for a bit, taking his time with his impressions. This woman appeared. High noon in his ever-scrolling melodrama. Draw the gun and shoot the past, something ridiculous like that. Even Eva was rolling her eyes, like how can she be jealous of something as histrionic as this?

He didn't know why he ducked down when Mary stared straight at the spot where he was crouched. Eyes closed, he lay down and waited for her to come to him through the fussing wheat.

Mary stood for a long moment, looking down at him. Jonas's eyes were closed. 'You hiding from me?'

Jonas said nothing and kept his eyes shut. The wheat crunkled as Mary shuffled on the ground and sat down cross-legged. His eye-lids were flickering. She studied the face, the lines round the eyes, wondering if she had ever looked at someone as closely as this. A tuft of hair blew across his face and she wanted to brush it behind his ear, with an affection she wasn't sure about. She looked away, into the sky. When she looked back he was squinting up at her.

'You're awake,' she said.

'I wasn't asleep.'

'I know.'

'I almost fell asleep.'

'Bit uncomfortable. I've got something poking my bum.'

She couldn't help thinking about the magazines. Her smile wavered. 'Why are you hiding here?'

'Cops.'

'You serious?'

'Angry locals with pitchforks?'

'Don't be stupid.'

'You know how many people came to my party? Twenty-two. How many people do you think will come next year?'

'C'mon. There'll be a few.'

'A few?'

'Maybe more.'

'Doubt it. They came again. The police.'

'When?'

'This morning. They wanted to know why Lacey came back after the party and why I hadn't told them.'

'She came back? What for?'

'Her jacket. She left it in the kitchen. I gave her a glass of lemonade.'

Mary felt her stomach turn. 'There's nothing wrong with that.' *But of course there was.*

'I know.'

She nodded vaguely.

'I know,' he repeated.

She closed her eyes. She felt his fingers seek hers and grasp them tightly. She resisted the urge to pull her hand away. She wanted to scream at him that you don't *do* those things, Jonas. You open the door and you leave her right there and you go back inside the house and find the jacket that you bring to her and *good night*. You do not invite her in. You just don't and you know you don't. Otherwise you would have told the police in the first place.

'What do you see up there, in the clouds?'

She turned her face. He was looking directly upwards.

'I think you see whatever you want to see.'

'I used to dream about this when I was a teenager. Alone in a field with a girl.' He sat up quickly and

213

turned to her. 'It was the expectation I looked forward to, I think, knowing something was about to happen but not knowing when. She'd look at me like you're looking at me and – '

He lunged at her and she let him briefly kiss her before pushing him away. He tried again and again she pushed him back, acutely aware, suddenly, of the remoteness of the field and her skimpy running gear. She wondered if she was frightened as she watched tears well in his eyes.

'I'm sorry, Jonas. It's just... I better go.'

Jonas nodded. He pulled his knees up to his chest and hugged himself.

'I think I need some space.'

'Mm.'

'It's nothing personal.'

'I get it.'

She had waded a few metres back through the wheat when he called out.

'I killed them, you know.'

When she turned she could only see the top of his head.

'My wife and daughter. I was the drunk driver. I wanted to tell you before someone else did.'

* * *

The doorbell rang just after 6 am. The sad-eyed detective presented a warrant. Jonas was free to stay while they carried out the search and was not under arrest. He was accompanied upstairs to get dressed by a jittery constable in a short-sleeved shirt, who frowned briefly when Jonas paused on the landing to look into Fletcher's room. It was empty, no sleeping mat or one-eyed doll, just the few cardboard boxes that had been there for years.

214

Thirty-three

The Skull was cool. Fletcher peered out the left eye at the overgrown golf course. The heavy green vegetation had thickened with the rain of the last few days. He imagined the End of Days to be just like this, weeds and plants pulsing unhindered in the ruins of civilisation. He used to read science fiction as a boy, projecting into the Apocalypse. But where he once fantasised about being the last human on earth, he now wondered about the vanity of survival.

He'd returned to The Skull the evening before, after removing all signs of himself from End Point.

The police were going to search the house. It would happen soon and it would be very early in the morning. He took no satisfaction in being right when he walked past End Point just after six that morning and saw a forensics van and three police cars pulled up outside.

Back in 1991 these tactics were bewildering, carefully designed – it seemed – to maximise his alienation: that odd way the police talked, a mix of procedural formality and exaggerated crassness, the occasional huddles in the corner and sometimes he heard those whispers, never sure if he was *meant* to. *Two minutes alone with him, two fuckin minutes is all I need...*

It would get so much worse for the Norwegian. The hostility would swell. If Mortensen had any sense, he would get out of the village. If he didn't then Fletcher could wait. His vicious little sister had taught him

215

patience long before the Marines. He let her kick and nip and scratch and put the anger someplace for later. On that last day she went crazy because he laughed at her for being fourteen and still playing with that creepy, one-eyed doll.

The police kept on about those scratches until Fletcher admitted they hadn't been caused by crashing his BMX. *You tell me what brother and sister don't fight*, he said, thinking that it sounded so grown-up to rationalise like this. *I can show you a scar where she bit me, if you want?*

They didn't. They exchanged angry glances because their absolutism made him guilty and his evasion outrageous. He respected it, now. An absolute imposed a discipline. The desert had taught him, the relentless sun burning off the flim-flam, the dust in his boots the last of his doubt, crumbled away to nothing. It made the killing easier. Maybe he'd tell the priest about the Taliban soldier, a teenager cursing him and refusing to die, Fletcher plunging his bayonet again and again, over thirty times, still thrusting after the boy finally died because his eyes retained their contempt until Fletcher stabbed them to a final blindness. *There's more than one absolute*, he would tell the priest, *and even you with all your cosmopolitan guilt will, come the end of your time, stress one truth to the detriment of all others.*

No one wanted McQueen's stories of traumatised, homeless veterans. They wanted Union Jacks by the side of the road as another cortege of heroes who couldn't be helped passed in the rain. They wanted red poppies on every lapel.

Fletcher lay down, drowsing to the distant thrum of the traffic on the bridge. He daydreamed of the girl in the blue jacket, saw her through murky water as he hovered overhead like a kestrel. When he opened his eyes a magpie was sitting on the eye socket of The Skull, looking at him. One for sorrow, and although he told himself not to, he couldn't help looking for a second as he crossed the golf course and walked into the village to *The Black Lion*.

He wondered if this, at the end of the day, was what it came down to, a simple search for joy.

'I'll murder the fucker!'

Fletcher saw the barwoman glance along the bar, where an old man pretended not to hear. He'd just opened the door. For an instant he wondered if John Smith was talking about him.

'Watch your language, John, or that's your last,' said the barwoman.

The face beneath the fuzzy hair was red and outraged. 'What, you *defending* him?'

She sighed and looked at Fletcher. 'What'll it be?'

'Bottle of Bud... and whatever he's having.'

'Serious?' she said.

Smith's gaze shifted. 'You're a gent!'

'That's me.'

They sat at a corner table and watched the live news broadcast from the village green. Councillor Bacon was being interviewed, sweating in a tweed suit and canary yellow shirt. He made clear to the interviewer that he would not speculate and then proceeded to speculate.

'There is mounting anecdotal evidence, it would seem.'

'What would you anticipate next?'

'I would expect an arrest.'

'Do you know the individual in question?'

'I know *of* him.'

Smith looked away from the TV. Leaned close to Fletcher. Told him Mortensen was responsible for Lacey's disappearance because he was a *foreigner, we know fuck all about him, nothing.*

217

When the TV anchor cut to the sports news Smith turned his attention to the old man at the bar.

'What about it, Sam? Not seeing you watching much of this? You know him, don't you, so what's the score?'

Sam spoke without turning. 'Never said a bad word to me.'

Smith was disgusted. 'It's not about you, you silly old fart. It's about Lacey and what he did to her.'

'So you say.'

'Watch the telly! It's not just me. It's everyone else, the whole world apart from you!'

'*Enough*, John, finish your drink and get out,' shouted Clara.

'The hell is wrong with you people.' Smith's attention suddenly shifted to the window. 'There's another, Mary Jackson. She's round his place all hours, probably gets a kick out of it, like those women who write to men on death row. What's all that about, eh?'

Fletcher watched Mary pass the window without glancing in. She was wearing her supermarket uniform. He thought about her childhood bedroom, the posters of those boy bands.

'I'd bang it, though,' said Smith.

Later, when Smith went to the toilet, Fletcher made up his mind. When Smith woke up on the toilet floor with a hand trailing in the stinking gutter of the urinal he had no idea who'd crept up behind him and smacked his face off the wall as he stood with his cock out. His first thought was old Sam. He had no way of knowing that Fletcher was a man of absolutes.

218

Thirty-four

The police were thorough. Quiet machines. Jonas waited in the kitchen. No one acknowledged him. It was perfectly feasible, he realised, to be the centre of attention yet completely invisible at the same time. They left at midday, leaving a small crowd on the pavement, nausea in his throat and a sense of exposure that reminded him of those last few months at the house in Christinegård when he returned to Bergen after being released from prison.

That day of return. A livid scar on his memory. Jonas wasn't doing well, back then.

All those white-painted wooden houses and oppressively neat gardens, it took so long to pass them, to get to his own front door, like in a troubling dream, that unknown something pulling you back. He was so tense, ready to apologise to anyone he saw, every neighbour known and unknown. But he met no one and the empty street seemed almost purposeful, as if word had been passed to stay out of sight, make sure Mortensen saw only ghosts.

He stood in the hallway, the house pressing, shrinking in, a quick falling of memories. He took off his shoes and socks. Then the rest of his clothes. And started slapping himself. Hard as he could on the face and body, again and again until his skin was red, singing with pain.

Still naked, he paced the rooms. The rugs too rough

219

and the polished floorboards too cold, as if the fibres were curling away and the pine somehow frosting over as he walked, appalled by his touch. He opened every window but the bright August sun transformed at the sill to a yellowing that fell on him like jaundice, fetal-curled on the couch and looking up and out at such an epic blue, the blue of freedom, but this just one confinement swapped for another.

Even in the back garden he was trapped, the flowers planted by Anya now spread and colonising. He had to get out of there. To stay was to become a recluse, peered at by children who came creeping at night, spying through the windows at *Killer J,* head in his hands and *it's such a spooky living room, Kjetil, it's like there's people in there only he can see.*

End Point felt the same. Compromised by Fletcher and now by the police. Trapped again.

He walked through to the sun room. Stood for a few moments, looking round at the surrounding houses. He turned his back to the garden, looking through the sun room and into the shadowed kitchen. Then he turned round again, looking up at the house directly opposite.

It was all a matter of trigonometry. Except he couldn't remember anything about High School maths. Still, he made the process relatively scientific. He pulled the kitchen table one foot back, one foot to the right, then sat at each chair. The angles said he could be seen through the kitchen window from the house on the left and from the second floor windows of the house opposite the sun room. Four more attempts and the table was now three feet back from its original position and two feet to the left. It was pushed almost up to the sink but Jonas couldn't be seen through any window, so long as he sat on the back right chair.

Crack open a beer. Crack another. Just because you're

paranoid doesn't mean they're not watching. The photographers would also find the angles. No question. They would pay the neighbours to poke long-lensed cameras from the windows and maybe *catch him*.

Doing what?

Didn't matter. Anything would make him seem guilty. A brief smile proof of the psychopath with no conscience.

He went to check the bedroom curtains were completely closed and did the same in the living room. He couldn't resist the urge to peek outside. A small crowd of peering locals had gathered on the opposite pavement, drawn by the search. And the media, of course, still circling, instantly recognisable by their bogus indifference; mobile-phoned and all a-strut.

Even Li Po was unsettled.

Jonas stared at the scroll painting. The little figure outside the temple seemed to shift in the half-light, as if looking over his shoulder, towards the distant mountains. Somewhere up there a refuge, as End Point had once been. He'd found it one morning when still bivvying down at Sycamore Camp, a quick recce all that was needed to tell him the house was long uninhabited. Three days later a rain-swept dawn allowed him to explore properly. Over the side fence and into the cypresses. The downpour hid the noise of the break-in.

And so much dust lifting from bare floorboards. It didn't catch his throat as back in Christinegård. This was the dust of someone else's past. The dirty marks on the kitchen lino when the light was right told stories he knew nothing about. Perhaps if he'd looked closer he'd have seen Fletcher's face in those shapes, the ghost that was yet to come. Not that there had seemed to be any danger of someone reclaiming that history anytime soon. The most recent letter in the pile under the letter box was nine years old. Clearly no inhabitant since.

So Jonas moved in.

A very private fitting of new locks and a very public cleaning of the ivy from the name plate beside the front door. Electricity? Jonas did as Asamoah showed him in that Harlesden squat he shared with seven others. On came the lights. Jonas started greeting his neighbours as the new owner of End Point, slipping himself into the village, another history emerging in the lino shapes, Jonas of the *Jonsok* parties, *the Viking*, an unfurling of a new life that was impossible in Bergen, where memories of Eva and Anya thundered like a winter waterfall and the neighbours all knew, whose contempt clung like leeches until he fled to Larvik once more.

That last home-coming. Thirteen months since the disastrous visit to Haakon, and thirteen months of avoiding contacting his father. Now Jonas stood outside his front door, winter-chilled and an even colder chill to come, feeling the slow fade of that final tenacious delusion, the thought he could build an elusive new life on the bones of another, more distant past.

It was why he stopped off en-route to buy a one-way ferry ticket to Denmark, leaving that evening.

His father opened the door and the performance began, a tour de force from the master: making his son face the sun so he had to squint; cupping his hands round the coffee mug, as if Jonas had brought an iciness to his home; a strained holding of his son's gaze after delivering the killer line, *how many times in your life are you going to be wrong... son?* There was genius in that pause, Jonas almost admired it. It held a lifetime, a *universe*. When the bells of Langestrand kirke began to toll he wondered if his father had somehow planned that too.

Nowhere to go but the sea, the fever roads of all Norway behind him and still pushing, into the salty water and in time, maybe, the salt would eat away at him, break him up to drift on blissful currents, away from Haakon's judgement and his father's incredulity, the same incredulity which leached from Mary the day before, there in the wheat with her head slightly angled, as his father's had been, face shadowed and an uncanny halo around his head, silver strands of hair so clear in the last of the light that Jonas could have counted them.

His father wanted Jonas to acknowledge his failure, he knew it, an apology to underline his inferiority. But because his father was such a manipulative bastard he didn't say anything, just seemed to project it, like a hypnotist, right into his hippofuckincampus. Jonas refused. There would be no forgive me for what I've done, father, for what I've become...

Any collapse would be for Big Haakon, not his father. It would pour uncontrollably if he happened to bump into Haakon, which was why he ran to the ferry terminal after leaving his father's house. No more traumatic an echo would there be to see Haakon in the streets of this emptied town, Haakon who would say *what became of you, Jonas?* Haakon the true fulcrum of his childhood, not his ever-crestfallen and long-dead mother or the semi-detached father who studied him with the indifference of a scientist to the object of a failed experiment.

Yet Jonas *expected* Haakon. He watched from the stern as the ferry eased into the harbour.

Somehow Haakon knew he was leaving and would appear, wave goodbye from the dock, there at the end of the white churning line of the ship's wake that glowed like phosphorescence and connected present to past and Jonas watching, following the froth of time back across the black sea, back to the dock until it all broke up in the white caps of a sudden squall.

But it wasn't Haakon he saw in the grey vagueness but two dark figures. An adult and a child. Eva and Anya,

223

standing but not waving, his father's words fogging his mind like the smirr that eventually obscured them. *How many times in your life are you going to be wrong?*

The words had goblin-squatted in his mind ever since, an epitaph for a grinning, clinging past.

Always the past.

Jonas needed and feared it. It followed him across Europe, to the building sites of Copenhagen and bunk-beds with Estonians who every night veered a drunken path through homeland stories and if Jonas never recip-rocated so what, exile imposing a camaraderie but also an impatience to get back to your own tale. It followed him to the vineyards of France and intelligent, bashful men from West Africa, who kept their heads down, like Sunny D, who stood on Dakar's terminal beach and paid the fortune to leave his wife and take the six-month journey to Morocco and north; to the strawberry fields of southern England where he slept in a fetid caravan with two hulking Romanians with photos of their children on the walls and when they asked him one evening as they demolished another bottle of vodka if he had children of his own out came a desperate but unwanted *yes*. So they knew not to ask any more questions and from then on it was football, *football* and the pretty farmer's daughter who always wore tight jeans. It followed him to the London restaurants and dishwashers ten a penny, like Asamoah, no job for six years so he paid a gang all his money and ended up in Berlin, an abattoir, and always blood under his nails until he got across the Channel beneath a lorry to work the sinks in twelve-hour shifts but at least his hands were always clean.

So many circling faces, constellations so bright in his private universe he had to turn from the glare. Sunny D and Kiev Dimitri, Asamoah and Wakaso, men who worked the Euro shadows and sent back the wages. Those men kept their heads down. They didn't befriend

224

fourteen-year-old girls. They understood that the window of self-preservation didn't stay open long.

Jonas left the living room and hurried up the stairs. His camping kit was in the loft, found again when he disinterred the one-eyed doll which was now gone with Fletcher to who knows where.

Twenty minutes later his rucksack was packed. Li Po was the last to go in, rolled into a cardboard cylinder. Jonas didn't bother with one last look around before exiting by the back door.

He took the same route as the day before when he met Mary. Through the cypresses and over the side fence.

Again, no one saw him. He kept his head low, hurrying through the housing estate to the woods, as if to look up would be to see whole families at their windows, staring back at him.

It took ten minutes to find Sycamore Camp. The sky darkened, deep lavender to grey-mauve, car headlights flicker-strobing through the leaves. He slung the fly sheet over a branch and pulled it taut with pegs stuck through the brass eyes of the fabric. He swept the ground under the tent free of twigs and stones and unrolled the bivvy bag, stuffing in the thermal mat.

Six years evaporated. Jonas lay on top of the bag, as then, head on the rucksack, looking through the open V of the tent, watching the lights, shapes, shifting shadows in quick-time.

The question, as ever, was where to go. London was the obvious choice and he still had Asamoah's mobile number. He could work the restaurants through winter, put some cash aside and then over to Europe for the fruit season. The world opened out and for a brief moment Jonas felt the lightness of freedom glimpsed. But when he tried Asamoah the phone told him the number was not recognised. Six years had passed, after all. He hoped that gentle Asamoah had made it home. That's what all the tabloid hacks couldn't comprehend, that the West wasn't some Shangri-La no one would ever want to leave but was full of men, women and children who only came because they desperately wanted to go home again.

There it was, the ever-troubling problem of home. You build it with such care. You give it stories. You tell others, time passes and your story takes root. Sunny D, Dimitri, Asamoah and all those stories, the common denominator was home, the need to get home, I miss home.

Except Jonas didn't have a tin shack in a Dakar slum or a breadline farmstead in the Romanian mountains. He climbed into his bivvy bag. He tried to convince himself he would be able to leave.

Thirty-five

'Are you screwing him?'

Mary turned over in bed. Tuesday morning. The alarm clock said 5.05. Her husband was looming over her. He seemed troubled. He might have been sitting there all night. Waiting for her to wake up until he couldn't wait anymore. She made him repeat his question.

'What?'

'Screwing him. As well as cleaning his house.'

'Who have you been talking to?'

'No one. Should I be?'

'Give it a rest, Andy.'

'You haven't answered my question.'

'Don't be ridiculous.' She turned back over and listened. Listened to him sitting. Sitting and looming and thinking. A few minutes later he got up. Her husband never got up this early.

Her daughter once asked why she didn't leave. A sunny August evening and just the two of them. They were half-drunk on the back patio, Andrea remaining true to the promise made on her eighteenth birthday to make a cocktail for them every Friday. That day it was Mojitos and they were halfway down their third when her daughter said *you need to get out of here.*

It was the gravity in Andrea's voice that upset her, something long considered that couldn't be contained any longer. *It's about faithfulness,* Mary said. *Not to marriage, and it isn't blind faith either, but faithfulness to who we were. The world moves in cycles. I want to be here when it spins round again.* Her daughter was scathing. *You can't possibly believe that crap.*

Now Mary couldn't sleep either.

Downstairs her husband was drinking tea. He was wearing a dressing gown. A sure signal of an argument. She wished she had put on a dressing gown as well. You can't have an argument while wearing a pink pyjama top that says *my other bed is a hammock*. No authority in it.

'I guess you've heard?' he said.

'The search?'

She made sure she was in bed when he got back the night before. He'd been away all day, some sales event. Texts and voice mails told him he was desperate to talk about the search. Then the thumping about in the bedroom trying to wake her, give him an excuse to start on about it. Mary kept her eyes shut. But she too was lying there thinking about the search.

'Yeah, the search. Be a lot for you to clean up after the cops turned the place upside down.'

'Give it a rest.'

'Just a matter of time till they find her.'

'You're the big expert then?'

'I'm just saying.'

'But you don't know a damn *thing*, do you?' She paused. 'Has he been charged?'

'Don't think so.'

'Well, don't go joining the lynch-mob just yet.'

'How can you be so sure? How well do you know this guy, eh?'

'For Christ's sake – '

'You *are* screwing him. Aren't you? How long for? Must be a real kick with all this going on. I want you to chuck that job in. *Now*. I don't want you going round there again. I want – '

228

'I want. I want. I *want*. You've not wanted anything for years and all of a sudden you're all demands. You know what I want? Eh? Do you know what *I* want? Go on then, do you?'

'No, I really – '

'Exactly!'

When Mary got upstairs she was shaking. She remembered the restless wheat. Jonas's lunging kiss. She'd slept with him and most enjoyed what she could only describe as the simplicity. She'd do it again, have sex with a man who killed his wife and child. The thought appalled her.

Now the search. She still wanted to believe him but something was resisting, something in a black hole, pushing back as she reached in her hand, refusing to let her find what she was grasping for. She hadn't told him about John Hackett and wondered if she could.

Thirty-six

On Tuesday morning Jonas almost went out. He made it to the front door. Out he would go, no problem, for a walk, nothing as normal as a walk, a jaunty step and click, click, click go the cameras but I'm only walking, I'm only walking. Hand on the door handle, he heard two things. First a ripple of laughter, the journos with their morning coffee. Then a metallic clanking, the pipes in the upstairs airing cupboard again. Then once more the laughter and again the pipes. There could be a problem with the pipes. He would have to stay in, see to it, see to the pipes before something burst, flooded the house and can you imagine the poor plumber who had to turn up, run the media gauntlet to fix his pipes? It was unfair, he couldn't ask the plumber to do that. So he got the tool box from under the kitchen sink and went upstairs to the airing cupboard to consider the decrepit heating system, the mysterious pipe-work leading from the giant boiler that looked like one of Saturn 5's fuel tanks. In his hand was a ratchet. That's what you needed, surely, to fix pipes. He peered for a long time, reached behind the water boiler, stood back with his arms folded and patted the ratchet against his palm, frowning and considering. In the silence he could still hear the laughter.

He stayed in all day. Made lentil and bacon soup and bread. Five loaves from the bags of flour he had in the cupboards. Then an over-hot bath and to bed, the boiling seas of the fever-dreams.

The rabbit came back. Tonight it was man-sized, like the one in that creepy film he couldn't remember. It walked right up to him, slow steps closer and closer until he was forced to shut his eyes, and then somehow through him, a crossing of dimensions he felt as coloured vibrations across his body. When Jonas opened his eyes again it was over by the window. A vaguely visible darkness on darkness but looking back at him, he knew. He saw that he was hanging out of bed and reaching towards it, a deep and permanent sadness in his chest.

As Jonas watched, the slow transformation began once more, the rabbit becoming smaller and smaller, morphing into that familiar child's shape. He had to get out of this occult darkness.

He came to at the window. A confused sense of time. Two seconds he may have been there. Two years.

His arms were wide and he was gripping each flung-open curtain. He stared at the dead flies on the windowsill, gaze moving up to the dusty window panes then outwards, beyond the glass, the houses across the street he may have been seeing for the first time. Then movement below, two figures under a streetlight, looking up. He realised he was naked.

Naked with his arms wide.

Like Jesus.

He laughed out loud as he stepped back from the window, pulling the curtains closed again. The dream was gone, the rabbit vanished and no Anya to see, lying at his feet, bleeding.

In the darkness, the fluorescent arms of the alarm clock said 3.33. He doubled it to 666 and started laughing

231

again. Halfway to the Beast. Normality had floated free. Just a speck now.

You can lose it in a thousand different ways. It's all dependent on the individual. To some extent you can even rationally lose it, like one part of you is watching another with curious detachment yet lacks the power to intervene, to say, *really, Jonas?* He wondered which one of him was the more real, the one rummaging in the garden shed or the one watching the rummaging?

He was still naked. The Petzl strapped to his forehead cast a thin and powerful beam, straight from the Third Eye of one of those two Jonases. It didn't matter which, all that mattered was the head-torch found his bow-drill kit on a shelf, the sycamore hearth board, and the bag of hay.

When Jonas finished there were five scorch patches on the lawn, like the five on a giant dice. Pink and yellow streaks had appeared behind the roofs to the east. One or two windows were lit. He felt dazed but better. His shoulder might ache and the tips of his fingers may be singed from the heat of the spindle turning in the bearing block but he felt better.

People had seen his firelighting frenzy. He'd heard their windows open, wakened by the screech of willow on sycamore. No one had shouted at him to shut up. They just watched from a silent, appraising distance, letting the maniac work through whatever he had to.

A third coffee told him to go back to work. Work meant normality. Meant nothing had changed. Hogg would be pleased. He was bound to need the labour. Jonas. He was here to help.

He phoned Eggers, who didn't answer, leaving a message to pick him up at the usual time. On his way for a shower, he checked the spare room. Fletcher still hadn't reappeared after the search and Jonas indulged the little part of him that wanted to believe he'd gone for good.

So he smiled as he showered and dressed and waited for Eggers to blast the horn. He felt better, remember? He would not be Jonas of the Cross. He would remember goodness where Big Haakon had forgotten. This was his home. This was where he'd met beautiful young Lacey. This was where he'd continue to smile, no matter the media camped outside his door.

Eggers didn't come.

Jonas paced the living room and peered through the gap in the curtain. He shrugged at Li Po, wondered what to do and decided. He strode into the hallway and there was the front door.

In Bergen, there had only been two or three journalists waiting for him when he returned to the house on Christinegård after being charged and released on bail. Outside End Point there were almost a dozen. Plus two TV cameras. All of them asked different questions at the same time, about Lacey, Eva and his daughter, fires in the night. But they wanted reaction, not answers, a spat-out *no comment*, a look of panic or a very public meltdown. So Jonas settled a beatific smile and pushed a way through the throng. He even managed a wave at the green-haired teenage hairdresser opening up another empty day in her salon. She lifted an automatic hand and dropped it like a stone but that was ok, at least she'd tried.

Two journalists got on the bus with him. One sat directly behind him and continued to jabber questions. The other sat a few seats back, trying to convince himself Jonas hadn't seen him. Both got off when he did, the last stop before the pedestrianised zone in the town centre.

He shook off the first in the market. In one door of

the fishmonger and out another. He lost the second by joining a group of Spanish tourists crowding along the High Street. When they reached St. Francis' church he ducked down Finstock Lane and didn't stop running until the park.

It took half an hour to walk to the ring road. Half an hour of faces on buses, cars, pavements. Quick looks, held looks, recognition flashes. He pulled his 49ers cap lower but felt more conspicuous than ever. Just needed to pull his collar up to complete the effect. So he did.

Because it was all a game. An unbelievable game. Two streets later he flung the cap in a bin.

It was just after 8 am. They were creating a new hamburger roundabout and the traffic was nose to tail, four lanes of dual-carriageway reduced to one each way as they built a relief lane through the centre of the old roundabout. A six- to eight-month job to relieve the traffic that would build exponentially until three years from now they'd have to think again.

He crossed the lanes to the work site, the ground where they'd scraped off the vegetation dry and rutted. Men in yellow bibs and red machines, like animals at a dried up watering hole, milling and shouting as a thousand engines revved. He headed for the Portakabins.

'Jonas?' Boss Hogg looked up with a classic double-take. He was sitting at his desk reading a newspaper.

'Hogg.'

'You're supposed to be on leave.'

'I guessed you might need me.'

'Did you now?'

'The team's a man down.'

'Not today. You guessed wrong, Jonas. Go home.'

'Come on Hogg, I – '

'The boys don't want you here, Jonas.'

'They might not want me here but it's my job.'

Hogg tapped his fingers on the desk. Thinking about something. Holding Jonas's gaze. 'Not for long.'

'What's that supposed to mean?'

He picked up the two-way radio on the desk. 'Eggers. You there? *Eggers.*'

The radio buzzed a few moments later. 'Boss man. What's up?'

'Get yourself in here.'

'Gimme ten, I'm on a break.'

'Just do it!'

Jonas looked down at the newspaper on the desk. *The Sun,* a double-page spread. He saw the word *Lacey.* Bold black letters. 'If this has got anything to do with her you're way off the line.'

'Off the *mark.* It's got nothing to do with that. There's a process there and there's a process here.'

'I don't know what you're talking about.'

The door handle turned and they both looked round. Eggers saw Jonas and stopped dead.

'Jackie,' said Hogg. 'What was that you were telling me this morning? Jonas using the work van for personal use.'

Eggers stared at him. 'You what?'

'Come *on,*' said Jonas, 'this is – '

'This morning. Remember? You said it was out of line how Jonas kept taking the van for personal use.'

Eggers frowned. He was still staring at Hogg. Then nodded, slowly then faster, a man in the process of making a decision. 'That's right. Personal use of the van. A few times he's taken it out.'

'You have to be joking!' said Jonas.

Hogg stood up and pointed Jonas towards the door. 'You heard it. There'll be a letter in the post.'

'About what?'

'The disciplinary.'

'That's what happens when you step out of line, mate,' Eggers blurted out. 'There's consequences.'

They followed him across the site. When Jonas crossed the lanes of traffic they were still watching, watching him all the way into the distance.

Eggers. He was doing a Haroldson and Mikke. Two teacher friends from Skillebekk High who kept a similar distance when Jonas was released. Neither would meet him and no chance of a reference. Not that he'd have got anywhere near a teaching post. A warehouse job was hard enough. They wanted to know about the long employment gap so Jonas started to lie. He turned himself into a fish packer from Lofoten, a trawler jock from Hammerfest...

It was startling, how it flowed, the details Jonas conjured. He almost convinced himself he had a gift for improvisation until he realised that most people weren't listening. They wanted to hear but they didn't want to listen. He could stretch his nonsense to higher planes of inanity before they finally twigged. It made him feel better about being shunned by old friends. In true connection was loyalty and forgiveness. In its absence there could have been no connection to begin with. He wondered what Haroldson and Mikke had *heard* when he had talked to them, joked with them, all those hours in the bar after parent evenings. What were they really thinking about when he was rambling on? And then he realised he couldn't remember a damn thing about what they had told *him*. It was a liberating moment, to know that every face was a mask and behind every mask was a stranger.

He headed back into town. To the bus station and a coffee while he waited for the B4, watching the orange scrolling digital destination screens, nine mins, six mins, two mins. DUE.

One of the place names drew his eye, something there he suddenly remembered. Longworth, the village where

236

the weapons expert, Dr David Kelly, was hounded to an alleged suicide after questioning Blair's weapons of mass destruction claims. Twenty-nine co-proxamol and the heart-breaking pathos of a childhood pocket knife. But if there is despair in killing yourself there is so much more in wanting the bliss of an escape you know you can't make.

That December afternoon at Christinegård. Mad as the blizzard outside. Staring into the bathroom mirror and shivering with soul-deep cold, more profound than the harshest winter. Fifty paracetamol and a bottle of vodka. He swallowed twenty before Eva touched his cheek.

Such forgiveness for what he had done to her and Anya. Or such pity for his lack of courage to follow through. He began to cry. Felt her stroke his head as he made himself throw up.

The B4 rolled in and Jonas got on. Ain't no one likes a killer. It's just a *thing*. Made you think twice about a handshake, never mind sex. But c'mon, Mary, what's a little killing between friends and lovers? Uncork that fine Burgundy and let's drink! Drink to the last images of a wife and daughter, to the blood on the floor of an old Saab and rain like in the movies, Jonas on his knees and he'd only had two beers, *two beers,* he wasn't drunk, the car skidded on slick moss at the side of the road is all, green and unseen but he was still over the limit.

No one forgave. Not Eva. Not one of the people who stared as he walked from the bus stop to the supermarket. Not Mary, who Jonas told himself he wasn't looking for as he walked the aisles. He just needed some food. Even the hunted needed baked beans. Baked beans meant normality. He picked up a tin and turned it in his hand. Supermarket brand. There was nothing as reassuring as a tin of beans. You may be lying in bed with the final fever but hey, be reassured that a few streets away there's a tin of beans on a supermarket shelf as there always would be. A tin of beans could save a man. A tin of beans was normalising in a way that making five little fires with a bow-drill in the middle of the night could never be.

He put nine tins in his trolley alongside the seven tins of tuna. Tuna was also normal though not as normal as beans, tuna being a little bit more aspirational. All in all, though, these were normal items. The abnormality came from the numbers, the till assistant would think it peculiar that he was buying seven tins of tuna and nine tins of beans. And why odd numbers? Why not eight of each? Jonas had no answer. The numbers were weird. He was weird.

They knew that already.

They peered at him round corners. Shop workers and shoppers, *members of the public*, he should call them, to distinguish them from himself, who was something else altogether.

Some people he recognised and some he didn't. They watched him choose his bread and meat and cheese, following it from shelf to hand to trolley, eyes lingering on each item, as if it could reveal something about him, or they were comparing themselves to him. He wondered if they put their own bread and meat and cheese back on the shelves after seeing that he'd chosen the same things. There could be no parallels with Killer J. Not even the most ordinary.

He didn't see Mary.

She couldn't be on shift. He gave up his hopeful dawdlings and joined the queue. Four assistants behind the tills. The man in front turned and stared. Looked away shaking his head.

It took five minutes to shuffle to the sweets and newspaper shelves that were the barrier between queue and tills. He saw the headline on the front page of *The*

238

Sun. Lacey suspect a killer! 2 am visit from missing girl. He picked the newspaper up and put it in his basket.

'No,' said the assistant, when Jonas stepped forward.

'Sorry?'

'Not serving you.'

The boy was about eighteen. Ginger hair. Jonas opened his arms wide. 'You can't just say no.'

'Just did, mate.'

Jonas moved to the till anyway and started piling up his items. The assistant glanced down at the newspaper. 'It wasn't murder, you know. Manslaughter.' The assistant seemed unnerved. He looked at his colleague with the bleached blonde hair and bright red lipstick who was doing her best to be a thousand miles away. 'And Lacey came round at midnight, not two.'

'Whatever you say.'

'Whatever I *say*. Don't you think it's important? Don't you think that it's important to know the facts?'

The assistant reached under the counter and a bell started ringing. 'You'll have to leave.'

'Yeah. Just leave!'

Jonas turned to the woman with the pram who'd shouted from the queue. 'They've got no right to do this.'

'Go back home!'

'This is my home.'

Danny from The Hub appeared. He'd tell his colleague to serve him. He'd *insist*. Or make a point of serving him himself. He was with a fat man whose badge said *Tim- Supervisor*.

'Sir,' said Tim.

'Don't call him sir!' shouted pram woman.

'*Sir*. I'm going to have to ask you to leave.'

Jonas stared. He wondered about the insistence on calling him *sir*. Then he looked to Danny, who looked him straight in the eye. No trace of embarrassment. No awkwardness at all.

239

'Just fuck off, Jonas.'

'C'mon, Danny.'

'Fuck… OFF!'

What do you do? There's no manual. You stare stupidly at your items and leave them on the counter. You shuffle as Jonas now shuffled. Red-faced. Back to the no-man's-land between queue and till, the supermarket revolving around him. Staring people and beeping tills.

Pram woman shoved past. She was buying twenty-four jam doughnuts, one apple and a copy of *The Sun*. There he was again, Front Page Jonas. Close up. Hands on hips. He looked arrogant. The journalist at the door had warned him there was a photographer in that Golf.

Norway's *Sun* equivalent, *Verdens Gang*, managed to photograph him twice at Christinegård.

The first was the worst, two weeks after he was released. Telephoto shot and another front page. Sat in the back garden in his shorts, laughing, but no right of reply to say what he was laughing at and why it was all so understandable if they had taken a little time to find out.

Thirty-seven

Mary saw Jonas come into the supermarket. She was stocking fruit when the automatic doors opened. Hurrying through to the back shop, she spent five minutes in the toilet, then five minutes unpacking boxes from the new delivery. This gave her the excuse to go to the manager's office, where they stacked the overflow. There was a bank of CCTV monitors in there.

Jonas was still in the supermarket. She picked him up in the tinned foods aisle and followed him from camera to camera. He was dawdling, obviously waiting for her to appear. Then he suddenly looked up at the camera and for an unsettling moment Mary was sure he could see her.

Tim the supervisor came into the office. She stared at him dumbly, unable to think of a reason for being there. Tim had a little crush and said nothing. A red sheen appeared on his forehead when he asked if she could help him check off the delivery. A moment later the counter bell rang.

Tim said *duty calls* and headed for the floor. Mary watched Jonas's humiliation and didn't know what to think. She'd read the article in *The Sun* again and again. Footsteps made her turn around and there was Daisy, a pinched smile as she looked from the screen to Mary.

She pushed past Daisy without a word and left the supermarket by the back entrance. The worst they could do was fire her. At least her husband would be happy.

But Tim wouldn't do that. He'd want to talk, a chance to be alone and sympathetic. *Is everything ok, Mary?*

She walked and walked and wanted to run. 10k, 20k, further and further and still in her uniform, running in her tights with her skirt round her waist, shoes in her hands. They'd all be watching, a bemused little crowd. Tim, Daisy, Meg and Mary's ever bewildered husband.

Daisy, she was *revelling* in it. But she didn't know a thing, neither about Jonas nor the fact that John Hackett was back. Surely she remembered John Hackett, what he did to his sister?

Mary could bring little to mind about John other than the sensation of the police investigation. The teenage romance may never have happened. As with so much in her life it had left no trace. An awkward boy is all that came back, over-keen, the kiss of death for seventeen-year-old Mary. When she dumped him she probably had a good laugh about it with her friends.

Two hours later, Mary turned up at End Point. She recognised a couple of the journalists she'd shouted at a few nights ago. They looked on impassively as a dozen lenses turned to her.

Jonas was sitting cross-legged in the living room with his back to the door. Buddha among a scatter of LPs. A deep, fractured voice was singing, the voice booming from the surround-sound speakers.

It's up in the morning and on the downs, little white clouds like gambolling lambs, and I am breathless without you...

She watched him stand up and put his arms around an imaginary partner, dancing with his eyes closed, slow spins and careful steps. A fragility of such perfection that tears came to her eyes.

'Jonas?'

He didn't seem surprised to see her. 'Nick Cave. *Breathless*. It's beautiful.'

'Are you ok?'

'The album's called the *Lyre of Orpheus*. A *lyre*. Like me eh? I feel like I'm in the underworld too.'

'There's something I have to tell you.'

'I'd put it number ten or eleven on my list. Albums, not songs. Song-wise it's in my top five. I've got a thing for Krautrock so I'd probably put Can and Harmonium ahead of it. And Neu, of course. In fact...' Jonas crouched down to the record shelves and ran a finger along the spines.

'Jonas – '

'You heard this? Neu, *Isi*.' He sat back down on the floor and again closed his eyes, nodding along to the driving beat and delicate keyboard rises. He was smiling, a thousand miles away.

When the track ended he lifted the needle into silence. 'I had to buy all my records again after I left. I'm almost there. A few more to go.' He cocked his head, listening. 'Is that rain?' His face brightened and he moved to the CD shelves, picking one out. 'Right. Come with me.'

She followed him into the kitchen. He put the CD into the portable player on top of the fridge.

'Howie B.'

The light was grey, becoming greyer as day became rain became dusk. He opened the sun room door as music filled the kitchen, an insistent bass line, off-kilter. She let him lead her, undone by his smile, out of the door and into the pouring rain, the music rising into each slackening, falling as the deluge returned. She was soaked and he was holding her so tightly, whispering the lyrics in her ear as they shuffled on the grass. *Take your partner by the hand. She's a woman, he's a man. What's so hard to understand? Take your partner by the hand.*

The affection she felt was very real. She thought of her honeymoon in Thailand, the rainforest cabin in the hills of Chiang Mai. Her husband couldn't stand it, moaning about the humidity.

Every night about seven there was a storm. On the third day she joined it, slowly twirling as he watched and laughed, refusing to join her. She was so disappointed as she walked away, down a winding path become a stream until she was alone in a secret monsoon, rain on a pond, quivering water plants edged in half-moons of ghost light, a lantern rocking in a tree and every shape with more depth than day, hibiscus dripping the night-beat.

Then, in place of affection, came a deep, alienating sadness. She pulled away from Jonas and sat in the sun room, listening to the song. *Wait a minute, where am I, on this elevator to nowhere.* Still he danced in the rain, as she had, watching him as her husband had watched her.

'Funny bugger, isn't he?'

She should have been startled but wasn't. Adam sat down beside her and looked out at Jonas, shaking his head. She stared at him for a long time. 'What did you do, John? To your sister.'

He turned with a half-smile, eyes wide. 'So you *do* think I had something to do with it?'

'Did you?'

The half-smile wavered and faded. He looked back at Jonas. 'I did whatever you think I did.'

She slapped him across the face and couldn't believe she'd done it. Then she did it again. 'What did you do?' She hit him again. 'What did you do to Lacey? What did you do, you bastard?' Still Adam let her hit him, again and again until she slumped onto the floor, crying.

Adam was gone when she sat up. Jonas was standing very still in the streaming rain, hair plastered across his face. He was staring at her oddly, a man returning from a far, far distance. The music was still blaring and she got up angrily, ran to the kitchen and switched it off.

When Jonas joined her she had the download ready on her mobile. She handed him her phone.

244

'*Cold Cases*?' He was frowning.

'It's a programme about unsolved crimes.'

'Why have you – ?'

'Just watch.'

They both did, Mary at his shoulder, the voiceover dramatic, interspersed with images of a dark-haired girl in a red and white polka-dot dress. *A sleepy village and twenty-three years have passed. No one would have thought it could happen again. When Iris Hackett disappeared...*

Jonas looked at her. 'Hackett was the name of Fletcher's grandfather.'

'It's Adam's sister. He changed his name. They arrested him but never found her. They had to let him go.'

'I saw them filming this. I thought it was a reconstruction about Lacey. They'd got it all wrong.'

'Lacey disappears in the same village. They roll out this old story. That's entertainment.'

'Is that what Eggers was on about?'

'I don't – '

'I thought he was talking rubbish.'

Jonas frowned. Opened his mouth and blinked a few times. Then came the torrent of questions.

She answered them all and asked none of her own, all those questions which had been nagging for days. She kept thinking of the photographers outside, Daisy and Meg, her husband; *are you screwing him?* Later, when Jonas went to the bathroom, she decided to just leave.

Thirty-eight

A Welshman was the last person to punch Fletcher in the face. Big ugly bugger with a fist like a hammer. An argument in a Taunton bar after England beat Wales in the Six Nations rugby.

Mary packed a fair whack as well. Fletcher stood in front of Mortensen's bathroom mirror, touching the bruise on his left cheek. He opened his mouth and pulled back the lips, holding a wide smile. He'd seen a corpse like that once, curled up on the ground with a grinning death mask, as if dying was the best joke he had ever heard, as if he'd died laughing.

He crossed to the window and peered out. The media crowd that followed the Norwegian across the street to the hairdresser had moved back to its usual position outside End Point.

Fletcher had waited until he saw Jonas sit down in the hairdresser's chair before he walked round the side of the house and jumped over the fence. He wanted to see how Jonas was getting on. The overflowing bins and stuffy, darkened rooms were a pretty decent guide.

An intelligence officer he met at Bastion called it the *pinch point*. The point where optimum pressure has been achieved and the subject becomes pliable, this last word said with a little wink Fletcher found troubling. He'd taken insurgents in and seen them come out, defiance become defeat. He remembered when it was him on the other side of the table. But he remembered without empathy. He knew the pinch point. As did Mortensen. A Google search in the library told him that the manslaughter trial had been a Norwegian media sensation.

The subject matter ticked all the boxes; Eva and Anya were beautiful, blonde and blue-eyed, Eva a well-known lawyer. It was the same back in 1991. His sister Iris was pretty and popular, his aunt a pillar of the community, chair of the Women's Institute, leader of the church choir...

Fletcher once read an article about how disappearances are reported, how race and class affect the vocabulary used in newspapers and TV reports, the length of prime-time exposure. A scale could probably be worked out. Two weeks for the Caucasian disappeared, five or six days for the black, less if you're Asian. Exposure could still be gained, it depended on how offbeat and *other* you were perceived, say a young boy who was removed from a hospital by his Jehovah's Witness parents, or a Muslim girl taken to a forced marriage in Pakistan.

Back in the kitchen he made a coffee and studied the mess on the table. A wine glass had Mary's lipstick on the rim. He touched the pinky-red smear, rubbing it between his fingers.

The night before she'd come in by the front door. He was impressed. Straight through the seethe of journalists. No one had stood by Fletcher like that. The story wasn't about Lacey anymore. It was about Mortensen, and this woman very publicly supporting him.

Like Lacey, Fletcher's sister Iris had quickly disappeared behind all that they said he had done. Both girls would be forever defined by that vanishing, lost in the shadows of the men who had taken them. Killed them, they said. A shallow grave in the woods, maybe, weighed down with stones at the bottom of the murky

247

river. Even if they magically re-appeared they would remain lost behind those men, who *must have* done it. Everyone knew it. Despite the psycho-babbling ambiguity of the shrinks, all the complexity of a situation, sometimes you just know. We need the other to convince ourselves of our normality. No smoke without fire.

So Fletcher could understand why Mary hit him again and again. It was why he didn't stop her.

As Mortensen would tell you, opinions become granite-hard are hard to shift. Fletcher wondered, as Mary slapped and punched him, whether beating him with her doubt was enough for her. Or whether she would tell others about him now. He didn't want to leave again. That would be the ultimate irony. Two troubled ghost-men. Two men who didn't want to leave End Point both forced to leave. He didn't feel sorry for the Norwegian, no chance of that. That meant allowing the return of a self-pity he had cast out a lifetime ago.

Thirty-nine

Jonas knew what he was going to do. He had a plan. Big Haakon would be pleased. *First rule of bushcraft, always have a plan.*

He considered telling the hairdresser. The words were on the tip of his tongue, almost out...

The mournful face stopped him. She wouldn't get it, too caught up in her misery to be interested in what Jonas was telling her. The lurid, tropic-green hair must have been a light-hearted attempt to leaven a depressive nature. It didn't seem to have worked. But Jonas didn't know her before the green hair. Perhaps she was completely transformed, if still miserable.

Also anxious from the moment Jonas walked through the door of the empty salon. She had immediately switched the radio off, as if this situation required her complete attention.

Jonas couldn't remember ever seeing anyone in the salon. Was it a front, a hobby, the hairdresser indulged by a *rich and smitten lover*? Someone of a more suspicious nature would make enquiries but Jonas just asked about the ten-pound wash and wet cut. She considered his request by running her eyes across the several people peering through the salon windows.

'I'm booked solid,' she said.

Jonas looked around. 'But there's no one here.'

'They're due.'

'When?'

'They're *due*.'

'Can't you fit me in? Look.' He put his hands to his head. 'Not much here anyway. It won't take long.'

She bit her lip and glanced at the window. So what'll it be, green-hair, a tenner's a tenner but is it worth the opprobrium of *serving the local paedophile*? Apparently yes, and Jonas so hangover-fragile that this simple little kindness almost set him blubbering like a child.

To begin with the hairdresser was rough, *hurrying*, scrubbing at his head like she was cleaning a pot. Maybe she noticed the grimace in his face, or the screw of his eyes where the shampoo was leaching in. Whatever it was she began to slow, the fingers relaxing, now gently pressing, massaging his scalp, making little yellow lights dance behind his stinging eyes.

Ah Jonas, he needed those gentle fingers. The hairdresser must be an understanding soul.

Maybe he'd tell her about the decisions he'd made the night before after all. Not for reassurance, just how they had suddenly clicked, the certainty still strong when he woke in the morning and found himself lying naked on his bedroom floor in the recovery position. Beside him was a half-eaten slice of toast and peanut butter. But the toast didn't matter, what did was his sense of enormous well-being, the euphoria of his decisions joined by that of a lingering booze-buzz. Straightaway, Jonas had decided to get a haircut. Why wouldn't he?

He gave the hairdresser twenty and *you can keep the change*. Again, she glanced at the window but the crowd was gone, no need to be cautious. 'Thanks,' she said, and looked at him brightly, *friendly*, the brightness that came from a normal transaction and if there was anything that Jonas would have paid much more than twenty pounds for, it was normality.

Too much to ask?

Probably, but a new haircut meant a fresh Jonas, one

distanced from what was happening all around him. Normal Jonas. The Viking. The Viking who had decided to have another party.

Mary had been horrified when he told her. *Really? Are you all right, Jonas? Are you sure you're coping?* He was, he was going about his normal life and normality meant doing what was expected of the Viking and that meant a party, everyone loved his parties. He didn't tell her about the second decision but she'd understand that as well, everyone would understand.

Jonas paused on the way out of the salon. He'd caught sight of himself in the mirror and it *truly was* a good haircut, the hairdresser should be congratulated. He also decided to tell her the story about the time Axel got a terrible bowl-cut from Camp Sven and stayed off school for *two weeks, can you believe it? As if two weeks was enough to heal that butcher's job!*

Because normal Jonas was also friendly Jonas, who'd fix a smile and let pass the tired old shouts of the media crowd which came hurrying over when they saw him coming out of the salon. When a photographer took a picture right in his face as he crossed the road to End Point that was fine too. He asked the photographer if he liked his new cut and the photographer could only open his mouth and frown, clearly no connoisseur of a decent haircut.

As soon as he closed the front door he broke down. Leaned back against the door and let it pour, slipping down to the floor until he was back in the recovery position he'd woken in. He told himself they were friendly people, all of them. They would come to his party and even Fletcher was welcome, even Fletcher, the man of smoke who came and went.

Jonas felt even better after he had made the phone call. Surprising, how easy it was to arrange.

He checked the clock. 11 am. Two hours to kill. He walked the rooms, *paced* the rooms, a restless meandering to a somewhere that turned out to be Old Sam. He hadn't seen Sam in a while and why not now, why not, surely the old guy would be in *The Black Lion*.

They followed him again. Occasional jostles, photographers running ahead to crouch down and point their cameras. Fewer questions about Lacey. More about Mary. *How's the affair. What's it like to have a woman who fights for you?*

He hesitated outside the door to *The Black Lion*. A sudden memory about Westerns, Sunday afternoons at Axel's, John Wayne and Henry Fonda. He felt like Henry Fonda now, wincing outside the saloon before stepping inside, the door swinging behind him in the stillness, gamblers staring and a honky-tonk piano abruptly stopped. Old Sam was there, thank God.

'Pint of Hooper's please.'

'Pint it is.'

Clara pulled the pint. Jonas heard the honky tonk start up, the drinkers returning to their conversations. But apart from Sam and Jonas the only other customers were a man in a motorised wheelchair and an unfeasibly fat dog. Even the damn dog looked at him with disdain.

'Sam.'

'Jonas.' The old man took another long drink of his pint before he turned. The eyes were troubled.

'Been a while.'

'Not really, son.'

'Seems like it.'

'Still a bloody circus out there. Not much wonder people start to lose their bearings.'

'That's one thing that can be guaranteed.'

'There's a lot more than that can be guaranteed, Jonas. You need to keep your eyes open.'

Jonas nodded to Clara to get Sam another pint. 'Funny thing. You were in my dream last night. We were sitting in a pub down Bergen harbour. We were fishermen, I think. It was winter.'

Sam chuckled and turned. The eyes had softened, become indulgent. 'Was I indeed? Bergen, eh? I never really fancied myself as a fisher. Rather be an engine-room jockey than stink of fish.'

And he told Sam the rest of a dream which hadn't happened, the details so easily pouring, how it was cold, must have been twenty below, snow in the streets and no light, 1942 and we were out after curfew, down by the warehouses, waiting for our Resistance contact, holding our breath and nervous, then crunching boots and a match lighting a cigarette and the face of a young German, lingering there, looking around as he smoked then flicking the butt that landed at our feet, hiding in the doorway not ten feet away... Sam gave a little laugh. When Jonas continued Sam put a hand on his. 'C'mon, you don't need to.'

'Don't need to what?' This was the dance. The dance of Sam and Jonas, with its cues and tells. Jonas needed a way back to Bergen, the Rosenkrantz Tower and the fantasy barmaid at *Logens*. He didn't want the old man to acknowledge a fake dream. He wanted him to *dance*.

Sam looked at him for a moment then smiled. Patted his hand. 'Bergen in winter. Helluva cold.'

'You never lived there!'

'I could have.'

'You and the barmaid, a cosy little house in Christinegård.'

'Now you're talking!'

'A little, white-painted wooden house.'

'Possibly, I would have – '

'It was a long walk from anywhere. A real pain if you've got the shopping. And a kid. Pushing a buggy up there.'

Sam shifted on his seat. 'Children? Well it might have been a – '

'Eva would call me to come and help her. I'd have to traipse down and push the buggy back. Then carry the damn thing up the steps. I'd complain to Anya all the way. I'd say *well the next time I think we should just leave her there.* And Anya would say *no, daddy, that's not fair* but Eva would agree and we'd keep it going, back and forth. Anya loved it. She loved it.'

He looked at Sam, who nodded vaguely. The troubled look was back. 'I read the papers, Jonas.'

'Do you now.' He didn't mean the harshness. He called to Clara for two whiskies. Doubles.

'Take it easy, son.'

Jonas clinked his glass against Sam's. 'I didn't fall in love like you. No fireworks, love at first sight. That's for lucky buggers like you. Eva and I just met in a bar, got talking and that was that.'

'You don't need to tell me this.'

He grabbed Sam's hand. Squeezed and smiled. 'It's what people want. Everyone wants to *know*. It's like they have a stake in me, and some of them would no doubt like to *stick* a stake in me!'

'C'mon now, that's – '

'Tell me about the barmaid at *Logens*. I've got this idea of her. I want to imagine her there with you.'

'It's maybe not the best – '

'Of course it is, c'mon Sam, tell it!'

So Sam did.

As Jonas listened and laughed and asked his occasional questions he wondered why Sam did. Maybe in the strangest of moments there's nothing as reassuring as our own fixations.

★ ★ ★

The presenter-journalist was celebrity-coiffed and bleach-toothed, exclusively clad in a suit that likely came with etiquette lessons. You can put on a Savile Row suit, old boy, but can you *wear* one?

He nodded, *sympathetically*, when Jonas said he felt bad about Sam. He agreed with a breathy *yes* when Jonas laid it on thick and said *life is a series of stage directions we can't quite hear*. All the while he scribbled in a notebook, leaning against the steering wheel of the big Lexus.

His eyes lit up when Jonas gave a flavour of what he'd told Sam. About his wife and daughter. Their life in Bergen. *This is just what the viewers want*, he said, *a man telling his story, telling the truth*. His demeanour said something different, the wariness in the eyes and the tension in the body giving away his nervousness about being in the presence of a *kidnapper*.

A *killer*.

'Do you tell people about this?' Jonas asked.

'What's that?'

'These secret meetings with your interviewees. People must be impressed.'

The presenter shifted in his seat. His face brightened. 'Sometimes I do. People are... interested, yes.'

'So I'll become a story.'

He laughed nervously and drummed his fingers on the steering wheel. 'You already are a story.'

'At your dinner parties, I mean. What'll you really say about me? The bits that won't get on TV.'

The fingers stopped drumming. The presenter stared out of the windscreen, Jonas following his gaze to the car park of Breckon Leisure Lake. A place of mid-range Fords and Nissans, their angler-owners hidden around the shore. Jonas didn't get it. There was something passive-aggressive in that unfathomable, over-equipped patience. Fishing was tailor-made for Slow TV, those ten-hour Norwegian epics; a fire burning in a grate, an old woman knitting. The presenter was unlikely to blaze that particular trail. His instinct was sensation, not slow, and if he seemed a bit nervy about sensation having brought him to a remote lake with the bogeyman he hid it well. He came back to the interview, the stark *drama*.

Live at eight.

Jonas Mortensen's living room.

'Your house is called *End Point*? Seriously? If we'd *scripted* this it couldn't have been better. There's so much tension having the partygoers there too. Genius! Can they ask questions?'

'Course they can, there's nothing to hide.' The J-Man would let it all just *flooow*, Norway to now and all subjects open, even Lacey Lewis. The presenter beamed, already composing the Bafta acceptance speech. Then Jonas said he wanted to finish with a *bombshell*.

'A revelation?'

'A revelation.'

'You gonna tell me what it is?'

'Where's the drama in that?'

The presenter almost glittered. He closed his notebook and pressed the ignition button, taking the revs higher as he drove off, couldn't resist hinting at that 300 hp Lexus engine.

* * *

The presenter dropped Jonas in the same lay-by down the road to the next village where he'd picked him up. Jonas watched the Lexus accelerate away and took the party posters from his rucksack. Purple felt-tip pen on mint green paper. He cringed again. No normal person wrote in purple, only wannabe maniacs knocking on the doors of the loony bin. Fight that urge to scream. Call Mary instead. But once more *the person you are calling is unavailable...*

Forty

Mary was unavailable to a whole range of people, not just Jonas. Names kept appearing on her mobile display, several numbers she didn't recognise. People known and unknown knocked at her door. She saw them from the bedroom, peering round the curtains as they walked away.

In the end she turned her phone off and snuck out to the garden shed. She had no intention of talking to anyone. Mary was frightened. If she couldn't disappear then she would hide.

She'd taken a book, which made it seem a bit more normal to skulk in a damp shed; it was just a quiet place to read, that's all, *Love in the Time of Cholera*, one of those books you're supposed to like but she'd never managed to get into. She'd been in there most of the day and hadn't even glanced at it. Instead, she sat in the broken easy chair and poured cup after plastic cup of cheap Chardonnay from the three-litre wine box she'd also taken with her.

Her husband used to like the shed. He'd tinker for hours with oily bits of car and motorbike. But he hadn't done that in an age and would no more think of looking for her in the shed than up the chimney. In fact, no one would think of looking for Mary in the shed. She hated it though, it stank of mould. For a while she considered burning it to the ground. People probably even expected it after last night's incident, which was why everyone was calling her.

It was the photographer's fault. He was in her face as soon as she opened the front door of End Point. The flash momentarily blinded her so she lashed out and caught him on the chin.

He stumbled backwards and fell over the garden wall to gasps and shouts from the onlookers.

Mary was jostled as she pushed on through, more camera flashes and shouted questions, followed all the way by a TV cameraman, who managed to dance his way out of trouble and keep the lens fixed on her, an excited-looking female presenter babbling into a furry microphone. When Mary felt wetness on her cheek and realised it was spit she started to run.

Again, the footage made the morning news. *More drama in the Lacey disappearance, the same woman who last week...* Mary watched on the bedroom TV. She could hear the TV in the living room but when she went downstairs her husband was watching cartoons. Daffy Duck. She burst into tears. Daffy bloody Duck. It made complete and perfect sense. Daffy Duck all noisy and frantic and her husband staring up at her from the couch. His gaze was hostile.

Then softening. He stood up and came over to her. He pulled her close. He was good at this. The way he could hold her so tight. She needed no words, no reassurance, just to be held.

The possibility of another bear hug would be gone by the time he got home. The last thing scrolling through his mind when he finally managed to track her down would be sympathy for his wife. Someone was bound to say something. He'd hear something on the radio...

She poured another plastic cup. Took one sip, two sips then downed it and refilled, the cups were tiny and the box of wine apparently bottomless. With a grimace she realised Andrea had probably been calling. Her daughter was following Lacey's disappearance like a soap opera, four or five texts a day. Mary doubted there would be a message like *way to go mum*, as after her haranguing of the journalists. In fact, she was more likely to turn up and ask what the hell was going on. Even now she might be dumping her bag on the floor of her old bedroom.

Mary stood up quickly and banged her head on a shelf, sending a tin of screws and a box of paintbrushes crashing to the floor. Then she fell over in the garden and decided to walk and not run back to the house. When she got upstairs there was no one in Andrea's room.

For a while she lay on the bed then crossed to the window. The two men with cameras round their necks were back again, standing under a lamp post on the other side of the street, just where she'd first seen them, that morning, just after her husband went to work.

She knew how Jonas must feel. She thought about him as she sat in the living room scrolling through her husband's Mega Satellite Package. But when the Norwegian's face appeared in a dramatic ITV trailer for *Morton Meets...* she knew she couldn't do this anymore.

Forty-one

Jonas was relieved. The assistant could have leaned across the counter, picked up the poster and ripped it up. She could have spat a big gob of phlegm right in his eyes. But the universe winked, she didn't know who he was. She just looked down at the poster and said a friendly *no problem, I'll do it later*. And only the vaguest of frowns when Jonas asked her to do it right away.

'It's Friday already. I need to get the word out fast so I'd really appreciate it if you could – '

'Of course!'

She stepped round the back of the till and pinned the poster on the small ads wall facing the window. Those ridiculous purple letters. Big bold stand-outs. At least people would notice.

Party at Jonas's!   All invited. Come on round. 7.30. Saturday 22nd.

Again, the presumption nagged him. Jonas. The Man Who Needed No Surname. He sat on the bench outside the Post Office and checked his phone. Still no Mary. He left a gabbled message about the famous presenter-journo, the TV interview and *please say that you'll come.*

The next forty minutes were spent hurrying round the streets with a stapler and attaching posters to telephone poles. *Laminated* posters and not just *any* telephone pole, selected telephone poles, *strategically placed* telephone poles that he'd marked on an A3 map of the village on the kitchen table. He put another poster in each of the four parish council notice-boards.

He was watched by a roving skulk of journalists and staring locals. Three people shouted at him, his only reaction an invitation to the party. He'd learned the hard way in Christinegård, rushing out of the door in his dressing gown, shouting at the kids who'd been throwing stones at his windows. And then the second *Verdens Gang* photo, page four the next day.

Abuse and shouts, all would pass; Li Po brushing the steps in front of the little temple.

Carlsberg and cherry schnapps would have to do, no time for the off-licence to order *akevitt* or Ringnes. *Denmark and Germany, not too bad, not too far away.* But this just met with a blank look. *From Norway I mean.* The assistant had already turned to another customer and no there wasn't a trolley to borrow, even though Jonas could see an empty one behind the counter in the store room. So he had to carry the booze home in three loads.

The food would be easier. He headed to the supermarket to pick up *smorgasbord* supplies, stopping at the newsagent across from the green to put up a poster. That was when the police appeared. An anxious tinkle from the doorbell that alerted the shopkeeper to school-kids (*only two allowed at a time...*) and there were two uniforms and the sad-eyed detective.

They had a few more questions. 'Would you be so kind as to come with us, Mr Mortensen?'

'Well, I am busy.'

'It won't take long.'

'How long?'

'Not long.'

'Jonas handed the poster to the shopkeeper, who reached out dumbly, taking it without a word. It was still in his hand as he stood in the door and watched Jonas get into the police car.

His mother never had to put up with this when planning *Jonsok* parties. He sat beside a uniform, fidgeting with the posters. The purple ink was annoying him again, the handwritten letters amateurish. He should have printed them. His mother would have been more organised. *Failing to prepare is preparing to fail, little Jonas.* She sure did love an irritating homily.

He nudged the uniform and told him he really didn't have time for this, had things to *do*, needed to buy a *new shirt for the TV cameras, I'm thinking white, maybe blue, what do you think?*

The uniform ignored him and Sad Eyes sniffed in the passenger seat. The detective had a cold, something else Jonas could do without. He asked if they could open the window but still no response. When the driver's eyes caught his in the rear-view mirror Jonas was suddenly shouting, *open the damn window*, then rising in his seat, sweat on his forehead and his neck itching, probably rogue hairs from his haircut and now a strong arm shoving him back down.

He breathed deeply when he left the police station. Stood on the steps in the sunshine and closed his eyes. To cartoon colours. Tom and Jerry and the theme from Looney Tunes. Here it finally was. That big cartoon snowball, rolling down the hill towards the police station, right at him.

The police said an allegation had been made by a friend of Lacey's. They asked other questions.

The snowball was huge and close. Jonas could run but there was no point, there never was, the snowball would outpace him, it always did, bigger and bigger behind him until he was finally caught, rolling and rolling and coming to a stop with arms and legs poking out.

That's all folks!

As he walked down the steps he remembered that he hadn't apologised for his behaviour in the police car and hurried back up to the reception. The desk sergeant looked at him closely, maybe even a flicker of amusement and amusement was always better than contempt.

'I will certainly pass on your apology... *sir.*'

The sarcasm rung in his ears all the way to the village hall. Friday. Another Hub night. Another attempt by Mark to reassert normality. But every week that passed was another tick of that very particular clock which started running the night Lacey disappeared. Two weeks now. You had to wonder how long the clock would run, or when people would realise they'd lost count.

In by the back entrance and no hanging around. Long enough to hand out a few invitations and make sure Mary was coming. He hoped to find her in the kitchen but she wasn't there, just a giggling Wendy and Greg, over by the cupboards, Wendy slapping Greg's hand away and *not here, Greg,* looking round warily, a pink face becoming red when she noticed Jonas.

There was no sign of Mary in the hall either, where everyone turned to look at him, as if choreographed. One of the girls, Sally, burst out crying, then Danny was running towards him and Mark holding him back as Danny shouted *get the hell out of here.* Jonas backed away, left a few flyers at the kitchen hatch and *remember you're all invited, 7.30 tomorrow!*

★ ★ ★

It rained all day Saturday. Third time in a week, summer on the quick-wane, the next swing of the year. Big Haakon loved the turns, season to season. When he remembered he would do a solstice ceremony: *water of autumn, sweeping in from the west, putting out the fires in the south.*

Behind Jonas water steamed into the bath, fogging the bathroom. He opened the window. Below him in the next garden the two children were screeching again, over-excited despite the rain. They marched round and round in a muddy circle, stamping their yellow Wellington boots, red and blue waterproofs covering their hands, hanging almost down to the knees.

One of them looked up and pointed. Jonas waved back and the other sprinted towards the house. The child looking up pushed her hood back and waved, uncertainly, making him think of time and great distances, how the most fleeting of moments can be the most touching.

He lay back in the water. A long listen to the patter on the window. A little tinny, like too much treble on his Marantz amplifier. Take it down, increase the bass and harmonise, the sound now rich and deep, a squall galloping across the Skagerrak, rain on the wheelhouse glass.

The tap dripped, Jonas sneezed. Someone, dozens of people, might be lying in other baths, listening to the gust of rain-wind that had just passed his window and was now reaching theirs. So many parallel lives. He took a deep breath and sank under the now cold water.

Both arms floated free. No bubbles from the mouth. A detective would think it the *classic bath suicide pose*, the lips slightly parted, hair drifting like seaweed. He would bring in a police photographer to record the scene. They would speculate, words punctuated by the flash of the camera, sudden brightness, how he just couldn't take it anymore. Too much pressure.

Jonas reached 130. The pain in the chest was beginning, a hot swelling and a voice that hadn't yet reached panic but was insisting that he should sit up. *Sit up, Jonas. Sit up now!*

Now the closing, peripheral vision shutting down. Sporadic colours flashed, orange-yellow and green, sight constricting to a fish-eye view, like looking into a child's kaleidoscope, the colours becoming shifting Escher symmetries and was it even possible to drown yourself in a bath? When would the detective and photographer realise that in the absence of compulsion the will to live is stronger than the will to die. *If no one was holding him down, sir, why didn't he just sit up? Why not indeed, Baker? Someone else was involved, we're looking at foul play. The game's afoot! Whodunnit?* Maybe one of the people now crowding the bath: Big Haakon peering down, Axel beside him with his gawky moon face and the pressure suddenly increasing in Jonas's chest, a few bubbles of precious air escaping and a spasm in the arm, rippling the water and dissolving Haakon and Axel, settling again to reveal Eva and Anya, Mary just behind them but none of them panicked in any way, more puzzled, slowly fading into a deeper dark and Jonas recognising one last face in the gloom, a smirk he had come to know and those hands about to reach out and hold him under.

Water tsunamied as he sat up, slopping from bath to floor. Fire in his chest, a ringing in his ears and shaking hands. Vision still dark on the periphery, probable and permanent brain damage. 150. Two minutes thirty seconds, a new record. And still the ringing, maybe his phone.

He clambered out of the bath and felt his legs buckle but when he picked up the mobile from his pile of clothes the screen was blank. No missed call. No Mary but still the ringing.

He went down the stairs, rubber legs giving way once or twice. In the kitchen he found an off-licence bag and swigged schnapps straight from the bottle, chasing it with a Carlsberg and wandering through to the living room. Li Po had a look of concern. Jonas raised the bottle and took another drink, spluttering it all down himself when his mobile buzzed.

He dropped the phone twice before he read the message. Mary. *I won't be there, Jonas. Good luck.*

The crush of disappointment was as pressing as his sudden uncertainty. He switched off the light and put on a record, a coal-dark living room with the curtains closed, Lou Reed singing and the bottle sinking lower. *Venus in Furs* then *Pale Blue Eyes*, Jonas mouthing along because he didn't want his voice to ruin that heart-breaking waver, just silently singing unto oblivion.

He woke to the same black. The ancient universe must have been like this. That first Being, alone in the ever-nothing. Black that didn't know it was black because light had yet to be born. And maybe a slow background *fuss, fuss, fuss*, the sound of a spinning record after the final track, amplified from the great Marantz at the end of the universe, no one else there to listen.

★ ★ ★

The TV crew arrived at six. Signalled in advance by a rising buzz from the crowd outside the front door as people parted, made way, *craned* to see the famed presenter. Then the doorbell.

Morton led the way. A stride to straddle the *ocean of truth* and a dazzling smile, sweeping round like a light-house beam. Jonas waited to see who else would follow presenter and crew into the house. Not one person. A couple of bouncers stood at the closed door.

'Got to keep the tabloids out,' the presenter said. 'You're big news. Have to guard the exclusive.'

Morton and Jonas sat at the kitchen table, the make-up woman dabbing and the presenter babbling. He went on about Jonas's blue shirt, *blue, are you sure, you might*

266

*sweat in the lights, patches under the armpits and that's bad,
have you got a white shirt, what do you think, Kate?*

Two tall stand-up lights had been set up in the living
room. They moved furniture around without asking
him. They took Li Po off the wall for some reason. They
told him to sit on the couch.

'How many viewers are you expecting?'

'2.5 million most weeks. This could get five plus.'
The presenter raised his eyebrows, emphasising both
the point and his popularity. They moved the easy
chair, *the judge's chair*, 90 degrees to the couch. Morton
could lean in, profile to the camera, show off that chis-
elled jawline.

At five minutes to air the stand-up lights flicked on.
Morton was doing mouth exercises. Showtime! Mikke
came to Jonas's mind, erstwhile director of the annual
show at Skillebekk High.

Mikke might be sitting back home in Åsane, trawling
the international channels, stumbling on this one, a
spoonful of cereal frozen at the mouth, Mikke was
always eating cereal, three boxes at any time in the staff
room. And there's Jonas, Jonas whom he completely
ignored when he got out of prison, Jonas he sometimes
wondered about and no way, it's *him*, blinking in British
TV lights and what had Mortensen done, what had
Mortensen done now? No sympathy there and none
from Sunny, shaking his head, sat on the Dakar beach
with a portable TV. Or Dimitri, screaming at him, drunk
in some Kiev bar. *What is this, Jonas, you gotta keep head
down and why you never learn, why you never learn, man?*

They all drifted and faded, into nothingness. Like the
people who came to his *Jonsok* party, no sign of any of
them.

It was the presenter's first question.

'Jonas. Many thanks for having us. But tell me, why
are our crew the only guests at your party?'

267

Jonas laughed, lightly, not too nervous, then told him about the challenge of belonging.

'You seem to have thought about this a lot.'

'No more than anyone else,' he said to the presenter. 'I just float. Everyone floats.'

'Everyone *floats*?'

'We tell ourselves that we swim when in fact we're just getting carried on the current.'

'Some people must drown.'

'I suppose they do.'

'Are you drowning, Jonas?'

'I've been in deep water.'

'You mean killing your wife and daughter?'

Jonas flinched. He saw those drinks in his hand. He saw his daughter, so peaceful on the back floor of the Saab, as if she was sleeping. 'I rewind every night. Sometimes in the morning, when I'm not sure if I'm awake or still asleep, I hear my wife saying *everything will be ok.*'

'Can you forgive yourself?'

'That is a stupid question.'

'Our viewers will be asking it.'

'You should give your viewers more credit. Of course I can't forgive myself. Let me tell you why...'

And he took Morton on a long trip. Larvik to Bergen to the side-worlds of migrant Europe, the faces from past and present looming out with troubling judgement, whether they knew what Jonas had done or not, because something *must* have happened, that way he always held back, severing the deeper connections but only because he felt worthless beside Kiev Dimitri, Asamoah, Sunny, those with only dignified reasons for drifting the Euro shadows.

'Don't misunderstand me, I am not seeking forgiveness.'

'And Lacey Lewis?'

Another flinch. The viewers would see it. A quick-wince of the eyes and then Jonas was crying.

The director mouthed *advert* but Morton waved his hand, out of shot. 'What was that mistake?'

The make-up woman watching from behind the camera put a hand to her mouth.'What happened?'

Jonas blinked.

'What happened, Jonas?'

'There's always something that goes wrong, Mr Morton. Always something you can't quite believe. Something happened. Something happened in this village and it's happening again.'

'Jonas Mortensen. A nation waits.' The presenter turned slowly, a grave look directly into the camera and then a pointing finger. 'And we ask *you* to wait. We'll be right back after this break.'

The director said *all clear* and the presenter leapt up from the chair. 'Sensational. *Sensational.*'

He squeezed Jonas's arm and then, as if it was a favourite pet, carefully patted his over-coiffed hair, hurrying over to down a schnapps, pick at Jonas's *smorgasbord* and congratulate him on the *fab-u-LOUS* food. He said Twitter was going mad with #*JonasandLacey* and explained that when they came back from the break he would recap the story of the disappearance then *over to you to bring... the... REVEAL.* He asked again for a hint and Jonas again refused.

'You're a natural Jonas, you know tension. Let's hope the ending doesn't fall off a cliff, eh?'

The adverts went on for five minutes, leaching from the sound-man's headphones: cars, cosmetics, cleaning products, cold remedies... something different for each demographic.

The John Hackett bombshell was the ultimate commodity, everyone wanted a piece of that.

A brief internet search in the library told him what

happened in the village in 1991. There was no vindictiveness here, Jonas wasn't a malicious man. Just someone doing a public service for his community and no blame attached to that. He'd walk out into the crowd, hands clean, head high. There would be another story in *The Sun* but a different headline this time, another man's picture on page two and they would thank him, slap him on the back and buy him a drink in *The Black Lion* and who knows, maybe even a syndicated story, taking it across the sea to Norway, to *Verdens Gang* and maybe Mikke would come across that too.

The director said *thirty seconds*.

Then noise.

The front door had been opened. He could hear it in the carrying of voices from the crowd outside.

Another couple of shouts and a vague thud, the slam of the front door. Jonas thought Mary but Eggers appeared. Clearly drunk, *disorientated* drunk and a little stumble back against the frame of the living room door. He stared at the TV camera. Frowned. Then Buzz Cut shoved past him, followed by Buzz Cut's snuffling friend and several men Jonas didn't know.

The director flustered, the presenter beamed and 'welcome, welcome gentlemen, have a drink.'

Eggers swayed, Buzz Cut sniffed and the snuffler giggled, swigging from a half bottle. Keystone Cop moments. They let the director shuffle them behind the couch and stood awkwardly behind Jonas. He looked round. Remembered snowballs in his face. *C'mon then, Thor, fight back!* Buzz Cut said *smile for the birdy* and winked. Eggers wouldn't look him in the eye, drumming his fingers on the top of the couch as the director mouthed five down to zero.

'Welcome back. My first question to Jonas Mortensen

270

was about a lack of guests at the party. He appears to have been vindicated, as you can see from these gentlemen just arrived.'

The face abruptly changed. Became grave and graver, a close-up to camera as he summarised the story of Lacey's disappearance and the allegations that had been put to Jonas.

'Jonas. Over to you.' He sat down again, *leaned in*. 'What do you want to tell the nation?'

As Jonas opened his mouth Psycho Dave appeared in the doorway. The viewers would see Jonas look out of shot and hear a voice shouting *are we going to listen to anymore of this bullshit?* Then the camera was on its side, showing feet, the bottom of the couch, shouts in the background and sudden black, a stuttering voice-over apologising for the loss of pictures.

Jonas thought about the viewers as he was dragged over the back of the couch. They would be frantic. *Let down*. They wanted to see this. The punches and the kicks. Pay per view was made for it. Public executions would have the biggest viewer numbers in history and this could have been the taster, Jonas Mortensen, the *Viking*, Jonas of the Parties getting the shit kicked out of him in his own living room, boots to the face, the stomach and most of all the balls, they were definitely favouring the balls and Jonas not even protecting himself anymore, his mouth bubbling with blood and maybe he was shouting something about John Hackett but maybe not, maybe it was all in his head, maybe Fletcher was a figment too and not actually appeared in the doorway, utterly nonplussed, arms folded and now grabbing Mary as she too materialised, horror on her face and lunging towards Jonas but held back by Fletcher.

She struggled so briefly.

271

That was the saddest thing. How she let herself be held back, the shoulders relaxing, concern becoming detachment as she just watched. He didn't think of anything then, he wasn't even aware of searching for something that he couldn't quite place. There was nothing.

Epilogue

Snow across the cypress. Thick, lazy fallings from epic black to yellow-orange; winter sky-glow.

He closed his eyes. Saw streetlights stretching into a silent white distance emptied of all people, past the subdued windows of Andrew Gladstone's café and the ever-empty hairdressing salon with the zebra-striped wallpaper, past the red-brick new-builds and the meandering lines of so many parked cars, hidden under snowy blankets, gone as if gone for good.

Midnight had passed. Hardly any lights in the overlooking windows, but a brighter glowing from the conservatory two houses down; imagine it lifting, a merry-go-round of fairground neon but no one on the plastic horses, spinning up and up and finally lost in black, dissonant Wurlitzer slowly fading. But the only sound was the occasional thrumming of a passing car, carrying over the roof of End Point to reach him where he sat in the back garden.

The fire was dying, dulling orange around the bony remnants of the beech logs, patterned in grey-white char like the ghost of the rainbow trout he'd wrapped in foil and cooked hours ago. The snow, too, was starting to falter. Soon, it would stop falling altogether.

He leaned forward on the deckchair. Poked the ashes with a stick. This was his third fire in just over a week, each lit only when the snow was actually falling. For obscure reasons it was necessary to simultaneously feel the heat of the flames and the cold of the snowflakes. This evening he'd thought about inviting people round. They would have only been confused by their host, who sat hunched and silent beside the fire, wrapped in an old blue puffer jacket, drawstring tight on the hood. He wore only a t-shirt underneath but was still sweating.

Today was the first in many he'd spoken to anyone. The connection was unsought. He just happened to be in the hall when the doorbell rang. Otherwise he'd have ignored it altogether. The man was collecting for the Red Cross Christmas appeal. Forty-five or so, kind eyes, an acne-scarred face that must have made adolescence an intolerable cruelty. He listened to the man's spiel then took his wallet from the hallway table and gave him seventy-two pounds, all the money he had. The man blustered, asking *are you sure, it's so generous?*

They talked about the weather then, the awkwardness of the interaction now over-ridden by his generosity. He thought about inviting the man in to sit beside his fire in the back garden. They could have talked some more. But the man would have refused, he was sure.

All these fires and still no decisions. He had even thought about becoming a postman. Everyone liked a postman, a postman was reassuring. He could join the football club too. His neighbour played. He'd seen him in his muddy strip, kit bag slung over his shoulder. It was because of football he'd switched on the radio tonight. There was a big Premiership match on somewhere. He couldn't remember the teams. But he remembered the news.

Lacey Lewis had come home. Five months to the day since her disappearance she walked into a London police station. A runaway and a return. A simple story, in the end. The news had played a clip of her mother. *It's wonderful, a Christmas miracle, even the snow is falling.*

Mortensen.

274

Pity the Norwegian.

He would have seen the report. In a boarding house maybe, a seaside bed and breakfast, standing at a window looking out on a black sea, Lacey behind him in vague TV reflection. Mortensen who spent three weeks in hospital, came back for a night then left again. He said nothing to Fletcher. Looked through him. Through the thin skein of this world into a troubled beyond.

He poked the fire again, sending orange embers dancing upwards, into the falling snow. He thought about getting up and going back into the house. It would be freezing. He'd left the sun room door open and the chill would have spread into every room. He didn't want to go inside. To go inside meant going to bed, knees to his chest under graveyard sheets. Instead, he threw another two logs on the fire, the bone-dry beech crackle-catching straightaway.

He leaned back and closed his eyes. The cold flakes landing on his eyelids were sporadic, then more regular, until he had to lick them from his lips, the snow coming down thickly again. He wondered if it would be possible to fall asleep like this. How long before hypothermia set in? Perhaps he would be smothered to death first, snow-clog in the nostrils. What about those last dreams, would they be cold and desolate or bask in longed-for heat?

When he sat up he saw them. Through the flurries and through the flames. On the other side of the fire. Lacey and his sister Iris in their blue jackets. The Afghan girl in her white qmis.

They seemed tired, made drowsy by the heat. They watched him throw on another log. Again the swelling sweetness of beech, flicker-flames wandering their faces, making shadows, their eyes that might be closed, might be open. He went to join them, undoing his hood and lying down beside them, looking up into the falling, settling snow that would bury all of them.

You have joined them, you who were never lost. Three of you, a Trinity, the triple aspect of a truth. Did any of you find peace? On nights of predators in cold London town, at that moment of abduction that became hours of terror, during that fall to dusty earth that may have lasted an eternity. What flashes of knowledge in those moments? Did you learn something, desperately sought by desert imams and hedgerow ministers, shamen and ascetics, pattern seekers in the digital flow? Because there must be God and if not God then explanation, hidden knowledge and transcendent esoteria that make a euphoric but utterly practical sense of the world. You snigger, you whisper and you will not tell. No reason you should and I do not care. I am no seeker. I know the opening of a hand to emptiness. I will not ask for lessons learned. I will not ask because you mock, you two become three, you of the soaring kite that day in the Sangin bazaar, the red of your blood as I shot you down, I know I did, did I really shoot you down, you of the miracle return and did I follow you home after Mortensen's party when you returned for your blue jacket, to hold you and touch you and make sure you were not my little sister, the same age as you and somehow returned, that other blue jacket that I followed twenty-three years ago, I think, down to the river and along by the woods where we fought again and I finally lost it, years of frustration the police said, hands on your throat, they said, arms straight out the way they held the SA80 which tore apart the Afghan girl. Is this what I did? I cannot tell now, the snow covers so much, it piles up like centuries.